Lessons in Fun and Frolic

Ruskin Bond is known for his signature simplistic and witty writing style. He is the author of several bestselling short stories, novellas, collections, essays and children's books; and has contributed a number of poems and articles to various magazines and anthologies. At the age of twenty-three, he won the prestigious John Llewellyn Rhys Prize for his first novel, *The Room on the Roof*. He was also the recipient of the Padma Shri in 1999, Lifetime Achievement Award by the Delhi Government in 2012 and the Padma Bhushan in 2014.

Born in 1934, Ruskin Bond grew up in Jamnagar, Shimla, New Delhi and Dehradun. Apart from three years in the UK, he has spent all his life in India, and now lives in Landour, Mussoorie, with his adopted family.

RUSKIN BOND

Lessons in Fun and Frolic

An Essential Collection for Children

RUPA

Published by
Rupa Publications India Pvt. Ltd 2023
7/16, Ansari Road, Daryaganj
New Delhi 110002

Sales centres:
Prayagraj Bengaluru Chennai
Hyderabad Jaipur Kathmandu
Kolkata Mumbai

Copyright © Ruskin Bond 2023

This is a work of fiction. Names, characters, places and incidents are either the product of the author's imagination or are used fictitiously and any resemblance to any actual person, living or dead, events or locales is entirely coincidental.

All rights reserved.
No part of this publication may be reproduced, transmitted, or stored in a retrieval system, in any form or by any means, electronic, mechanical, photocopying, recording or otherwise, without the prior permission of the publisher.

P-ISBN: 978-93-5702-230-9
E-ISBN: 978-93-5702-226-2

First impression 2023

10 9 8 7 6 5 4 3 2 1

The moral right of the author has been asserted.

Printed in India

This book is sold subject to the condition that it shall not, by way of trade or otherwise, be lent, resold, hired out, or otherwise circulated, without the publisher's prior consent, in any form of binding or cover other than that in which it is published.

CONTENTS

Introduction — vii

1. At Sea with Uncle Ken — 1
2. The Ugly Prince and the Heartless Princess — 8
3. The Tiger King's Gift — 17
4. Panther's Moon — 27
5. A Tiger in the House — 60
6. The Tunnel — 65
7. Ranji's Wonderful Bat — 73
8. Mukesh Starts a Zoo — 82
9. The Boy Who Broke the Bank — 88
10. Koki Plays the Game — 95
11. The Great Train Journey — 101
12. The Room of Many Colours — 108
13. A Case for Inspector Lal — 133
14. Our Great Escape — 142
15. The Trouble with Djinns — 149
16. The Blue Umbrella — 154
17. Sita and the River — 177
18. The Story of Madhu — 222

19. Miss Babcock's Big Toe	227
20. The Zigzag Walk	230
21. Four Boys on a Glacier	233
22. The Leopard	239
23. My Failed Omelettes and Other Disasters	247
24. The School among the Pines	250
25. The Thief's Story	274
26. When the Trees Walked	279
27. King Bharata	283
28. Nala and Damayanti	287
29. Children of India	290
30. Adventures in Reading	296
31. Miss Ramola and Others	305

INTRODUCTION

Would you rather spend a fun day with a friend learning to swim or frolicing around the house with an adorable little tiger cub? Tough choice, isn't it? You may often find yourself choosing between enjoyable escapades in the great outdoors or cooking up some naughty shenanigans inside the house. In fact, you may want to do it all at once: have a romp with cute animals, climb trees, bask in the sun, run around town with friends, steal sweets from the local shops, and above all, make fun of adults!

Growing up in the mountains, I had my share of childhood misadventures that have inspired many of my stories: of mischievous pets, eccentric friends, kind townsfolk, wonderful journeys and fun games. Through these joyous and gleeful experiences, I have learnt lessons that have left a mark on me.

This book is a window into those carefree childhood days, filled with laughter and excitement; curiosity and imagination; friendship and love. From the quirky innocence of Timothy the Tiger Cub to the mind-boggling mystery of Inspector Keemat Lal's latest case, the stories in this book will take you on amusing and intriguing quests.

I hope these stories of fun and frolic not only excite and entertain you, dear reader, but leave you with insightful life lessons to mull over.

Ruskin Bond

AT SEA WITH UNCLE KEN

With uncle Ken you always had to expect the unexpected. Even in the most normal circumstances, something unusual would happen to him and to those around him. He was a catalyst for confusion.

My mother should have known better than to ask him to accompany me to England the year after I'd finished school. She felt that a boy of sixteen was a little too young to make the voyage on his own; I might get lost or lose my money or fall overboard or catch some dreadful disease. She should have realized that Uncle Ken, her only brother (well spoilt by his five sisters), was more likely to do all these things.

Anyway, he was put in charge of me and instructed to deliver me safely to my aunt in England, after which he could either stay there or return to India, whichever he preferred. Granny had paid for his ticket; so in effect he was getting a free holiday which included a voyage on a posh P&O liner.

Our train journey to Bombay passed off without incident, although Uncle Ken did manage to misplace his spectacles, getting down at the station wearing someone else's. This left him a little short-sighted, which might have accounted for his mistaking the stationmaster for a porter and instructing him to look after our luggage.

We had two days in Bombay before boarding the *S.S. Strathnaver* and Uncle Ken vowed that we would enjoy ourselves. However, he was a little constrained by his budget and took me to a rather seedy hotel on Lamington Road, where we had to share a toilet with over twenty other people.

'Never mind,' he said. 'We won't spend much time in this dump.' So he took me to Marine Drive and the Gateway of India and to an Irani restaurant in Colaba, where we enjoyed a super dinner of curried prawns and scented rice. I don't know if it was the curry, the prawns or the scent, but Uncle Ken was up all night, running back and forth to that toilet, so that no one else had a chance to use it. Several dispirited travellers simply opened their windows and ejected into space, cursing Uncle Ken all the while.

He had recovered by morning and proposed a trip to the Elephanta Caves. After a breakfast of fish pickle, Malabar chilli chutney and sweet Gujarati puris, we got into a launch, accompanied by several other tourists and set off on our short cruise. The sea was rather choppy and we hadn't gone far before Uncle Ken decided to share his breakfast with the fishes of the sea. He was as green as a seaweed by the time we were ashore. Uncle Ken collapsed on the sand and refused to move, so we didn't see much of the caves. I brought him some coconut water and he revived a bit and suggested we go on a fast until it was time to board our ship.

We were safely on board the following morning, and the ship sailed majestically out from Ballard Pier, Bombay, and India receded into the distance, quite possibly forever as I wasn't sure that I would ever return. The sea fascinated me and I remained on deck all day, gazing at small crafts, passing steamers, sea birds, the distant shoreline, salt water smells, the surge of the waves and, of course, my fellow passengers. I could well understand the fascination it held for writers such as Conrad, Stevenson, Maugham and others.

Uncle Ken, however, remained confined to his cabin. The rolling of the ship made him feel extremely ill. If he had been looking green in Bombay, he was looking yellow at sea. I took my meals in the dining saloon, where I struck up an acquaintance with a well-known palmist and fortune teller who was on his way to London to make his fortune. He looked at my hand and told me I'd never be rich, but that I'd help other people get rich!

When Uncle Ken felt better (on the third day of the voyage), he struggled up on the deck, took a large lungful of sea air and subsided into a deck chair. He dozed the day away, but was suddenly wide awake when an attractive blonde strode past us on her way to the lounge. After some time we heard the tinkling of a piano. Intrigued, Uncle Ken rose and staggered into the lounge. The girl was at the piano, playing something classical which wasn't something that Uncle Ken normally enjoyed, but he was smitten by the girl's good looks and stood enraptured, his eyes brightly gleaming, his jaw sagging. With his nose pressed against the glass of the lounge door, he reminded me of a goldfish who had fallen in love with an angelfish that had just been introduced into the tank.

'What is she playing?' he whispered, aware that I had grown up on my father's classical record collection.

'Rachmaninoff,' I made a guess. 'Or maybe Rimsky Korsakov.'

'Something easier to pronounce,' he begged.

'Chopin,' I said.

'And what's his most famous composition?'

'Polonaise in E flat. Or maybe it's E minor.'

LESSONS IN FUN AND FROLIC

He pushed open the lounge door, walked in, and when the girl had finished playing, applauded loudly. She acknowledged his applause with a smile and then went on to play something else. When she had finished he clapped again and said, 'Wonderful! Chopin never sounded better!'

'Actually, it's Tchaikovsky,' said the girl. But she didn't seem to mind.

Uncle Ken would turn up at all her practice sessions and very soon they were strolling the decks together. She was Australian, on her way to London to pursue a musical career as a concert pianist. I don't know what she saw in Uncle Ken, but he knew all the right people. And he was quite good-looking in an effete sort of way.

Left to my own devices, I followed my fortune-telling friend around and watched him study the palms of our fellow passengers. He foretold romance, travel, success, happiness, health, wealth and longevity, but never predicted anything that might upset anyone. As he did not charge anything (he was, after all, on holiday) he proved to be a popular passenger throughout the voyage. Later he was to become quite famous as a palmist and mind reader, an Indian 'Cheiro', much in demand in the capitals of Europe.

The voyage lasted eighteen days, with stops for passengers and cargo at Aden, Port Said and Marseilles, in that order. It was at Port Said that Uncle Ken and his friend went ashore, to look at the sights and do some shopping.

'You stay on the ship,' Uncle Ken told me. 'Port Said isn't safe for young boys.'

He wanted the girl all to himself, of course. He couldn't have shown off with me around. His 'man of the world' manner would not have been very convincing in my presence.

The ship was due to sail again that evening and passengers had to be back on board an hour before departure. The hours passed easily enough for me as the little library kept me engrossed. If there are books around, I am never bored. Towards evening, I went up on deck and saw Uncle Ken's friend coming up the gangway; but of Uncle Ken there was no sign.

'Where's Uncle?' I asked her.

'Hasn't he returned? We got separated in a busy marketplace and I thought he'd get here before me.'

We stood at the railings and looked up and down the pier, expecting to see Uncle Ken among the other returning passengers. But he did not turn up.

'I suppose he's looking for you,' I said. 'He'll miss the boat if he doesn't hurry.'

The ship's hooter sounded. 'All aboard!' called the captain on his megaphone. The big ship moved slowly out of the harbour. We were on our way! In the distance I saw a figure that looked like Uncle Ken running along the pier, frantically waving his arms. But there was no turning back.

A few days later my aunt met me at Tilbury Dock.

'Where's your Uncle Ken?' she asked.

'He stayed behind at Port Said. He went ashore and didn't get back in time.'

'Just like Ken. And I don't suppose he has much money with him. Well, if he gets in touch we'll send him a postal order.'

But Uncle Ken failed to get in touch. He was a topic of discussion for several days, while I settled down in my aunt's house and looked for a job. At sixteen, I was working in an office, earning a modest salary and contributing towards my aunt's housekeeping expenses. There was no time to worry about Uncle Ken's whereabouts.

My readers know that I longed to return to India, but it was nearly four years before that became possible. Finally I did come home and as the train drew into Dehra's little station, I looked out of the window and saw a familiar figure on the platform. It was Uncle Ken!

He made no reference to his disappearance at Port Said, and greeted me as though we had last seen each other the previous day.

'I've hired a cycle for you,' he said. 'Feel like a ride?'

'Let me get home first, Uncle Ken. I've got all this luggage.'

The luggage was piled into a tonga, I sat on top of everything and we went clip-clopping down an avenue of familiar litchi trees (all gone now, I fear). Uncle Ken rode behind the tonga, whistling cheerfully.

'When did you get back to Dehra?' I asked.

'Oh, a couple of years ago. Sorry I missed the boat. Was the girl upset?'

'She said she'd never forgive you.'

'Oh well, I expect she's better off without me. Fine piano player. Chopin and all that stuff.'

'Did Granny send you the money to come home?'

'No, I had to take a job working as a waiter in a Greek restaurant. Then I took tourists to look at the pyramids. I'm an expert on pyramids now. Great place, Egypt. But I had to leave when they found I had no papers or permit. They put me on a boat to Aden. Stayed in Aden six months teaching English to the son of a shiekh. Shiekh's son went to England, I came back to India.'

'And what are you doing now, Uncle Ken?'

'Thinking of starting a poultry farm. Lots of space behind your Gran's house. Maybe you can help with it.'

'I couldn't save much money, Uncle.'

'We'll start in a small way. There is a big demand for eggs, you know. Everyone's into eggs—scrambled, fried, poached, boiled. Egg curry for lunch. Omelettes for dinner. Egg sandwiches for tea. How do you like your egg?'

'Fried,' I said. 'Sunny side up.'

'We shall have fried eggs for breakfast. Funny side up!'

The poultry farm never did happen, but it was good to be back in Dehra, with the prospect of limitless bicycle rides with Uncle Ken.

THE UGLY PRINCE AND THE HEARTLESS PRINCESS

In the kingdom of Malla, there was once a young prince named Kusa, who was famed for his great kindness and wisdom, but unfortunately, he was very ugly.

In spite of his ugliness, everyone in the kingdom was extremely fond of the prince, but Kusa himself was sensitive about his appearance, and when his father, King Okkaka, urged him to marry, he said, 'Don't ask me to get married. How could a beautiful princess love such an ugly fellow?'

But the king insisted, and at last Kusa grew so tired of refusing to choose a bride, he hit upon a scheme by which he hoped to free himself forever from the problem of his marriage. He was very skilful with his hands, and he fashioned a golden image, and showing the king his handiwork, he said, 'If a princess as beautiful as this image can be found for me, I will make her my bride. Otherwise I will remain single.'

Kusa felt sure that there was no princess who could compare with his statue, but the king was determined to find such a beauty, and he sent messengers far and wide.

The messengers visited many kingdoms, carrying the statue with them. Whenever they arrived at a city or a village, they asked the inhabitants whether they knew of anyone who resembled the golden image. But nowhere was such a beauty to be found until the messengers reached the kingdom of Madda.

THE UGLY PRINCE AND THE HEARTLESS PRINCESS

The King of Madda had eight lovely daughters, and the eldest of them, Pabhavati, bore an extraordinary resemblance to the golden image. When the messengers saw her, they went straight to the king and said that they had come to ask the hand of Princess Pabhavati for Prince Kusa, the son of King Okkaka.

The King of Madda knew that Okkaka was a rich and powerful king, and he was pleased at the idea of being allied to him through marriage.

'If King Okkaka will visit me,' he said, 'I will give him the hand of Princess Pabhavati for his son, Prince Kusa.'

The messengers hurried back to Malla with the good news, and King Okkaka was delighted at the outcome of their mission; but poor Kusa was dismayed.

'But, my dear Father,' he said to the king, 'how will such a beautiful princess behave when she sees how ugly I am? She will surely flee from me at once.'

'Do not worry, my son,' said King Okkaka. 'I will revive an ancient custom in order to protect you. According to this custom, a bride may not look upon the face of her husband until one year after the marriage. Therefore, for one whole year, you must only meet your bride in a darkened room.'

'But how will that help me in the end?' asked Kusa doubtfully. 'My looks will not have improved by the end of the year. She will have to see me some day.'

'True, but during that year your bride will have learned to love you so much that, when she sees you at last, you will not be ugly in her eyes!'

Prince Kusa still had his doubts, but the king was insistent and wasted no time in visiting the kingdom of Madda and returning with the beautiful Princess Pabhavati. Soon after, the marriage ceremony was performed in a darkened chamber, by order of the king.

Princess Pabhavati was surprised to discover that she was not to look upon the face of her husband for one year after the marriage had taken place.

This is a strange custom, she thought, but she accepted the condition without protest, and settled down in a magnificent suite of apartments, one room of which was always to be kept in complete darkness.

Kusa came daily to this room to visit his bride, and as his voice and manners were kind and gentle, Pabhavati soon grew to love him, although she did not get a glimpse of his face. He spent many hours playing to her upon his sitar, and she would listen to him, enthralled.

Was there ever a prince like this husband of mine?, she thought. How I long for the day when I shall see his face! Surely he must be as handsome as he is kind and wise.

All might have been well if Pabhavati had been content to wait for a year; but, after she had been married for only a month, she grew impatient and found herself constantly wondering about Prince Kusa's appearance. During the second month she could conceal her curiosity no longer. One day, when Kusa was with her in the darkened room, she said: 'Dear husband, it makes me sad that I must wait so long before I can look upon your face. I beg you to meet me in the light of day.'

'No, Pabhavati, that is impossible,' said the prince. 'I cannot disobey my father, the king. Be patient a little longer. The months will pass quickly.'

But the quality of patience was absent in the princess, and soon she began to question the maidservants and others about her husband's appearance. As she never received a clear answer, she became even more curious. Finally, she bribed one of her attendants to help her obtain a glimpse of Kusa.

One day, when the prince was due to ride through the city at the head of a procession, the waiting woman concealed the princess in a corner room of the palace, a window of which looked out upon the highway.

When the procession came by, Pabhavati hurried to the window. She heard the sound of music and shouting, and saw gay banners and garlands thrown at the feet of the elephant upon which Prince Kusa was riding in state.

'Long live Kusa, our noble prince!' cried the people on the streets.

As the elephant passed beneath the window, Pabhavati caught a glimpse of the prince's face. She shrank back in horror.

'Oh, no!' she cried. 'Can that hideous creature be my husband? No, that is not Kusa!'

Her attendant assured her that it was indeed the prince, whereupon Pabhavati decided that she would flee instantly from such an ugly husband. She demanded that an escort be provided for her return to the kingdom of Madda, declaring that she would not be bound by marriage to a husband who was so different from the man she had imagined!

King Okkaka could have forced the princess to remain in the palace, but Kusa shook his head sadly and said, 'No, let her do as she wishes.'

Then, forgetful of all the love and tenderness that she had received from Kusa, and thinking only of his ugly face, Pabhavati left the palace and returned to her father's kingdom.

Prince Kusa was terribly unhappy; but one day, the thought

occurred to him that if he were to visit Pabhavati in her own land, he might find that her attitude had changed. He changed his princely robes for simple clothes, and, taking his sitar, he set out on foot for the kingdom of Madda.

After a journey of several days, Kusa arrived one evening at the chief city of Madda.

It was midnight when he reached the royal palace. He crept beneath the walls, then began playing softly upon his sitar. He played so sweetly that the sleepers in the palace stirred and smiled in their dreams. But Pabhavati wakened with a start and tensed as she listened to the familiar music.

That is Kusa below, she thought, afraid and angry at the same time. *If my father knows that he is here, I will be forced to return to that hideous husband.*

But Kusa had no intention of appealing to the king. He would rather lose Pabhavati forever than have her return against her will. He was determined to keep his presence in the city a secret from everyone except the princess.

When morning came he went to the chief potter in the city and asked to become his apprentice.

'If I do good work for you, will you display my wares in the palace?' asked Kusa.

'Certainly,' said the potter. 'But show me what you can do.'

Kusa set to work at the potter's wheel, and the bowls he produced were so beautifully formed that the potter was delighted.

'I am sure the king will purchase such dainty bowls for his daughters,' he said, and taking some of the bowls made by Kusa, he went straight to the palace.

The King took a great fancy to the potter's new wares.

When he learned that they had been made by a new apprentice, he said, 'Give the young man a thousand gold pieces, and tell him that from now on he must work only for my daughters. Now take eight of these beautiful bowls to the princesses as my gifts to them.'

The potter did as he was told, and the king's daughters were thrilled with their presents; but Pabhavati knew in her heart that they had been fashioned by Kusa. She returned her bowl to the potter and said, 'Take this bowl back to your apprentice and tell him that it is as ugly as he is.'

When the potter passed on these remarks to Kusa, the prince sighed and thought, *how can I touch her hard heart? If I could speak to her, it might make a difference. Tomorrow I will seek service in the palace.*

He gave the potter the king's gold pieces and said goodbye; then, hearing that the palace cook needed an assistant, he presented himself at the royal kitchens.

The cook took Kusa into his service, and the prince proved to be as good a cook as he was a potter—so much so, that a dish specially prepared by him was sent straight to the king.

The king thoroughly enjoyed the dish, and when he heard that it had been prepared by the cook's new assistant, he said, 'Give him a thousand pieces of gold, and from now on let him prepare and serve all the food for myself and my daughters.'

Kusa was happy to give the king's gold pieces to the chief cook, then set to work to prepare a delicious meal.

At dinner, Pabhavati was horrified to see her husband, disguised as a cook, stagger into the banquet hall with a heavy load of dishes. He gave no sign of recognition, but the princess was angry and, staring at him with contempt, said, 'I do not care for these dishes. Bring me food that someone else has prepared.'

Her sisters protested, crying out that they had never tasted such delicious cooking. But although Kusa came day after day, serving a variety of tasty dishes, Pabhavati would not touch any of them.

At last, the prince decided that there was no way in which he could touch the heart of the princess.

Nothing that I do pleases her, he thought. *Now I must leave her forever.*

While he was preparing to leave the palace, he heard that the King of Madda was greatly troubled. The king had received news that seven kings were riding towards the city with seven armies, and that each of these kings, having heard of the beauty of Pabhavati, was anxious to make her his wife.

The king was in a quandary, because he felt sure that if he chose one of these kings as the husband of Pabhavati, the other six would attack his kingdom in revenge.

If only Pabhavati had not left her rightful husband, thought the king, *these troubles would not have arisen.*

Realizing that it was useless to spend his time in regrets, the king summoned his advisers and asked them which king he should choose for the princess.

'Not one of them alone,' declared the wise men. 'The princess has endangered the kingdom. Therefore she must suffer the consequences. She must be executed, her body divided into seven pieces, and one portion presented to each of the seven kings. Only in this way can a terrible war be avoided.'

The king was horrified by this advice from his men of wisdom; but while he was sitting alone, deep in thought, Kusa, still in the guise of a cook, came to him and said, 'Your Majesty, let me deal with these kings. Give me your army, and I will crush them or die in the attempt.'

'What!' cried the astonished king. 'Shall a cook do battle with kings?'

'If a cook knows how to fight, why not? But I must confess that I am not really a servant, but Prince Kusa, to whom you once entrusted your daughter. Although she has rejected me, I still love her, and it is only right that I should deal with these suitors.'

The king could hardly believe that it was Kusa who stood before him. He had Pabhavati brought to him, and when she admitted that the cook's apprentice was her royal husband, he cried, 'You should be ashamed, daughter, for allowing your husband to be treated as a servant in the palace.'

He dismissed Pabhavati from his presence, and begged Kusa's pardon for the way in which he had been insulted.

Kusa replied that all he wanted was freedom to deal with the seven invading kings, and the king immediately placed him at the head of an army. The fate of the kingdom lay in Kusa's hands.

The seven kings were taken by surprise when they saw Kusa and his forces advancing towards them, for they had not expected any resistance. In spite of their superior numbers, they were soon routed by an inspired force under Kusa's command. They laid down their arms and surrendered, and the prince led them as captives to the king.

'Deal with these prisoners as you will,' said Kusa.

'They are your captives,' said the king. 'It is for you to decide their fate.'

'Then,' said the prince, 'since each of these kings wishes to marry a beautiful princess, why do you not marry them all to the sisters of Pabhavati?'

The king was delighted with this solution to his problem; it would guarantee the safety of his kingdom forever. The seven kings were bowled over by the beauty and grace of Pabhavati's sisters. And the seven sisters thought their prospective husbands looked very handsome indeed.

But Pabhavati sat alone, weeping bitter tears. She now realized how heartlessly she had treated Kusa, and what a noble man and lover she had scorned.

He will never forgive me, she thought sadly.

She went to him, and threw herself at his feet, crying, 'Forgive me, my husband, and take me back, even if you decide to treat me as a slave.'

Kusa raised her gently from the ground.

'Do you really wish to return to me?' he asked. 'Look at me, Pabhavati. I am still as ugly as when you ran away from me.' Pabhavati gazed at him steadfastly, and instead of the loathing which Kusa had seen in her eyes before, he now saw only wonder and tenderness.

'You have changed!' she cried. 'You are no longer ugly!'

'No,' said Kusa. 'I haven't changed. It is you who has changed.'

THE TIGER KING'S GIFT

Long ago, in the days of the ancient Pandya kings of South India, a father and his two sons lived in a village near Madura. The father was an astrologer, but he had never become famous, and so was very poor. The elder son was called Chellan; the younger Gangan. When the time came for the father to put off his earthly body, he gave his few fields to Chellan, and a palm leaf with some words scratched on it to Gangan.

These were the words that Gangan read:

'From birth, poverty;
For ten years, captivity;
On the seashore, death.
For a little while happiness shall follow.'

'This must be my fortune,' said Gangan to himself, 'and it doesn't seem to be much of a fortune. I must have done something terrible in a former birth. But I will go as a pilgrim to Papanasam and do penance. If I can expiate my sin, I may have better luck.'

His only possession was a water jar of hammered copper, which had belonged to his grandfather. He coiled a rope round the jar, in case he needed to draw water from a well. Then he put a little rice into a bundle, said farewell to his brother, and set out.

As he journeyed, he had to pass through a great forest. Soon he had eaten all his food and drunk all the water in his jar. In the heat of the day he became very thirsty.

At last he came to an old, disused well. As he looked down into it, he could see that a winding stairway had once gone round it down to the water's edge, and that there had been four landing places at different heights down this stairway, so that those who wanted to fetch water might descend the stairway to the level of the water and fill their water pots with ease, regardless of whether the well was full, or three-quarters full, or half full or only one-quarter full.

Now the well was nearly empty. The stairway had fallen away. Gangan could not go down to fill his water jar so he uncoiled his rope, tied his jar to it and slowly let it down. To his amazement, as it was going down past the first landing place, a huge striped paw shot out and caught it, and a growling voice called out: 'Oh Lord of Charity, have mercy! The stair is fallen. I die unless you save me! Fear me not. Though King of Tigers, I will not harm you.'

Gangan was terrified at hearing a tiger speak, but his kindness overcame his fear, and with a great effort, he pulled the beast up.

The Tiger King—for it was indeed the Lord of All Tigers—bowed his head before Gangan, and reverently paced around him thrice from right to left as worshippers do round a shrine.

'Three days ago,' said the Tiger King, 'a goldsmith passed by, and I followed him. In terror he jumped down this well and fell on the fourth landing place below. He is there still. When I leaped after him I fell on the first landing place. On the third landing is a rat who jumped in when a great snake chased him. And on the second landing, above the rat, is the snake who followed him. They will all clamour for you to draw them up.

'Free the snake, by all means. He will be grateful and will not harm you. Free the rat, if you will. But do not free the goldsmith, for he cannot be trusted. Should you free him, you will surely repent of your kindness. He will do you an injury for his own profit. But remember that I will help you whenever you need me.'

Then the Tiger King bounded away into the forest.

Gangan had forgotten his thirst while he stood before the Tiger King. Now he felt it more than before, and again let down his water jar.

As it passed the second landing place on the ruined staircase, a huge snake darted out and twisted itself round the rope. 'Oh, Incarnation of Mercy, save me!' it hissed. 'Unless you help me, I must die here, for I cannot climb the sides of the well. Help me, and I will always serve you!'

Gangan's heart was again touched, and he drew up the snake. It glided round him as if he were a holy being. 'I am the Serpent King,' it said. 'I was chasing a rat. It jumped into the well and fell on the third landing below. I followed, but fell on the second landing. Then the goldsmith leaped in and fell on the fourth landing place, while the tiger fell on the top landing. You saved the Tiger King. You have saved me. You may save the rat, if you wish. But do not free the goldsmith. He is not to be trusted. He will harm you if you help him. But I will not forget you, and will come to your aid if you call upon me.'

Then the King of Snakes disappeared into the long grass of the forest.

Gangan let down his jar once more, eager to quench his thirst. But as the jar passed the third landing, the rat leaped into it.

'After the Tiger King, what is a rat?' said Gangan to himself, and pulled the jar up.

Like the tiger and the snake, the rat did reverence, and offered his services if ever they were needed. And like the tiger and the snake, he warned Gangan against the goldsmith. Then the Rat King—for he was none other—ran off into a hole among the roots of a banyan tree.

By this time, Gangan's thirst was becoming unbearable. He almost flung the water jar down the well. But again the rope was seized, and Gangan heard the goldsmith beg piteously to be hauled up.

'Unless I pull him out of the well, I shall never get any water,' groaned Gangan. 'And after all, why not help the unfortunate man?' So with a great struggle—for he was a very fat goldsmith—Gangan got him out of the well and on to the grass beside him.

The goldsmith had much to say. But before listening to him, Gangan let his jar down into the well a fifth time. And then he drank till he was satisfied.

'Friend and deliverer!' cried the goldsmith. 'Don't believe what those beasts have said about me! I live in the holy city of Tenkasi, only a day's journey north of Papanasam. Come and visit me whenever you are there. I will show you that I am not an ungrateful man.' And he took leave of Gangan and went his way.

'From birth, poverty.'

Gangan resumed his pilgrimage, begging his way to Papanasam. There he stayed many weeks, performing all the ceremonies which pilgrims should perform, bathing at the waterfall, and watching the Brahmin priests feeding the fishes in the sacred stream. He visited other shrines, going as far as Cape Comorin, the southernmost tip of India, where he bathed in the sea. Then he came back through the jungles of Travancore.

He had started on his pilgrimage with his copper water jar and nothing more. After months of wanderings, it was still the only thing he owned. The first prophecy on the palm leaf had already come true: 'From birth, poverty.'

During his wanderings Gangan had never once thought of the Tiger King and the others, but as he walked wearily along in his rags, he saw a ruined well by the roadside, and it reminded him of his wonderful adventure. And just to see if the Tiger King was genuine, he called out: 'Oh King of Tigers, let me see you!'

No sooner had he spoken than the Tiger King leaped out of the bushes, carrying in his mouth a glittering golden helmet, embedded with precious stones.

It was the helmet of King Pandya, the monarch of the land.

The king had been waylaid and killed by robbers, for the sake of the jewelled helmet; but they in turn had fallen prey to the tiger, who had walked away with the helmet.

Gangan, of course, knew nothing about all this, and when the Tiger King laid the helmet at his feet, he stood stupefied at its splendour and his own good luck.

After the Tiger King had left him, Gangan thought of the goldsmith. *He will take the jewels out of the helmet, and I will sell some of them. Others I will take home.* So he wrapped the helmet in a rag and made his way to Tenkasi.

In the Tenkasi bazaar he soon found the goldsmith's shop. When they had talked a while, Gangan uncovered the golden helmet. The goldsmith—who knew its worth far better than Gangan—gloated over it, and at once agreed to take out the jewels and sell a few so that Gangan might have some money to spend.

'Now let me examine this helmet at leisure,' said the goldsmith. 'You go to the shrines, worship, and come back. I will then tell you what your treasure is worth.'

Gangan went off to worship at the famous shrines of Tenkasi. And as soon as he had gone, the goldsmith went off to the local magistrate.

'Did not the herald of King Pandya's son come here only yesterday and announce that he would give half his kingdom to anyone who discovered his father's murderer?' he asked. 'Well, I have found the killer. He has brought the king's jewelled helmet to me this very day.'

The magistrate called his guards, and they all hurried to the goldsmith's shop and reached it just as Gangan returned from his tour of the temples.

'Here is the helmet!' exclaimed the goldsmith to the magistrate. 'And here is the villain who murdered the king to get it!'

The guards seized poor Gangan and marched him off to Madura, the capital of the Pandya kingdom, and brought him before the murdered king's son. When Gangan tried to explain about the Tiger King, the goldsmith called him a liar, and the new king had him thrown into the death cell, a deep, well-like pit, dug into the ground in a courtyard of the palace. The only entrance to it was a hole in the pavement of the courtyard. Here Gangan was left to die of hunger and thirst.

At first Gangan lay helpless where he had fallen. Then, looking around him, he found himself on a heap of bones, the bones of those who before him had died in the dungeon; and he was watched by an army of rats who were waiting to gnaw his dead body. He remembered how the Tiger King had warned him against the goldsmith, and had promised help if ever it was needed.

'I need help now,' groaned Gangan, and shouted for the Tiger King, the Snake King, and the Rat King.

For some time nothing happened. Then all the rats in the dungeon suddenly left him and began burrowing in a corner between some of the stones in the wall. Presently Gangan saw that the hole was quite large, and that many other rats were coming and going, working at the same tunnel. And then the Rat King himself came through the little passage, and he was followed by the Snake King, while a great roar from outside told Gangan that the Tiger King was there.

'We cannot get you out of this place,' said the Snake King. 'The walls are too strong. But the armies of the Rat King will bring rice cakes from the palace kitchens, and sweets from the shops in the bazaars, and rags soaked in water. They will not let you die. And from this day on the tigers and the snakes will slay tenfold, and the rats will destroy grain and cloth as never before. Before long the people will begin to complain. Then, when you hear anyone passing in front of your cell, shout: 'These disasters are the results of your ruler's injustice! But I can save you from them!' At first they will pay no attention. But after some time they will take you out, and at your word we will stop the sacking and the slaughter. And then they will honour you.'

'For ten years, captivity.'

For ten years the tigers killed. The serpents struck. The rats destroyed. And at last the people wailed, 'The gods are plaguing us.'

All the while Gangan cried out to those who came near his cell, declaring that he could save them; they thought he was a madman. So ten years passed, and the second prophecy on the palm leaf was fulfilled.

At last, the Snake King made his way into the palace and bit the king's only daughter. She was dead in a few minutes.

The king called for all the snake charmers and offered half his kingdom to any one of them who would restore his daughter to life. None of them was able to do so. Then the king's servants remembered the cries of Gangan and remarked that there was a madman in the dungeons who kept insisting that he could bring an end to all their troubles. The king at once ordered the dungeon to be opened. Ladders were let down. Men descended and found Gangan, looking more like a ghost than a man. His hair had grown so long that none could see his face. The king did not remember him, but Gangan soon reminded the king of how he had condemned him without enquiry, on the word of the goldsmith.

The king grovelled in the dust before Gangan, begged forgiveness, and entreated him to restore the dead princess to life.

'Bring me the body of the princess,' said Gangan.

Then he called on the Tiger King and the Snake King to come and give life to the princess. As soon as they entered the royal chamber, the princess was restored to life.

Glad as they were to see the princess alive, the king and his courtiers were filled with fear at the sight of the Tiger King and the Snake King. But the tiger and the snake hurt no one, and at a second prayer from Gangan, they brought life to all those they had slain.

And when Gangan made a third petition, the Tiger, the

Snake and the Rat Kings ordered their subjects to stop pillaging the Pandya kingdom, so long as the king did no further injustice.

'Let us find that treacherous goldsmith and put him in the dungeon,' said the Tiger King.

But Gangan wanted no vengeance. That very day he set out for his village to see his brother, Chellan, once more. But when he left the Pandya king's capital, he took the wrong road. After much wandering, he found himself on the seashore.

Now it happened that his brother was also making a journey in those parts, and it was their fate that they should meet by the sea. When Gangan saw his brother, his gladness was so sudden and so great that he fell down dead.

And so the third prophecy was fulfilled:

'On the seashore, death.'

Chellan, as he came along the shore road, had seen a half-ruined shrine of Pillaiyar, the elephant-headed god of good luck. Chellan was a very devout servant of Pillaiyar, and, the day being a festival day, he felt it was his duty to worship the god. But it was also his duty to perform the funeral rites for his brother.

The seashore was lonely. There was no one to help him. It would take hours to collect fuel and driftwood enough for a funeral pyre. For a while Chellan did not know what to do. But at last he took up the body and carried it to Pillaiyar's temple.

Then he addressed the god. 'This is my brother's body,' he said. 'I am unclean because I have touched it. I must go and bathe in the sea. Then I will come and worship you, and afterwards I will burn my brother's body. Meanwhile, I leave it in your care.'

Chellan left, and the god told his attendant *Ganas* (goblins) to watch over the body. These *Ganas* are inclined to be mischievous, and when the god wasn't looking, they gobbled up the body of Gangan.

When Chellan came back from bathing, he reverently worshipped Pillaiyar. He then looked for his brother's body. It was not to be found. Anxiously he demanded it of the god. Pillaiyar called on his goblins to produce it. Terrified, they confessed to what they had done.

Chellan reproached the god for the misdeeds of his attendants. And Pillaiyar felt so much pity for him that by his divine power he restored dead Gangan's body to Chellan, and brought Gangan to life again.

The two brothers then returned to King Pandya's capital, where Gangan married the princess and became king when her father died.

And so the fourth prophecy was fulfilled:

'For a little while happiness shall follow.'

But there are wise men who say that the lines of the prophecy were wrongly read and understood, and that the whole should run:

'From birth, poverty;
For ten years, captivity;
On the seashore, death for a little while;
Happiness shall follow.'

It is the last two lines that are different. And this must be the correct version, because when happiness came to Gangan it was not 'for a little while.' When the goddess of good fortune did arrive, she stayed in his palace for many, many years.

PANTHER'S MOON

I

In the entire village, he was the first to get up. Even the dog, a big hill mastiff called Sheroo, was asleep in a corner of the dark room, curled up near the cold embers of the previous night's fire. Bisnu's tousled head emerged from his blanket. He rubbed the sleep from his eyes and sat up on his haunches. Then, gathering his wits, he crawled in the direction of the loud ticking that came from the battered little clock which occupied the second most honoured place in a niche in the wall. The most honoured place belonged to a picture of Ganesha, the god of learning, who had an elephant's head and a fat boy's body.

Bringing his face close to the clock, Bisnu could just make out the hands. It was five o'clock. He had half an hour in which to get ready and leave.

He got up, in vest and underpants, and moved quietly towards the door. The soft tread of his bare feet woke Sheroo, and the big black dog rose silently and padded behind the boy. The door opened and closed, and then the boy and the dog were outside in the early dawn. The month was June, and the nights were warm, even in the Himalayan valleys; but there was fresh dew on the grass. Bisnu felt the dew beneath his feet. He took a deep breath and began walking down to the stream.

LESSONS IN FUN AND FROLIC

The sound of the stream filled the small valley. At that early hour of the morning, it was the only sound; but Bisnu was hardly conscious of it. It was a sound he lived with and took for granted. It was only when he had crossed the hill, on his way to the town—and the sound of the stream grew distant—that he really began to notice it. And it was only when the stream was too far away to be heard that he really missed its sound.

He slipped out of his underclothes, gazed for a few moments at the goose pimples rising on his flesh, and then dashed into the shallow stream. As he went further in, the cold mountain water reached his loins and navel, and he gasped with shock and pleasure. He drifted slowly with the current, swam across to a small inlet which formed a fairly deep pool and plunged into the water. Sheroo hated cold water at this early hour. Had the sun been up, he would not have hesitated to join Bisnu. Now he contented himself with sitting on a smooth rock and gazing placidly at the slim brown boy splashing about in the clear water, in the widening light of dawn.

Bisnu did not stay long in the water. There wasn't time. When he returned to the house, he found his mother up, making tea and chapattis. His sister, Puja, was still asleep. She was a little older than Bisnu, a pretty girl with large black eyes, good teeth and strong arms and legs. During the day, she helped her mother in the house and in the fields. She did not go to the school with Bisnu. But when he came home in the evenings, he would try teaching her some of the things he had learnt. Their father was dead. Bisnu, at twelve, considered himself the head of the family.

He ate two chapattis, after spreading butter-oil on them. He drank a glass of hot sweet tea. His mother gave two thick chapattis to Sheroo, and the dog wolfed them down in a few minutes. Then she wrapped two chapattis and a gourd curry in some big green leaves, and handed these to Bisnu. This was his lunch packet. His mother and Puja would take their meal afterwards.

When Bisnu was dressed, he stood with folded hands before the picture of Ganesha. Ganesha is the god who blesses all beginnings. The author who begins to write a new book, the banker who opens a new ledger, the traveller who starts on a journey, all invoke the kindly help of Ganesha. And as Bisnu made a journey every day, he never left without the goodwill of the elephant-headed god.

How, one might ask, did Ganesha get his elephant's head?

When born, he was a beautiful child. Parvati, his mother, was so proud of him that she went about showing him to everyone. Unfortunately, she made the mistake of showing the child to that envious planet, Saturn, who promptly burnt off poor Ganesha's head. Parvati in despair went to Brahma, the Creator, for a new head for her son. He had no head to give her, but advised her to search for some man or animal caught in a sinful or wrong act. Parvati wandered about until she came upon an elephant sleeping with its head the wrong way, that is, to the south. She promptly removed the elephant's head and planted it on Ganesha's shoulders, where it took root.

Bisnu knew this story. He had heard it from his mother.

Wearing a white shirt and black shorts, and a pair of worn white keds, he was ready for his long walk to school, five miles up the mountain.

His sister woke up just as he was about to leave. She pushed the hair away from her face and gave Bisnu one of her rare smiles.

LESSONS IN FUN AND FROLIC

'I hope you have not forgotten,' she said.

'Forgotten?' said Bisnu, pretending innocence. 'Is there anything I am supposed to remember?'

'Don't tease me. You promised to buy me a pair of bangles, remember? I hope you won't spend the money on sweets, as you did last time.'

'Oh, yes, your bangles,' said Bisnu. 'Girls have nothing better to do than waste money on trinkets. Now, don't lose your temper! I'll get them for you. Red and gold are the colours you want?'

'Yes, Brother,' said Puja gently, pleased that Bisnu had remembered the colours. 'And for your dinner tonight we'll make you something special. Won't we, Mother?'

'Yes. But hurry up and dress. There is some ploughing to be done today. The rains will soon be here, if the gods are kind.'

'The monsoon will be late this year,' said Bisnu. 'Mr Nautiyal, our teacher, told us so. He said it had nothing to do with the gods.'

'Be off, you are getting late,' said Puja, before Bisnu could begin an argument with his mother. She was diligently winding the old clock. It was quite light in the room. The sun would be up any minute.

Bisnu shouldered his school bag, kissed his mother, pinched his sister's cheeks and left the house. He started climbing the steep path up the mountainside. Sheroo bounded ahead; for he, too, always went with Bisnu to school.

Five miles to school. Every day, except Sunday, Bisnu walked five miles to school; and in the evening, he walked home again. There was no school in his own small village of Manjari, for the village consisted of only five families. The nearest school was at Kemptee, a small township on the bus route through the district of Garhwal. A number of boys walked to school, from distances of two or three miles; their villages were not quite as remote as Manjari. But Bisnu's village lay right at the bottom of the mountain, a drop of over two thousand feet from Kemptee. There was no proper road between the village and the town.

In Kemptee there was a school, a small mission hospital, a post office and several shops. In Manjari village there were none of these amenities. If you were sick, you stayed at home until you got well; if you were very sick, you walked or were carried to the hospital, up the five mile path. If you wanted to buy something, you went without it; but if you wanted it very badly, you could walk the five miles to Kemptee.

Manjari was known as the Five Mile Village.

Twice a week, if there were any letters, a postman came to the village. Bisnu usually passed the postman on his way to and from school.

There were other boys in Manjari village, but Bisnu was the only one who went to school. His mother would not have fussed if he had stayed at home and worked in the fields. That was what the other boys did; all except lazy Chittru, who preferred fishing in the stream or helping himself to the fruit of other people's trees. But Bisnu went to school. He went because he wanted to. No one could force him to go; and no one could stop him from going. He had set his heart on receiving a good schooling. He wanted to read and write as well as anyone in the big world, the world that seemed to begin only where the mountains ended. He felt cut off from the world in his small valley. He would rather live at the top of a mountain than at the bottom of one. That was why he liked climbing to Kemptee, it took him to the top of the mountain; and from its ridge he could look down on his own valley to the north, and on the wide endless plains stretching towards the south.

The plainsman looks to the hills for the needs of his spirit but the hill man looks to the plains for a living.

Leaving the village and the fields below him, Bisnu climbed steadily up the bare hillside, now dry and brown. By the time the sun was up, he had entered the welcome shade of an oak and rhododendron forest. Sheroo went bounding ahead, chasing squirrels and barking at langoors.

A colony of langoors lived in the oak forest. They fed on oak leaves, acorns and other green things, and usually remained in the trees, coming down to the ground only to play or bask in the sun. They were beautiful, supple-limbed animals, with black faces and silver-grey coats and long, sensitive tails. They leapt from tree to tree with great agility. The young ones wrestled on the grass like boys.

A dignified community, the langoors did not have the cheekiness or dishonest habits of the red monkeys of the plains; they did not approach dogs or humans. But they had grown used to Bisnu's comings and goings, and did not fear him. Some of the older ones would watch him quietly, a little puzzled. They did not go near the town, because the Kemptee boys threw stones at them. And anyway, the oak forest gave them all the food they required.

Emerging from the trees, Bisnu crossed a small brook. Here he stopped to drink the fresh clean water of a spring. The brook tumbled down the mountain and joined the river a little below Bisnu's village. Coming from another direction was a second path, and at the junction of the two paths Sarru was waiting for him.

Sarru came from a small village about three miles from Bisnu's and closer to the town. He had two large milk cans slung over his shoulders. Every morning he carried this milk to town, selling one can to the school and the other to Mrs Taylor, the lady doctor at the small mission hospital. He was a little older than Bisnu but not as well-built.

They hailed each other, and Sarru fell into step beside Bisnu. They often met at this spot, keeping each other company for the remaining two miles to Kemptee.

'There was a panther in our village last night,' said Sarru.

This information interested but did not excite Bisnu. Panthers were common enough in the hills and did not usually present a problem except during the winter months, when their natural prey was scarce. Then, occasionally, a panther would take to haunting the outskirts of a village, seizing a careless dog or a stray goat.

'Did you lose any animals?' asked Bisnu.

'No. It tried to get into the cowshed but the dogs set up an alarm. We drove it off.'

'It must be the same one which came around last winter. We lost a calf and two dogs in our village.'

'Wasn't that the one the shikaris wounded? I hope it hasn't become a cattle lifter.'

'It could be the same. It has a bullet in its leg. These hunters are the people who cause all the trouble. They think it's easy to shoot a panther. It would be better if they missed altogether, but they usually wound it.'

'And then the panther's too slow to catch the barking deer, and starts on our own animals.'

'We're lucky it didn't become a man-eater. Do you remember

the man-eater six years ago? I was very small then. My father told me all about it. Ten people were killed in our valley alone. What happened to it?'

'I don't know. Some say it poisoned itself when it ate the headman of another village.'

Bisnu laughed. 'No one liked that old villain. He must have been a man-eater himself in some previous existence!' They linked arms and scrambled up the stony path. Sheroo began barking and ran ahead. Someone was coming down the path.

It was Mela Ram, the postman.

II

'Any letters for us?' asked Bisnu and Sarru together.

They never received any letters but that did not stop them from asking. It was one way of finding out who had received letters.

'You're welcome to all of them,' said Mela Ram, 'if you'll carry my bag for me.'

'Not today,' said Sarru. 'We're busy today. Is there a letter from Corporal Ghanshyam for his family?'

'Yes, there is a postcard for his people. He is posted on the Ladakh border now and finds it very cold there.'

Postcards, unlike sealed letters, were considered public property and were read by everyone. The senders knew that too, and so Corporal Ghanshyam Singh was careful to mention that he expected a promotion very soon. He wanted everyone in his village to know it.

Mela Ram, complaining of sore feet, continued on his way, and the boys carried on up the path. It was eight o'clock when they reached Kemptee. Dr Taylor's outpatients were just beginning to trickle in at the hospital gate. The doctor was trying to prop up a rose creeper which had blown down during the night. She liked attending to her plants in the mornings, before starting on her patients. She found this helped her in her work. There was a lot in common between ailing plants and ailing people.

Dr Taylor was fifty, white-haired but fresh in the face and full of vitality. She had been in India for twenty years, and ten of these had been spent working in the hill regions.

She saw Bisnu coming down the road. She knew about the boy and his long walk to school and admired him for his keenness and sense of purpose. She wished there were more like him.

Bisnu greeted her shyly. Sheroo barked and put his paws up on the gate.

'Yes, there's a bone for you,' said Dr Taylor. She often put aside bones for the big black dog, for she knew that Bisnu's people could not afford to give the dog a regular diet of meat—though he did well enough on milk and chapattis.

She threw the bone over the gate and Sheroo caught it before it fell. The school bell began ringing and Bisnu broke into a run. Sheroo loped along behind the boy.

When Bisnu entered the school gate, Sheroo sat down on the grass of the compound. He would remain there until the lunch break. He knew of various ways of amusing himself during school hours and had friends among the bazaar dogs. But just then he didn't want company. He had his bone to get on with.

Mr Nautiyal, Bisnu's teacher, was in a bad mood. He was a keen rose grower and only that morning, on getting up and looking out of his bedroom window, he had been horrified to see a herd of goats in his garden. He had chased them down the road with a stick but the damage had already been done. His prize roses had all been consumed.

Mr Nautiyal had been so upset that he had gone without his breakfast. He had also cut himself whilst shaving. Thus, his mood had gone from bad to worse. Several times during the day, he brought down his ruler on the knuckles of any boy who irritated him. Bisnu was one of his best pupils. But even Bisnu irritated him by asking too many questions about a new sum which Mr Nautiyal didn't feel like explaining.

That was the kind of day it was for Mr Nautiyal. Most school teachers know similar days.

Poor Mr Nautiyal, thought Bisnu. *I wonder why he's so upset. It must be because of his pay. He doesn't get much money. But he's a good teacher. I hope he doesn't take another job.*

But after Mr Nautiyal had eaten his lunch, his mood improved (as it always did after a meal), and the rest of the day passed serenely. Armed with a bundle of homework, Bisnu came out from the school compound at four o'clock, and was immediately joined by Sheroo. He proceeded down the road in the company of several of his classfellows. But he did not linger long in the bazaar. There were five miles to walk, and he did not like to get home too late. Usually, he reached his house just as it was beginning to get dark.

Sarru had gone home long ago, and Bisnu had to make the return journey on his own. It was a good opportunity to memorize the words of an English poem he had been asked to learn.

Bisnu had reached the little brook when he remembered the bangles he had promised to buy for his sister.

'Oh, I've forgotten them again,' he said aloud. 'Now I'll catch it—and she's probably made something special for my dinner!'

Sheroo, to whom these words were addressed, paid no attention but bounded off into the oak forest. Bisnu looked around for the monkeys but they were nowhere to be seen.

Strange, he thought, *I wonder why they have disappeared.*

He was startled by a sudden sharp cry, followed by a fierce yelp. He knew at once that Sheroo was in trouble. The noise came from the bushes down the khud, into which the dog had rushed but a few seconds previously.

Bisnu jumped off the path and ran down the slope towards the bushes. There was no dog and not a sound. He whistled and called, but there was no response. Then he saw something lying on the dry grass. He picked it up. It was a portion of a dog's collar, stained with blood. It was Sheroo's collar and Sheroo's blood.

Bisnu did not search further. He knew, without a doubt, that Sheroo had been seized by a panther. No other animal could have attacked so silently and swiftly and carried off a big dog without a struggle. Sheroo was dead—must have been dead within seconds of being caught and flung into the air. Bisnu knew the danger that lay in wait for him if he followed the blood trail through the trees. The panther would attack anyone who interfered with its meal.

With tears starting in his eyes, Bisnu carried on down the path to the village. His fingers still clutched the little bit of bloodstained collar that was all that was left to him of his dog.

III

Bisnu was not a very sentimental boy, but he sorrowed for his dog who had been his companion on many a hike into the hills and forests. He did not sleep that night, but turned restlessly from side to side moaning softly. After some time he felt Puja's hand on his head. She began stroking his brow. He took her hand in his own and the clasp of her rough, warm familiar hand gave him a feeling of comfort and security.

Next morning, when he went down to the stream to bathe, he missed the presence of his dog. He did not stay long in the water. It wasn't as much fun when there was no Sheroo to watch him.

When Bisnu's mother gave him his food, she told him to be careful and hurry home that evening. A panther, even if it is only a cowardly lifter of sheep or dogs, is not to be trifled with. And this particular panther had shown some daring by seizing the dog even before it was dark.

Still, there was no question of staying away from school. If Bisnu remained at home every time a panther put in an appearance, he might as well stop going to school altogether.

He set off even earlier than usual and reached the meeting of the paths long before Sarru. He did not wait for his friend, because he did not feel like talking about the loss of his dog. It was not the day for the postman, and so Bisnu reached Kemptee without meeting anyone on the way. He tried creeping past the hospital gate unnoticed, but Dr Taylor saw him and the first thing she said was: 'Where's Sheroo? I've got something for him.'

When Dr Taylor saw the boy's face, she knew at once that something was wrong.

'What is it, Bisnu?' she asked. She looked quickly up and down the road. 'Is it Sheroo?'

He nodded gravely.

'A panther took him,' he said.

'In the village?'

'No, while we were walking home through the forest. I did not see anything—but I heard.'

Dr Taylor knew that there was nothing she could say that would console him, and she tried to conceal the bone which she had brought out for the dog, but Bisnu noticed her hiding it behind her back and the tears welled up in his eyes. He turned away and began running down the road.

His schoolfellows noticed Sheroo's absence and questioned Bisnu. He had to tell them everything. They were full of sympathy, but they were also quite thrilled at what had happened and kept pestering Bisnu for all the details. There was a lot of noise in the classroom, and Mr Nautiyal had to call for order. When he learnt what had happened, he patted Bisnu on the head and told him that he need not attend school for the rest of the day. But Bisnu did not want to go home. After school, he got into a fight with one of the boys, and that helped him forget.

IV

The panther that plunged the village into an atmosphere of gloom and terror may not have been the same panther that took Sheroo. There was no way of knowing, and it would have made no difference, because the panther that came by night and struck at the people of Manjari was that most feared of wild creatures, a man-eater.

Nine-year-old Sanjay, son of Kalam Singh, was the first child to be attacked by the panther.

Kalam Singh's house was the last in the village and nearest the stream. Like the other houses, it was quite small, just a room above and a stable below, with steps leading up from outside the house. He lived there with his wife, two sons (Sanjay was the youngest) and little daughter Basanti who had just turned three.

Sanjay had brought his father's cows home after grazing them on the hillside in the company of other children. He had also brought home an edible wild plant, which his mother cooked into a tasty dish for their evening meal. They had their food at dusk, sitting on the floor of their single room, and soon after, settled down for the night. Sanjay curled up in his favourite spot, with his head near the door, where he got a little fresh air. As the nights were warm, the door was usually left a little ajar. Sanjay's mother piled ash on the embers of the fire and the family was soon asleep.

No one heard the stealthy padding of a panther approaching the door, pushing it wide open. But suddenly there were sounds of a frantic struggle, and Sanjay's stifled cries were mixed with the grunts of the panther. Kalam Singh leapt to his feet with a shout. The panther had dragged Sanjay out of the door and was pulling him down the steps, when Kalam Singh started battering at the animal with a large stone. The rest of the family screamed in terror, rousing the entire village. A number of men came to Kalam Singh's assistance, and the panther was driven off. But Sanjay lay unconscious.

Someone brought a lantern and the boy's mother screamed when she saw her small son with his head lying in a pool of blood. It looked as if the side of his head had been eaten off by the panther. But he was still alive, and as Kalam Singh plastered ash on the boy's head to stop the bleeding, he found that though the scalp had been torn off one side of the head, the bare bone was smooth and unbroken.

'He won't live through the night,' said a neighbour. 'We'll have to carry him down to the river in the morning.'

The dead were always cremated on the banks of a small river which flowed past Manjari village.

Suddenly the panther, still prowling about the village, called out in rage and frustration, and the villagers rushed to their homes in panic and barricaded themselves in for the night.

Sanjay's mother sat by the boy for the rest of the night, weeping and watching. Towards dawn he started to moan and show signs of coming round. At this sign of returning consciousness, Kalam Singh rose determinedly and looked around for his stick.

He told his elder son to remain behind with the mother and daughter, as he was going to take Sanjay to Dr Taylor at the hospital.

'See, he is moaning and in pain,' said Kalam Singh. 'That means he has a chance to live if he can be treated at once.'

With a stout stick in his hand, and Sanjay on his back, Kalam Singh set off on the two miles of hard mountain track to the hospital at Kemptee. His son, a bloodstained cloth around his head, was moaning but still unconscious. When at last Kalam Singh climbed up through the last fields below the hospital, he asked for the doctor and stammered out an account of what had happened.

It was a terrible injury, as Dr Taylor discovered. The bone over almost one-third of the head was bare and the scalp was torn all round. As the father told his story, the doctor cleaned and dressed the wound, and then gave Sanjay a shot of penicillin to prevent sepsis. Later, Kalam Singh carried the boy home again.

V

After this, the panther went away for some time. But the people of Manjari could not be sure of its whereabouts. They kept to their houses after dark and shut their doors. Bisnu had to stop going to school, because there was no one to accompany him and it was dangerous to go alone. This worried him, because his final exam was only a few weeks off and he would be missing important classwork. When he wasn't in the fields, helping with the sowing of rice and maize, he would be sitting in the shade of a chestnut tree, going through his well-thumbed second-hand school books. He had no other reading, except for a copy of the Ramayana and a Hindi translation of *Alice's Adventures in Wonderland*. These were well-preserved, read only in fits and starts, and usually kept locked in his mother's old tin trunk.

Sanjay had nightmares for several nights and woke up screaming. But with the resilience of youth, he quickly recovered. At the end of the week he was able to walk to the hospital, though his father always accompanied him. Even a desperate panther will hesitate to attack a party of two. Sanjay, with his thin little face and huge bandaged head, looked a pathetic figure, but he was getting better and the wound looked healthy.

Bisnu often went to see him, and the two boys spent long hours together near the stream. Sometimes Chittru would join them, and they would try catching fish with a home-made net. They were often successful in taking home one or two mountain trout. Sometimes, Bisnu and Chittru wrestled in the shallow water or on the grassy banks of the stream. Chittru was a chubby boy with a broad chest, strong legs and thighs, and when he used his weight he got Bisnu under him. But Bisnu was hard and wiry and had very strong wrists and fingers. When he had Chittru in a vice, the bigger boy would cry out and give up the struggle. Sanjay could not join in these games.

He had never been a very strong boy and he needed plenty of rest if his wounds were to heal well.

The panther had not been seen for over a week, and the people of Manjari were beginning to hope that it might have moved on over the mountain or further down the valley.

'I think I can start going to school again,' said Bisnu. 'The panther has gone away.'

'Don't be too sure,' said Puja. 'The moon is full these days and perhaps it is only being cautious.'

'Wait a few days,' said their mother. 'It is better to wait. Perhaps you could go the day after tomorrow when Sanjay goes to the hospital with his father. Then you will not be alone.'

And so, two days later, Bisnu went up to Kemptee with Sanjay and Kalam Singh. Sanjay's wound had almost healed over. Little islets of flesh had grown over the bone. Dr Taylor told him that he need come to see her only once a fortnight, instead of every third day.

Bisnu went to his school, and was given a warm welcome by his friends and by Mr Nautiyal.

'You'll have to work hard,' said his teacher. 'You have to catch up with the others. If you like, I can give you some extra time after classes.'

'Thank you, sir, but it will make me late,' said Bisnu. 'I must get home before it is dark, otherwise my mother will worry. I think the panther has gone but nothing is certain.'

'Well, you mustn't take risks. Do your best, Bisnu. Work hard and you'll soon catch up with your lessons.'

Sanjay and Kalam Singh were waiting for him outside the school. Together they took the path down to Manjari, passing the postman on the way. Mela Ram said he had heard that the panther was in another district and that there was nothing to fear. He was on his rounds again.

Nothing happened on the way. The langoors were back in their favourite part of the forest. Bisnu got home just as the kerosene lamp was being lit. Puja met him at the door with a winsome smile.

'Did you get the bangles?' she asked.

But Bisnu had forgotten again.

VI

There had been a thunderstorm and some rain—a short, sharp shower which gave the villagers hope that the monsoon would arrive on time. It brought out the thunder lilies—pink, crocus-like flowers which sprang up on the hillsides immediately after a summer shower.

Bisnu, on his way home from school, was caught in the rain. He knew the shower would not last, so he took shelter in a small cave and, to pass the time, began doing sums, scratching figures in the damp earth with the end of a stick.

When the rain stopped, he came out from the cave and continued down the path. He wasn't in a hurry. The rain had made everything smell fresh and good. The scent from fallen pine needles rose from wet earth. The leaves of the oak trees had been washed clean and a light breeze turned them about, showing their silver undersides. The birds, refreshed and high-spirited, set up a terrific noise. The worst offenders were the yellow-bottomed bulbuls who squabbled and fought in the blackberry bushes. A barbet, high up in the branches of a deodar, set up its querulous, plaintive call. And a flock of bright green parrots came swooping down the hill to settle in a wild plum tree and feast on the unripe fruit. The langoors, too, had been revived by the rain. They leapt friskily from tree to tree greeting Bisnu with little grunts.

He was almost out of the oak forest when he heard a faint bleating. Presently, a little goat came stumbling up the path towards him. The kid was far from home and must have strayed from the rest of the herd. But it was not yet conscious of being lost. It came to Bisnu with a hop, skip and a jump and started nuzzling against his legs like a cat.

'I wonder who you belong to,' mused Bisnu, stroking the little creature. 'You'd better come home with me until someone claims you.'

He didn't have to take the kid in his arms. It was used to humans and followed close at his heels. Now that darkness was coming on, Bisnu walked a little faster.

He had not gone very far when he heard the sawing grunt of a panther.

The sound came from the hill to the right, and Bisnu judged the distance to be anything from 100 to 200 yards. He hesitated on the path, wondering what to do. Then he picked the kid up in his arms and hurried on in the direction of home and safety.

The panther called again, much closer now. If it was an ordinary panther, it would go away on finding that the kid was with Bisnu. If it was the man-eater, it would not hesitate to attack the boy, for no man-eater fears a human. There was no time to lose and there did not seem much point in running. Bisnu looked up and down the hillside. The forest was far behind him and there were only a few trees in his vicinity. He chose a spruce.

The branches of the Himalayan spruce are very brittle and snap easily beneath a heavy weight. They were strong enough to support Bisnu's light frame. It was unlikely they would take the weight of a full-grown panther. At least that was what Bisnu hoped.

Holding the kid with one arm, Bisnu gripped a low branch and swung himself up into the tree. He was a good climber. Slowly but confidently he climbed halfway up the tree, until he was about twelve feet above the ground. He couldn't go any higher without risking a fall.

He had barely settled himself in the crook of a branch when the panther came into the open, running into the clearing at a brisk trot. This was no stealthy approach, no wary stalking of its prey. It was the man-eater, all right. Bisnu felt a cold shiver run down his spine. He felt a little sick.

The panther stood in the clearing with a slight thrusting forward of the head. This gave it the appearance of gazing intently and rather short-sightedly at some invisible object in the clearing. But there is nothing short-sighted about a panther's vision. Its sight and hearing are acute.

Bisnu remained motionless in the tree and sent up a prayer to all the gods he could think of. But the kid began bleating. The panther looked up and gave its deep-throated, rasping grunt—a fearsome sound, calculated to strike terror in any treeborne animal. Many a monkey, petrified by a panther's roar, has fallen from its perch to make a meal for Mr Spots. The man-eater was trying the same technique on Bisnu. But though the boy was trembling with fright, he clung firmly to the base of the spruce tree.

The panther did not make any attempt to leap into the tree. Perhaps, it knew instinctively that this was not the type of tree that it could climb. Instead, it described a semicircle round the tree, keeping its face turned towards Bisnu. Then it disappeared into the bushes.

The man-eater was cunning. It hoped to put the boy off his guard, perhaps entice him down from the tree. For, a few seconds later, with a half-humorous growl, it rushed back into the clearing and then stopped, staring up at the boy in some surprise. The panther was getting frustrated. It snarled, and putting its forefeet up against the tree trunk began scratching at the bark in the manner of an ordinary domestic cat. The tree shook at each thud of the beast's paw.

Bisnu began shouting for help.

The moon had not yet come up. Down in Manjari village, Bisnu's mother and sister stood in their lighted doorway, gazing anxiously up the pathway. Every now and then, Puja would turn to take a look at the small clock.

Sanjay's father appeared in a field below. He had a kerosene lantern in his hand.

'Sister, isn't your boy home as yet?' he asked.

'No, he hasn't arrived. We are very worried. He should have been home an hour ago. Do you think the panther will be about tonight? There's going to be a moon.'

'True, but it will be dark for another hour. I will fetch the other menfolk, and we will go up the mountain for your boy. There may have been a landslide during the rain. Perhaps the path has been washed away.'

'Thank you, brother. But arm yourselves, just in case the panther is about.'

'I will take my spear,' said Kalam Singh. 'I have sworn to spear that devil when I find him. There is some evil spirit dwelling in the beast and it must be destroyed!'

'I am coming with you,' said Puja.

'No, you cannot go,' said her mother. 'It's bad enough that Bisnu is in danger. You stay at home with me. This is work for men.'

'I shall be safe with them,' insisted Puja. 'I am going, Mother!' And she jumped down the embankment into the field and followed Sanjay's father through the village.

Ten minutes later, two men armed with axes had joined Kalam Singh in the courtyard of his house, and the small party moved silently and swiftly up the mountain path. Puja walked in the middle of the group, holding the lantern. As soon as the village lights were hidden by a shoulder of the hill, the men began to shout—both to frighten the panther, if it was about, and to give themselves courage.

Bisnu's mother closed the front door and turned to the image of Ganesha, the god for comfort and help.

Bisnu's calls were carried on the wind, and Puja and the men heard him while they were still half a mile away. Their own shouts increased in volume and, hearing their voices, Bisnu felt strength return to his shaking limbs. Emboldened by the approach of his own people, he began shouting insults at the snarling panther, then throwing twigs and small branches at the enraged animal. The kid added its bleats to the boy's shouts, the birds took up the chorus. The langoors squealed and grunted, the searchers shouted themselves hoarse, and the panther howled with rage. The forest had never before been so noisy.

As the search party drew near, they could hear the panther's savage snarls, and hurried, fearing that perhaps Bisnu had been seized. Puja began to run.

'Don't rush ahead, girl,' said Kalam Singh. 'Stay between us.'

The panther, now aware of the approaching humans, stood still in the middle of the clearing, head thrust forward in a familiar stance. There seemed too many men for one panther. When the animal saw the light of the lantern dancing between the trees, it turned, snarled defiance and hate, and without another look at the boy in the tree, disappeared into the bushes. It was not yet ready for a showdown.

VII

Nobody turned up to claim the little goat, so Bisnu kept it. A goat was a poor substitute for a dog, but, like Mary's lamb, it followed Bisnu wherever he went, and the boy couldn't help being touched by its devotion. He took it down to the stream, where it would skip about in the shallows and nibble the sweet grass that grew on the banks.

As for the panther, frustrated in its attempt on Bisnu's life, it did not wait long before attacking another human.

It was Chittru who came running down the path one afternoon, bubbling excitedly about the panther and the postman.

Chittru, deeming it safe to gather ripe bilberries in the daytime, had walked about half a mile up the path from the village, when he had stumbled across Mela Ram's mailbag lying on the ground. Of the postman himself there was no sign. But a trail of blood led through the bushes.

Once again, a party of men headed by Kalam Singh and accompanied by Bisnu and Chittru, went out to look for the postman. But though they found Mela Ram's bloodstained clothes, they could not find his body. The panther had made no mistake this time.

It was to be several weeks before Manjari had a new postman.

A few days after Mela Ram's disappearance, an old woman was sleeping with her head near the open door of her house. She had been advised to sleep inside with the door closed, but the nights were hot and anyway the old woman was a little deaf, and in the middle of the night, an hour before moonrise, the panther seized her by the throat. Her strangled cry woke her grown-up son, and all the men in the village woke up at his shouts and came running.

The panther dragged the old woman out of the house and down the steps, but left her when the men approached with their axes and spears, and made off into the bushes. The old woman was still alive, and the men made a rough stretcher of bamboo and vines and started carrying her up the path. But they had not gone far when she began to cough, and because of her terrible throat wounds, her lungs collapsed and she died.

It was the 'dark of the month'—the week of the new moon when nights are darkest.

Bisnu, closing the front door and lighting the kerosene lantern, said, 'I wonder where that panther is tonight!'

The panther was busy in another village: Sarru's village.

A woman and her daughter had been out in the evening bedding the cattle down in the stable. The girl had gone into the house and the woman was following. As she bent down to go in at the low door, the panther sprang from the bushes. Fortunately, one of its paws hit the doorpost and broke the force of the attack, or the woman would have been killed.

When she cried out, the men came round shouting and the panther slunk off. The woman had deep scratches on her back and was badly shocked.

The next day, a small party of villagers presented themselves in front of the magistrate's office at Kemptee and demanded that something be done about the panther. But the magistrate was away on tour, and there was no one else in Kemptee who had a gun. Mr Nautiyal met the villagers and promised to write to a well-known shikari, but said that it would be at least a fortnight before the shikari would be able to come.

Bisnu was fretting because he could not go to school. Most boys would be only too happy to miss school, but when you are living in a remote village in the mountains and having an education is the only way of seeing the world, you look forward to going to school, even if it is five miles from home. Bisnu's exams were only two weeks off, and he didn't want to remain in the same class while the others were promoted. Besides, he knew he could pass even though he had missed a number of lessons. But he had to sit for the exams. He couldn't miss them.

'Cheer up, Bhaiya,' said Puja, as they sat drinking glasses of hot tea after their evening meal. 'The panther may go away once the rains break.'

'Even the rains are late this year,' said Bisnu. 'It's so hot and dry. Can't we open the door?'

'And be dragged down the steps by the panther?' said his mother. 'It isn't safe to have the window open, let alone the door.' And she went to the small window—through which a cat would have found difficulty in passing—and bolted it firmly.

With a sigh of resignation, Bisnu threw off all his clothes

except his underwear and stretched himself out on the earthen floor.

'We will be rid of the beast soon,' said his mother. 'I know it in my heart. Our prayers will be heard, and you shall go to school and pass your exams.'

To cheer up her children, she told them a humorous story which had been handed down to her by her grandmother. It was all about a tiger, a panther and a bear, the three of whom were made to feel very foolish by a thief hiding in the hollow trunk of a banyan tree. Bisnu was sleepy and did not listen very attentively. He dropped off to sleep before the story was finished.

When he woke, it was dark and his mother and sister were asleep on the cot. He wondered what it was that had woken him. He could hear his sister's easy breathing and the steady ticking of the clock. Far away an owl hooted—an unlucky sign, his mother would have said; but she was asleep and Bisnu was not superstitious.

And then he heard something scratching at the door, and the hair on his head felt tight and prickly. It was like a cat scratching, only louder. The door creaked a little whenever it felt the impact of the paw—a heavy paw, as Bisnu could tell from the dull sound it made.

'It's the panther,' he muttered under his breath, sitting up on the hard floor.

The door, he felt, was strong enough to resist the panther's weight. And if he set up an alarm, he could rouse the village. But the middle of the night was no time for the bravest of men to tackle a panther.

In a corner of the room stood a long bamboo stick with a sharp knife tied to one end, which Bisnu sometimes used for spearing fish. Crawling on all fours across the room, he grasped the home-made spear, and then scrambling on to a cupboard, he drew level with the skylight window. He could get his head and shoulders through the window.

'What are you doing up there?' said Puja, who had woken up at the sound of Bisnu shuffling about the room.

'Be quiet,' said Bisnu. 'You'll wake Mother.'

Their mother was awake by now. 'Come down from there, Bisnu. I can hear a noise outside.'

'Don't worry,' said Bisnu, who found himself looking down on the wriggling animal which was trying to get its paw in under the door. With his mother and Puja awake, there was no time to lose. He had got the spear through the window, and though he could not manoeuvre it so as to strike the panther's head, he brought the sharp end down with considerable force on the animal's rump.

With a roar of pain and rage the man-eater leapt down from the steps and disappeared into the darkness. It did not pause to see what had struck it. Certain that no human could have come upon it in that fashion, it ran fearfully to its lair, howling until the pain subsided.

VIII

A panther is an enigma. There are occasions when it proves himself to be the most cunning animal under the sun, and yet the very next day it will walk into an obvious trap that no self-respecting jackal would ever go near. One day a panther will prove itself to be a complete coward and run like a hare from a couple of dogs, and the very next it will dash in amongst half a dozen men sitting round a camp fire and inflict terrible injuries on them.

It is not often that a panther is taken by surprise, as its power of sight and hearing are very acute. It is a master at the art of camouflage, and its spotted coat is admirably suited for the purpose. It does not need heavy jungle to hide in. A couple of bushes and the light and shade from surrounding trees are enough to make it almost invisible.

Because the Manjari panther had been fooled by Bisnu, it did not mean that it was a stupid panther. It simply meant that it had been a little careless. And Bisnu and Puja, growing in confidence since their midnight encounter with the animal, became a little careless themselves.

Puja was hoeing the last field above the house and Bisnu, at the other end of the same field, was chopping up several branches of green oak, prior to leaving the wood to dry in the loft. It was late afternoon and the descending sun glinted in patches on the small river. It was a time of day when only the most desperate and daring of man-eaters would be likely to show itself.

Pausing for a moment to wipe the sweat from his brow, Bisnu glanced up at the hillside, and his eye caught sight of a rock on the brown of the hill which seemed unfamiliar to him. Just as he was about to look elsewhere, the round rock began to grow and then alter its shape, and Bisnu watching in fascination was at last able to make out the head and forequarters of the panther. It looked enormous from the angle at which he saw it, and for a moment he thought it was a tiger. But Bisnu knew instinctively that it was the man-eater.

Slowly, the wary beast pulled itself to its feet and began to walk round the side of the great rock. For a second it disappeared and Bisnu wondered if it had gone away. Then it reappeared and the boy was all excitement again. Very slowly and silently the panther walked across the face of the rock until it was in direct line with the corner of the field where Puja was working.

With a thrill of horror Bisnu realised that the panther was stalking his sister. He shook himself free from the spell which had woven itself round him and shouting hoarsely ran forward.

'Run, Puja, run!' he called. 'It's on the hill above you!'

Puja turned to see what Bisnu was shouting about. She saw him gesticulate to the hill behind her, looked up just in time to see the panther crouching for his spring.

With great presence of mind, she leapt down the banking of the field and tumbled into an irrigation ditch.

The springing panther missed its prey, lost its foothold on the slippery shale banking and somersaulted into the ditch a few feet away from Puja. Before the animal could recover from its surprise, Bisnu was dashing down the slope, swinging his axe and shouting, *'Maro, maro!* (Kill, kill!)'

Two men came running across the field. They, too, were armed with axes. Together with Bisnu they made a half-circle around the snarling animal, which turned at bay and plunged at them in order to get away. Puja wriggled along the ditch on her stomach. The men aimed their axes at the panther's head, and Bisnu had the satisfaction of getting in a well-aimed blow between the eyes. The animal then charged straight at one of the men, knocked him over and tried to get at his throat. Just then Sanjay's father arrived with his long spear. He plunged the end of the spear into the panther's neck.

The panther left its victim and ran into the bushes, dragging the spear through the grass and leaving a trail of blood on the ground. The men followed cautiously—all except the man who had been wounded and who lay on the ground, while Puja and the other womenfolk rushed up to help him.

The panther had made for the bed of the stream and Bisnu, Sanjay's father and their companion were able to follow it quite easily. The water was red where the panther had crossed the stream, and the rocks were stained with blood. After they had gone downstream for about a furlong, they found the panther lying still on its side at the edge of the water. It was mortally wounded, but it continued to wave its tail like an angry cat. Then, even the tail lay still.

'It is dead,' said Bisnu. 'It will not trouble us again in this body.'

'Let us be certain,' said Sanjay's father, and he bent down and pulled the panther's tail.

There was no response.

'It is dead,' said Kalam Singh. 'No panther would suffer such an insult were it alive!'

They cut down a long piece of thick bamboo and tied the panther to it by its feet. Then, with their enemy hanging upside down from the bamboo pole, they started back for the village.

'There will be a feast at my house tonight,' said Kalam Singh. 'Everyone in the village must come. And tomorrow we will visit all the villages in the valley and show them the dead panther, so that they may move about again without fear.'

'We can sell the skin in Kemptee,' said their companion. 'It will fetch a good price.'

'But the claws we will give to Bisnu,' said Kalam Singh, putting his arm around the boy's shoulders. 'He has done a man's work today. He deserves the claws.'

A panther's or tiger's claws are considered to be lucky charms.

'I will take only three claws,' said Bisnu. 'One each for my mother and sister, and one for myself. You may give the others to Sanjay and Chittru and the smaller children.'

As the sun set, a big fire was lit in the middle of the village of Manjari and the people gathered round it, singing and laughing. Kalam Singh killed his fattest goat and there was meat for everyone.

IX

Bisnu was on his way home. He had just handed in his first paper, arithmetic, which he had found quite easy. Tomorrow it would be algebra, and when he got home he would have to practice square roots and cube roots and fractional coefficients.

Mr Nautiyal and the entire class had been happy that he had been able to sit for the exams. He was also a hero to them for his part in killing the panther. The story had spread through the villages with the rapidity of a forest fire, a fire which was now raging in Kemptee town.

When he walked past the hospital, he was whistling cheerfully. Dr Taylor waved to him from the veranda steps.

'How is Sanjay now?' she asked.

'He is well,' said Bisnu.

'And your mother and sister?'

'They are well,' said Bisnu.

'Are you going to get yourself a new dog?'

'I am thinking about it,' said Bisnu. 'At present I have a baby goat—I am teaching it to swim!'

He started down the path to the valley. Dark clouds had gathered and there was a rumble of thunder. A storm was imminent.

'Wait for me!' shouted Sarru, running down the path behind Bisnu, his milk pails clanging against each other. He fell into step beside Bisnu.

'Well, I hope we don't have any more man-eaters for some time,' he said. 'I've lost a lot of money by not being able to take milk up to Kemptee.'

'We should be safe as long as a shikari doesn't wound another panther. There was an old bullet wound in the man-eater's thigh. That's why it couldn't hunt in the forest. The deer were too fast for it.'

'Is there a new postman yet?'

'He starts tomorrow. A cousin of Mela Ram's.'

When they reached the parting of their ways it had begun to rain a little.

'I must hurry,' said Sarru. 'It's going to get heavier any minute.' 'I feel like getting wet,' said Bisnu. 'This time it's the monsoon, I'm sure.'

Bisnu entered the forest on his own, and at the same time the rain came down in heavy opaque sheets. The trees shook in the wind, the langoors chattered with excitement.

It was still pouring when Bisnu emerged from the forest, drenched to the skin. But the rain stopped suddenly, just as the village of Manjari came in view. The sun appeared through a rift in the clouds. The leaves and the grass gave out a sweet, fresh smell.

Bisnu could see his mother and sister in the field transplanting the rice seedlings. The menfolk were driving the yoked oxen through the thin mud of the fields, while the children hung on to the oxen's tails, standing on the plain wooden harrows and with weird cries and shouts sending the animals almost at a gallop along the narrow terraces.

Bisnu felt the urge to be with them, working in the fields. He ran down the path, his feet falling softly on the wet earth. Puja saw him coming and waved to him. She met him at the edge of the field.

'How did you find your paper today?' she asked.

'Oh, it was easy.' Bisnu slipped his hand into hers and together they walked across the field. Puja felt something smooth and hard against her fingers, and before she could see what Bisnu was doing, he had slipped a pair of bangles over her wrist.

'I remembered,' he said, with a sense of achievement. Puja looked at the bangles and burst out: 'But they are blue, Bhai, and I wanted red and gold bangles!' And then, when she saw him looking crestfallen, she hurried on: 'But they are very pretty, and you did remember... Actually, they're just as nice as red and gold bangles! Come into the house when you are ready. I have made something special for you.'

'I am coming,' said Bisnu, turning towards the house. 'You don't know how hungry a man gets, walking five miles to reach home!'

A TIGER IN THE HOUSE

Timothy, the tiger cub, was discovered by Grandfather on a hunting expedition in the Terai jungle near Dehra.

Grandfather was no shikari, but as he knew the forests of the Siwalik hills better than most people, he was persuaded to accompany the party—it consisted of several Very Important Persons from Delhi—to advise on the terrain and the direction the beaters should take once a tiger had been spotted.

The camp itself was sumptuous—seven large tents (one for each shikari), a dining tent and a number of servants' tents. The dinner was very good, as Grandfather admitted afterwards; it was not often that one saw hot-water plates, finger glasses and seven or eight courses in a tent in the jungle! But that was how things were done in the days of the viceroys… There were also some fifteen elephants, four of them with howdahs for the shikaris, and the others specially trained for taking part in the beat.

The sportsmen never saw a tiger, nor did they shoot anything else, though they saw a number of deer, peacock and wild boar. They were giving up all hope of finding a tiger and were beginning to shoot at jackals, when Grandfather, strolling down the forest path at some distance from the rest of the party, discovered a little tiger about eighteen inches long, hiding among the intricate roots of a banyan tree. Grandfather picked him up and brought him home after the camp had broken up. He had the distinction of being the only member of the party to have bagged any game, dead or alive.

At first the tiger cub, who was named Timothy by Grandmother, was brought up entirely on milk given to him in a feeding bottle by our cook, Mahmoud. But the milk proved too rich for him, and he was put on a diet of raw mutton and cod liver oil, to be followed later by a more tempting diet of pigeons and rabbits.

Timothy was provided with two companions—Toto the monkey, who was bold enough to pull the young tiger by the tail, and then climb up the curtains if Timothy lost his temper; and a small mongrel puppy, found on the road by Grandfather.

At first Timothy appeared to be quite afraid of the puppy and darted back with a spring if it came too near. He would make absurd dashes at it with his large forepaws and then retreat to a ridiculously safe distance. Finally, he allowed the puppy to crawl on his back and rest there!

One of Timothy's favourite amusements was to stalk anyone who would play with him, and so, when I came to live with Grandfather, I became one of the tiger's favourites. With a crafty look in his glittering eyes, and his body crouching, he would creep closer and closer to me, suddenly making a dash for my feet, rolling over on his back and kicking with delight, and pretending to bite my ankles.

He was by this time the size of a full-grown retriever, and when I took him out for walks, people on the road would give us a wide berth. When he pulled hard on his chain, I had difficulty in keeping up with him. His favourite place in the house was the drawing room, and he would make himself comfortable on the long sofa, reclining there with great dignity and snarling at anybody who tried to get him off.

Timothy had clean habits, and would scrub his face with his paws exactly like a cat. At night, he slept in the cook's quarters and was always delighted at being let out by him in the morning.

'One of these days,' declared Grandmother in her prophetic manner, 'we are going to find Timothy sitting on Mahmoud's bed, and no sign of the cook except his clothes and shoes!'

Of course, it never came to that, but when Timothy was about six months old a change came over him; he grew steadily less friendly. When out for a walk with me, he would try to steal away to stalk a cat or someone's pet Pekingese. Sometimes at night we would hear frenzied cackling from the poultry house, and in the morning there would be feathers lying all over the veranda. Timothy had to be chained up more often. And, finally, when he began to stalk Mahmoud about the house with what looked like villainous intent, Grandfather decided it was time to transfer him to a zoo.

The nearest zoo was at Lucknow, two hundred miles away. Reserving a first-class compartment for himself and Timothy—no one would share a compartment with them—Grandfather took him to Lucknow where the zoo authorities were only too glad to receive as a gift a well-fed and fairly civilized tiger.

About six months later, when my grandparents were visiting relatives in Lucknow, Grandfather took the opportunity of calling at the zoo to see how Timothy was getting on. I was not there to accompany him, but I heard all about it when he returned to Dehra.

Arriving at the zoo, Grandfather made straight for the

particular cage in which Timothy had been interned. The tiger was there, crouched in a corner, full-grown and with a magnificent striped coat.

'Hello, Timothy!' said Grandfather and, climbing the railing with ease, he put his arm through the bars of the cage.

The tiger approached the bars and allowed Grandfather to put both hands around his head. Grandfather stroked the tiger's forehead and tickled his ear, and, whenever he growled, smacked him across the mouth, which was his old way of keeping him quiet.

He licked Grandfather's hands and only sprang away when a leopard in the next cage snarled at him. Grandfather 'shooed' the leopard away and the tiger returned to lick his hands; but every now and then the leopard would rush at the bars and the tiger would slink back to his corner.

A number of people had gathered to watch the reunion when a keeper pushed his way through the crowd and asked Grandfather what he was doing.

'I'm talking to Timothy,' said Grandfather. 'Weren't you here when I gave him to the zoo six months ago?'

'I haven't been here very long,' said the surprised keeper. 'Please continue your conversation. But I have never been able to touch him myself, he is always very bad tempered.'

'Why don't you put him somewhere else?' suggested Grandfather. 'That leopard keeps frightening him. I'll go and see the superintendent about it.'

Grandfather went in search of the superintendent of the zoo, but found that he had gone home early; and so, after wandering about the zoo for a little while, he returned to Timothy's cage to say goodbye. It was beginning to get dark.

He had been stroking and slapping Timothy for about five minutes when he found another keeper observing him with some alarm. Grandfather recognized him as the keeper who had been there when Timothy had first come to the zoo.

'*You* remember me,' said Grandfather. 'Now why don't you transfer Timothy to another cage, away from this stupid leopard?'

'But—sir—' stammered the keeper, 'it is not your tiger.'

'I know, I know,' said Grandfather testily. 'I realize he is no longer mine. But you might at least take a suggestion or two from me.'

'I remember your tiger very well,' said the keeper. 'He died two months ago.'

'Died!' exclaimed Grandfather.

'Yes, sir, of pneumonia. This tiger was trapped in the hills only last month, and he is very dangerous!'

Grandfather could think of nothing to say. The tiger was still licking his arm, with increasing relish. Grandfather took what seemed to him an age to withdraw his hand from the cage.

With his face near the tiger's he mumbled, 'Goodnight, Timothy,' and giving the keeper a scornful look, walked briskly out of the zoo.

THE TUNNEL

It was almost noon, and the jungle was very still, very silent. Heat waves shimmered along the railway embankment where it cut a path through the tall evergreen trees. The railway lines were two straight black serpents disappearing into the tunnel in the hillside.

Suraj stood near the cutting, waiting for the mid-day train. It wasn't a station, and he wasn't catching a train. He was waiting so that he could watch the steam-engine come roaring out of the tunnel.

He had cycled out of the town and taken the jungle path until he had come to a small village. He had left the cycle there, and walked over a low, scrub-covered hill and down to the tunnel exit.

Now he looked up. He had heard, in the distance, the shrill whistle of the engine. He couldn't see anything, because the train was approaching from the other side of the hill; but presently a sound, like distant thunder, issued from the tunnel, and he knew the train was coming through.

A second or two later, the steam-engine shot out of the tunnel, snorting and puffing like some green, black and gold dragon, some beautiful monster out of Suraj's dreams. Showering sparks left and right, it roared a challenge to the jungle.

Instinctively, Suraj stepped back a few paces. And then the train had gone, leaving only a plume of smoke to drift lazily over tall shisham trees.

LESSONS IN FUN AND FROLIC

The jungle was still again. No one moved. Suraj turned from his contemplation of the drifting smoke and began walking along the embankment towards the tunnel.

The tunnel grew darker as he walked further into it. When he had gone about twenty yards, it became pitch black. Suraj had to turn and look back at the opening to reassure himself that there was still daylight outside. Ahead of him, the tunnel's other opening was just a small round circle of light.

The tunnel was still full of smoke from the train, but it would be several hours before another train came through. Till then, it belonged to the jungle again.

Suraj didn't stop, because there was nothing to do in the tunnel and nothing to see. He had simply wanted to walk through, so that he would know what the inside of a tunnel was really like. The walls were damp and sticky. A bat flew past. A lizard scuttled between the lines.

Coming straight from the darkness into the light, Suraj was dazzled by the sudden glare. He put a hand up to shade his eyes and looked up at the tree-covered hillside. He thought he saw something moving between the trees.

It was just a flash of orange and gold, and a long swishing tail. It was there between the trees for a second or two, and then it was gone.

About fifty feet from the entrance to the tunnel stood the watchman's hut. Marigolds grew in front of the hut, and at the back there was a small vegetable patch. It was the watchman's duty to inspect the tunnel and keep it clear of obstacles. Every day, before the train came through, he would walk the length of the tunnel. If all was well, he would return to his hut and take a nap. If something was wrong, he would walk back up

THE TUNNEL

the line and wave a red flag and the engine-driver would slow down. At night, the watchman lit an oil lamp and made a similar inspection of the tunnel. Of course, he could not stop the train if there was a porcupine on the line. But if there was any danger to the train, he'd go back up the line and wave his lamp to the approaching engine. If all was well, he'd hang his lamp at the door of the hut and go to sleep.

He was just settling down on his cot for an afternoon nap when he saw the boy emerge from the tunnel. He waited until Suraj was only a few feet away and then said: 'Welcome, welcome, I don't often have visitors. Sit down for a while, and tell me why you were inspecting my tunnel.'

'Is it your tunnel?' asked Suraj.

'It is,' said the watchman. 'It is truly my tunnel, since no one else will have anything to do with it. I have only lent it to the government.'

Suraj sat down on the edge of the cot.

'I wanted to see the train come through,' he said. 'And then, when it had gone, I thought I'd walk through the tunnel.'

'And what did you find in it?'

'Nothing. It was very dark. But when I came out, I thought I saw an animal—up on the hill—but I'm not sure, it moved away very quickly.'

'It was a leopard you saw,' said the watchman. 'My leopard.'

'Do you own a leopard too?'

'I do.'

'And do you lend it to the government?'

'I do not.'

'Is it dangerous?'

'No, it's a leopard that minds its own business. It comes

to this range for a few days every month.'

'Have you been here a long time?' asked Suraj.

'Many years. My name is Sunder Singh.'

'My name's Suraj.'

'There's one train during the day. And another during the night. Have you seen the night mail come through the tunnel?'

'No. At what time does it come?'

'About nine o'clock, if it isn't late. You could come and sit here with me, if you like. And after it has gone, I'll take you home.'

'I shall ask my parents,' said Suraj. 'Will it be safe?'

'Of course. It's safer in the jungle than in the town. Nothing happens to me out here, but last month when I went into the town, I was almost run over by a bus.'

Sunder Singh yawned and stretched himself out on the cot. 'And now I'm going to take a nap, my friend. It is too hot to be up and about in the afternoon.'

'Everyone goes to sleep in the afternoon,' complained Suraj. 'My father lies down as soon as he's had his lunch.'

'Well, the animals also rest in the heat of the day. It is only the tribe of boys who cannot, or will not, rest.'

Sunder Singh placed a large banana-leaf over his face to keep away the flies, and was soon snoring gently. Suraj stood up, looking up and down the railway tracks. Then he began walking back to the village.

The following evening, towards dusk, as the flying foxes swooped silently out of the trees, Suraj made his way to the watchman's hut.

It had been a long hot day, but now the earth was cooling, and a light breeze was moving through the trees. It carried with it a scent of mango blossoms, the promise of rain.

THE TUNNEL

Sunder Singh was waiting for Suraj. He had watered his small garden, and the flowers looked cool and fresh. A kettle was boiling on a small oil-stove.

'I'm making tea,' he said. 'There's nothing like a glass of hot tea while waiting for a train.'

They drank their tea, listening to the sharp notes of the tailorbird and the noisy chatter of the seven-sisters. As the brief twilight faded, most of the birds fell silent. Sunder Singh lit his oil-lamp and said it was time for him to inspect the tunnel. He moved off towards the tunnel, while Suraj sat on the cot, sipping his tea. In the dark, the trees seemed to move closer to him. And the night life of the forest was conveyed on the breeze—the sharp call of a barking-deer, the cry of a fox, the quaint tonk-tonk of a nightjar. There were some sounds that Suraj couldn't recognise—sounds that came from the trees, creakings and whisperings, as though the trees were coming alive, stretching their limbs in the dark, shifting a little, reflexing their fingers.

Sunder Singh stood inside the tunnel, trimming his lamp. The night sounds were familiar to him and he did not give them much thought; but something else—a padded footfall, a rustle of dry leaves—made him stand alert for a few seconds, peering into the darkness. Then, humming softly to himself, he returned to where Suraj was waiting. Another ten minutes remained for the night mail to arrive.

As Sunder Singh sat down on the cot beside Suraj, a new sound reached both of them quite distinctly—a rhythmic sawing sound, as if someone was cutting through the branch of a tree.

'What's that?' whispered Suraj.

'It's the leopard,' said Sunder Singh.

'I think it's in the tunnel.'

'The train will soon be here,' reminded Suraj.

'Yes, my friend. And if we don't drive the leopard out of the tunnel, it will be run over and killed. I can't let that happen.'

'But won't it attack us if we try to drive it out?' asked Suraj, beginning to share the watchman's concern.

'Not this leopard. It knows me well. We have seen each other many times. It has a weakness for goats and stray dogs, but it won't harm us. Even so, I'll take my axe with me. You stay here, Suraj.'

'No, I'm going with you. It'll be better than sitting here alone in the dark!'

'All right, but stay close behind me. And remember, there's nothing to fear.'

Raising his lamp high, Sunder Singh advanced into the tunnel, shouting at the top of his voice to try and scare away the animal. Suraj followed close behind, but he found he was unable to do any shouting. His throat was quite dry.

They had gone just about twenty paces into the tunnel when the light from the lamp fell upon the leopard. It was crouching between the tracks, only fifteen feet away from them. It was not a very big leopard, but it looked lithe and sinewy. Baring its teeth and snarling, it went down on its belly, tail twitching.

Suraj and Sunder Singh both shouted together. Their voices rang through the tunnel. And the leopard, uncertain as to how many terrifying humans were there in the tunnel with him, turned swiftly and disappeared into the darkness.

To make sure that it had gone, Sunder Singh and Suraj walked the length of the tunnel. When they returned to the entrance, the rails were beginning to hum. They knew the train was coming.

THE TUNNEL

Suraj put his hand to the rails and felt its tremor. He heard the distant rumble of the train. And then the engine came round the bend, hissing at them, scattering sparks into the darkness, defying the jungle as it roared through the steep sides of the cutting. It charged straight at the tunnel, and into it, thundering past Suraj like the beautiful dragon of his dreams.

And when it had gone, the silence returned and the forest seemed to breathe, to live again. Only the rails still trembled with the passing of the train.

And they trembled to the passing of the same train, almost a week later, when Suraj and his father were both travelling in it.

Suraj's father was scribbling in a notebook, doing his accounts. Suraj sat at an open window staring out at the darkness. His father was going to Delhi on a business trip and had decided to take the boy along. 'I don't know where he gets to, most of the time,' he'd complained. 'I think it's time he learnt something about my business.'

The night mail rushed through the forest with its hundreds of passengers. Tiny flickering lights came and went, as they passed small villages on the fringe of the jungle.

Suraj heard the rumble as the train passed over a small bridge. It was too dark to see the hut near the cutting, but he knew they must be approaching the tunnel. He strained his eyes looking out into the night; and then, just as the engine let out a shrill whistle, Suraj saw the lamp.

He couldn't see Sunder Singh, but he saw the lamp, and he knew that his friend was out there.

The train went into the tunnel and out again; it left the jungle behind and thundered across the endless plains; and Suraj stared out at the darkness, thinking of the lonely cutting in the forest, and the watchman with the lamp who would always remain a firefly for those travelling thousands, as he lit up the darkness for steam-engines and leopards.

RANJI'S WONDERFUL BAT

'How's that!' shouted the wicketkeeper, holding the ball up in his gloves.

'How's that!' echoed the slip fielders.

'How?' growled the fast bowler, glaring at the umpire.

'Out!' said the umpire.

And Suraj, the captain of the school team, was walking slowly back to the pavilion—which was really a toolshed at the end of the field.

The score stood at 53 runs for 4 wickets. Another 60 runs had to be made for victory, and only one good batsman remained. All the rest were bowlers who couldn't be expected to make many runs.

It was Ranji's turn to bat.

He was the youngest member of the team, only eleven, but sturdy and full of pluck. As he walked briskly to the wicket, his unruly black hair was blown about by a cool breeze that came down from the hills.

Ranji had a good eye and strong wrists, and had made lots of runs in some of the minor matches. But in the last two inter-school games, his scores had been poor, the highest being 12 runs. Today he was determined to make enough runs to take his side to victory.

Ranji took his guard and prepared to face the bowler. The fielders moved closer, in anticipation of another catch. The tall fast bowler scowled and began his long run. His arm whirled over, and the hard, shiny red ball came hurtling towards Ranji.

Ranji was going to lunge forward and play the ball back to the bowler, but at the last moment he changed his mind and stepped back, intending to push the ball through the ring of fielders on his right or offside.

'How's that!' screamed the bowler hopping about like a kangaroo.

'How?' shouted the wicketkeeper.

The umpire slowly raised a finger.

'Out,' he said.

'Never mind,' said Suraj, patting Ranji on the back. 'You'll do better next time. You're out of form just now, that's all.'

'You'll have to make more runs in the next game,' he told Ranji, 'or you'll lose your place in the side!'

Avoiding the other players, Ranji slowly walked homewards, his head down, his hands in his pockets. He was very upset. He had been trying so hard and practising so regularly, but when an important game came along he failed to make a big score. It seemed that there was nothing he could do about it. But he loved playing cricket, and he couldn't bear the thought of being out of the school team.

On his way home he had to pass the clock tower, where he often stopped at Mr Kumar's Sports Shop, to chat with the owner or look at all the things on the shelves: footballs, cricket balls, badminton rackets, hockey sticks, balls of various shapes and sizes—it was a wonderland where Ranji liked to linger every day.

But this was one day when he didn't feel like stopping. He looked the other way and was about to cross the road when Mr Kumar's voice stopped him.

'Hello, Ranji! Off in a hurry today? And why are you looking so sad?'

So Ranji had to stop and say namaste. He couldn't ignore Mr Kumar, who had always been so kind and helpful, often giving him advice on how to bowl in different styles. Mr Kumar had been a state-level player once, and had scored a century in a match against Tanzania. Now he liked encouraging young players and he thought Ranji would make a good cricketer.

'What's the trouble?' he asked as Ranji stepped into the shop. Because Mr Kumar was so friendly, the sports merchandise also seemed friendly. The bats and balls and shuttlecocks all seemed to want to be helpful.

'We lost the match,' said Ranji.

'Never mind,' said Mr Kumar. 'Where would we be without losers? There wouldn't be any games without them—no cricket or football or hockey or tennis! No carom or marbles. No sports shop for me! Anyway, how many runs did you make?'

'None, I made a big, round egg.'

Mr Kumar rested his hand on Ranji's shoulder. 'Never mind. All good players have a bad day now and then.'

'But I haven't made a good score in my last three matches,' said Ranji. 'I'll be dropped from the team if I don't do something in the next game.'

'Well, we can't have that happening,' mused Mr Kumar. 'Something will have to be done about it.'

'I'm just unlucky,' said Ranji.

'Maybe, maybe... But in that case, it's time your luck changed.'

'It's too late now,' said Ranji.

'Nonsense. It's never too late. Now, you just come with

me to the back of the shop and I'll see if I can do something about your luck.'

Puzzled, Ranji followed Mr Kumar through the curtained partition at the back of the shop. He found himself in a badly-lit room stacked to the ceiling with all kinds of old and second-hand sporting goods—torn football bladders, broken bats, rackets without strings, broken darts, and tattered badminton nets. Mr Kumar began examining a number of old cricket bats, and after a few minutes he said, 'Ah!' Picking up one of the bats, he held it out to Ranji.

'This is it!' he said. 'This is the luckiest of all my old bats. This is the bat I made a century with!' He gave it a twirl and started hitting an imaginary ball to all corners of the room.

'Of course it's an old bat, but it hasn't lost any of its magic,' said Mr Kumar, pausing in his stroke-making to recover his breath. He held it out to Ranji. 'Here, take it!' I'll lend it to you for the rest of the cricket season. You won't fail with this with you.'

Ranji took the bat and looked at it with awe and delight.

'Is it really the bat you made a century with?' he asked.

'It is,' said Mr Kumar. 'And it may get you a hundred runs too!'

Ranji spent a nervous week waiting for Saturday's match. His school team would be playing against a strong side from another town. There was a lot of classwork that week, so Ranji did not get much time to practise with the other boys. As he had no brothers or sisters he asked Koki, the girl next door, to bowl to him in the garden. Koki bowled quite well, but Ranji liked to hit the ball hard—'just to get used to the bat,' he told her—and she soon got tired of chasing the ball all over the garden.

At last Saturday arrived, bright and sunny and just right for cricket.

Suraj won the toss for the school and chose batting first.

The opening batsmen put on 30 runs without being separated. The visiting fast bowlers couldn't do much. Then the spin bowlers came on, and immediately there was a change in the game. Two wickets fell in one over, and the score was 33 for 2. Suraj made a few quick runs, then he too was out to one of the spinners, caught behind the wicket. The next batsman was clean bowled—46 for 4—and it was Ranji's turn to bat.

He walked slowly to the wicket. The fielders crowded around him. He took guard and prepared for the first ball.

The bowler took a short run and then the ball was twirling towards Ranji, looking as though it would spin away from his bat as he leaned forward into his stroke.

And then a thrill ran through Ranji's arm as he felt the ball meet the springy willow of the bat.

Crack!

The ball, hit firmly with the middle of Ranji's bat, streaked past the helpless bowler and sped towards the boundary. Four runs!

The bowler was annoyed, with the result that his next ball was a loose full toss. Ranji swung it to the onside boundary for another four.

And that was only the beginning. Now, Ranji began to play all the strokes he knew: late cuts and square cuts, straight drives, on drives and off drives. The rival captain tried all his bowlers, fast and spin, but none of them could remove Ranji. Instead, he sent the fielders scampering to all corners of the field.

By the lunch break he had scored 40 runs. And twenty minutes after lunch, when Suraj closed the innings, Ranji was not out with 58.

The rival team was bowled out for a poor score, and Ranji's school won the match.

On his way home, Ranji stopped at Mr Kumar's shop to give him the good news.

'We won!' he said. 'And I made 58—my highest score so far. It really is a lucky bat!'

'I told you so,' said Mr Kumar, giving Ranji a warm handshake. 'There will be bigger scores yet.'

Ranji went home in high spirits. He was so pleased that he stopped at the Jumma Sweet Shop and bought two laddus for Koki. She was crazy about laddus.

Mr Kumar was right. It was only the beginning of Ranji's success with the bat. In the next game he scored 40, and was out when he grew careless and allowed himself to be stumped by the wicketkeeper. The game that followed was a two-day match, and Ranji, who was now batting at Number 3, made 45 runs. He hit a number of boundaries before being caught. In the second innings, when the school team needed only 6 runs for victory, Ranji was batting at 25 when the winning runs were hit.

Everyone was pleased with him—his coach, his captain, Suraj, and Mr Kumar—but only one knew about the lucky bat. That was a secret between Ranji and Mr Kumar.

One evening, during an informal game on the maidan, Ranji's friend Bhim slipped while running after the ball, and cut his hand on a sharp stone. Ranji took him to a doctor near the clock tower, where the wound was washed and bandaged. As it was getting late, he decided to go straight home. Usually he walked, but that evening he caught a bus near the clock tower.

When he got home, his mother brought him a cup of tea, and while he was drinking it, Koki walked in, and the first thing she said was, 'Ranji, where's your bat?'

'Oh, I must have left it at the maidan when Bhim got hurt,' said Ranji, starting up and spilling his tea. 'I'd better go and get it now, or it will disappear.'

'You can fetch it tomorrow,' said his mother. 'It's getting dark.'

'I'll take a torch,' said Ranji.

He was worried about the bat.

Without it, his luck might desert him.

He hadn't the patience to wait for a bus, and ran all the way to the maidan.

The maidan was deserted, and there was no sign of the bat. And then Ranji remembered that he'd had it with him on the bus, after saying goodbye to Bhim at the clock tower. He must have left it on the bus!

Well, he'd never find it now. The bat was lost forever. And on Saturday Ranji's school would be playing their last and most important match of the cricket season against a public school team from Delhi.

Next day he was at Mr Kumar's shop, looking very sorry for himself.

'What's the matter?' asked Mr Kumar.

'I've lost the bat,' said Ranji. 'Your lucky bat. The one I made all my runs with! I left it in the bus. And the day after tomorrow we are playing the Delhi school, and I'll be out for a duck, and we'll lose our chance of being the champion school.'

LESSONS IN FUN AND FROLIC

Mr Kumar looked a little anxious at first; then he smiled and said, 'You can still make all the runs you want.'

'But I don't have the bat any more,' said Ranji.

'Any bat will do,' said Mr Kumar.

'What do you mean?'

'I mean it's the batsman and not the bat that matters. Shall I tell you something? That old bat I gave you was no different from any other bat I've used. True, I made a lot of runs with it, but I made runs with other bats too. A bat has magic only when the batsman has magic! What you needed was confidence, not a bat. And by believing in the bat, you got your confidence back!'

'What's confidence?' asked Ranji. It was a new word for him.

'Confidence,' said Mr Kumar slowly, 'confidence is knowing you are good.'

'And I can be good without the bat?'

'Of course. You have always been good. You are good now. You will be good the day after tomorrow. Remember that. If you remember it, you'll make the runs.'

On Saturday, Ranji walked to the wicket with a bat borrowed from Bhim.

The school team had lost its first wicket with only 2 runs on the board. Ranji went in at this stage. The Delhi school's opening bowler was sending down some really fast ones. Ranji faced up to him.

The first ball was very fast but it wasn't on a good length. Quick on his feet, Ranji stepped back and pulled it hard to the onside boundary. The ball soared over the heads of the fielders and landed with a crash in a crate full of cold drink bottles.

A six! Everyone stood up and cheered.

And it was only the beginning of Ranji's wonderful innings.

The match ended in a draw, but Ranji's 75 was the talk of the school.

On his way home he bought a dozen laddus. Six for Koki and six for Mr Kumar.

MUKESH STARTS A ZOO

On a visit to Delhi with his parents, Mukesh spent two crowded hours at the zoo. He was dazzled by the many colourful birds, fascinated by the reptiles, charmed by the gibbons and chimps, and awestruck by the big cats—the lions, tigers and leopards. There was no zoo in the small town of Dehra where he lived, and the jungle was some way across the river-bed. So, as soon as he got home, he decided that he would have a zoo of his own.

'I'm going to start a zoo,' he announced at breakfast, the day after his return.

'But you don't have any birds or animals,' said Dolly, his little sister.

'I'll soon find them,' said Mukesh. 'That's what a zoo is all about—collecting animals.'

He was gazing at the white-washed walls of the verandah, where a gecko, a small wall lizard, was in pursuit of a fly. A little later Mukesh was trying to catch the lizard. But it was more alert than it looked, and always managed to keep a few inches ahead of his grasp.

'That's not the way to catch a lizard,' said Teju, appearing on the verandah steps. Teju and his sister Koki lived next door.

'You catch it, then,' said Mukesh.

Teju fetched a stick from the garden, where it had been used to prop up sweet-peas. He used the stick to tip the lizard off the wall and into a shoe-box.

'You'll be my Head Keeper,' said Mukesh, and soon he and Teju were at work in the back garden setting up enclosures with a roll of wire-netting they had found in the poultry shed.

'What else can we have in the zoo?' asked Teju. 'We need more than a lizard.'

'There's your grandmother's parrot,' said Mukesh.

'That's a good idea. But we won't tell her about it—not yet. I don't think she'd lend it to us. You see, it's a *religious* parrot. She's taught it lots of prayers and chants.'

'Then people are sure to come and listen to it. They'll pay, too.'

'We must have the parrot, then. What else?'

'Well, there's my dog,' said Mukesh. 'He's very fierce.'

'But a dog isn't a zoo animal.'

'Mine is—he's a wild dog. Look, he's black all over and he's got yellow eyes. There's no other dog like him.'

Mukesh's dog, who spent most of his time sleeping on the verandah, raised his head and obligingly revealed his yellow eyes.

'He's got jaundice,' said Teju. 'They've always been yellow.'

'All right, then, we've got a lizard, a parrot and a black dog with yellow eyes.'

'Koki has a white rabbit. Will she lend it to us?'

'I don't know. She thinks a lot of her rabbit. Maybe we can rent it from her.'

'And there's Sitaram's donkey.'

Sitaram, the dhobi-boy, usually used a donkey to deliver and collect the laundry from the houses along this particular street.

'Do you really want a donkey?' asked Teju doubtfully.

'Why not? It's a wild donkey. Haven't you heard of them?'

'I've heard of a wild ass, but not a wild donkey.'

'Well, they're all related to each other—asses, donkeys and mules.'

'Why don't you paint black stripes on it and call it a zebra?'

'No, that's cheating. It's got to be a proper zoo. No tricks—it's not a circus!'

On Saturday afternoon, a large placard with corrected spelling announced the opening of the zoo. It hung from the branches of the jack-fruit tree. Children were allowed in free but grown-ups had to buy tickets at fifty paise each, and Koki and Dolly were selling home-made tickets to the occasional passer-by or parent who happened to look in. Mukesh and his friends had worked hard at making notices for the various enclosures and each resident of the zoo was appropriately named.

The first attraction was a large packing-case filled with an assortment of house-lizards. They looked rather sluggish, having been generously fed with a supply of beetles and other insects.

Then came an enclosure in which Koki's white rabbit was on display. Freshly washed and brushed, it looked very cuddly and was praised by all.

Staring at it with evil intent from behind wire-netting was Mukesh's dog—RARE BLACK DOG WITH YELLOW EYES read the notice. Those yellow eyes were now trying hard to hypnotize the pink eyes of Koki's nervous rabbit. The dog pawed at the ground, trying to dig its way out from under the fence to get at the rabbit.

Tethered to a mango tree was Sitaram's small donkey. And tacked to the tree was a placard saying WILD ASS FROM KUTCH. A distant relative it may have been, but everyone recognized it as the local washerman's beast of burden. Every now and then it tried to break loose, for it was long past its feeding time.

There was also a duck that did not seem to belong to anyone, and a small cow that had strayed in on its own; but the star attraction was the parrot. As it could recite three different prayers, over and over again, it was soon surrounded by a group of admiring parents, all of whom wished they had a parrot who could pray, or rather, do their praying for them. Oddly enough, Koki's grandmother had chosen that day for visiting the temple, so she was unaware of the fuss that was being made of her pet, or even that it had been made an honorary member of the zoo. Teju had convinced himself she wouldn't mind.

While Mukesh and Teju were escorting visitors around the zoo, lecturing them on wild dogs and wild asses, Koki and Dolly were doing a brisk trade at the ticket counter. They had collected about ten rupees and were hoping for yet more, when there was a disturbance in the enclosures.

The black dog with yellow eyes had finally managed to dig his way out of his cage, and was now busy trying to dig his way into the rabbit's compartment. The rabbit was running round and round in panic-stricken circles. Meanwhile, the donkey had finally snapped the rope that held it and, braying loudly, scattered the spectators and made for home.

Koki went to the rescue of her rabbit and soon had it cradled in her arms. The dog now turned his attention to the duck. The duck flew over the packing-case, while the dog landed in it, scattering lizards in all directions.

In all this confusion, no one noticed that the door of the parrot's cage had slipped open. With a squawk and a whirr of wings, the bird shot out of the cage and flew off into a nearby orchard.

'The parrot's gone!' shouted Dolly, and almost immediately a silence fell upon the assembled visitors and children. Even the dog stopped barking. Granny's praying parrot had escaped! How could they possibly face her? Teju wondered if she would believe him if he told her it had flown off to heaven.

'Can anyone see it?' he asked tearfully.

'It's in a mango tree,' said Dolly. 'It won't come back.'

The crowd fell away, unwilling to share any of the blame when Koki's grandmother came home and discovered what had happened.

'What are we going to do now?' asked Teju, looking to Koki for help; but Koki was too upset to suggest anything. Mukesh had an idea.

'I know!' he said. 'We'll get another one!'

'How?'

'Well, there's the ten rupees we've collected. We can buy a new parrot for ten rupees!'

'But won't Granny know the difference?' asked Teju.

'All these hill parrots look alike,' said Mukesh.

So, taking the cage with them, they hurried off to the bazaar, where they soon found a bird-seller who was happy to sell them a parrot not unlike Granny's. He assured them it would talk.

'It looks like your grandmother's parrot,' said Mukesh on the way home. 'But can it pray?'

'Of course not,' said Koki. 'But we can teach it.'

Koki's grandmother, who was short-sighted, did not notice the substitution; but she complained bitterly that the bird had stopped repeating its prayers and was instead making rude noises and even swearing occasionally.

Teju soon remedied this sad state of affairs.

Every morning he stood in front of the parrot's cage and repeated Granny's prayers. Within a few weeks the bird had learnt to repeat one of them. Granny was happy again—not only because her parrot had started praying once more, but because Teju had started praying too!

THE BOY WHO BROKE THE BANK

Nathu, the sweeper-boy, grumbled to himself as he swept the steps of a small local bank, owned for the most part by Seth Govind Ram, a man of wealth whose haphazard business dealings had often brought him to the verge of ruin. Nathu used the small broom hurriedly and carelessly; the dust, after rising in a cloud above his head, settled down again on the steps. As Nathu was banging his pan against a dustbin, Sitaram, the washerman's son, passed by.

Sitaram was on his delivery round. He had a bundle of pressed clothes balanced on his head.

'Don't raise such a dust!' he called out to Nathu. 'Are you annoyed because they are still refusing to pay you another five rupees a month?'

'I don't want to talk about it,' complained the sweeper-boy. 'I haven't even received my regular pay. And this is the end of the month. Soon two months' pay will be due. Who would think this was a bank, holding up a poor man's salary? As soon as I get my money, I'm off! Not another week will I work in the place.'

And Nathu banged his pan against the dustbin two or three times more, just to emphasize his point and give himself confidence.

'Well, I wish you luck,' said Sitaram. 'I'll be on the look-out for a new job for you.' And he plodded barefoot along the road, the big bundle of clothes hiding most of his head and shoulders.

At the fourth house he visited, delivering the washing, Sitaram overheard the woman of the house saying how difficult it was to get someone to sweep the courtyard. Tying up his bundle, Sitaram said: 'I know a sweeper-boy who's looking for work. He might be able to work for you from next month. He's with Seth Govind Ram's bank just now, but they are not giving him his pay, and he wants to leave.'

'Oh, is that so?' said Mrs Prakash. 'And why aren't they paying him?'

'They must be short of money,' said Sitaram with a shrug. Mrs Prakash laughed, 'Well, tell him to come and see me when he's free.'

Sitaram, glad that he had been of some service both to a friend and to a customer, hoisted his bag on his shoulders and went on his way.

Mrs Prakash had to do some shopping. She gave instructions to her maidservant with regard to the baby and told the cook what she wanted for lunch. Her husband worked for a large company, and they could keep servants and do things in style. Having given her orders, she set out for the bazaar to make her customary tour of the cloth shops.

A large, shady tamarind tree grew near the clock tower, and it was here that Mrs Prakash found her friend, Mrs Bhushan, sheltering from the heat. Mrs Bhushan was fanning herself with a large peacock's feather. She complained that the summer was the hottest in the history of the town. She then showed Mrs Prakash a sample of the cloth she was going to buy, and for five minutes they discussed its shade, texture and design.

When they had exhausted the subject, Mrs Prakash said:

'Do you know, my dear, Seth Govind Ram's bank can't even pay its employees. Only this morning I heard a complaint from their sweeper-boy, who hasn't received his pay for two months!'

'It's disgraceful!' exclaimed Mrs Bhushan. 'If they can't pay their sweeper, they must be in a bad way. None of the others can be getting paid either.'

She left Mrs Prakash at the tamarind tree and went in search of her husband, who was found sitting under the fan in Jugal Kishore's electrical goods shop, playing cards with the owner.

'So there you are!' cried Mrs Bhushan. 'I've been looking for you for nearly an hour. Where did you disappear to?'

'Nowhere,' replied Mr Bhushan. 'Had you remained stationary in one shop, you might have found me. But you go from one to another, like a bee in a flower-garden.'

'Now don't start grumbling. The heat is bad enough. I don't know what's happening to this town. Even the bank is going bankrupt.'

'What did you say?' said Mr Jugal Kishore, sitting up suddenly. 'Which bank?'

'Why, Seth Govind Ram's bank, of course. I hear they've stopped paying their employees—no salary for over three months! Don't tell me you have an account with them, Mr Kishore?'

'No, but my neighbour has!' he said, and he called out to the keeper of the barber shop next door: 'Faiz Hussain, have you heard the latest? Seth Govind Ram's bank is about to collapse! You'd better take your money out while there's still time.'

Faiz Hussain, who was cutting the hair of an elderly gentleman, was so startled that his hand shook and he nicked his customer's ear. The customer yelped with pain and distress:

pain, because of the cut, and distress, because of the awful news he had just heard. With one side of his neck still unshorn, he leapt out of his chair and sped across the road to a general merchant's store, where there was a telephone. He dialled Seth Govind Ram's number. The Seth was not at home. Where was he, then? The Seth was holidaying in Kashmir. Oh, was that so? The elderly gentleman did not believe it. He hurried back to the barber shop and told Faiz Hussain: 'The bird has flown! Seth Govind Ram has left town. Definitely, it means a collapse. I'll have the rest of my haircut another time.' And he dashed out of the shop and made a bee-line for his office and cheque book.

◆

The news spread through the bazaar with the rapidity of a forest fire. From the general merchant's it travelled to the tea-shop, circulated amongst the customers, and then spread with them in various directions, to the paan-seller, the tailor, the fruit-vendor, the jeweller, the beggar sitting on the pavement .

Old Ganpat, the beggar, had a crooked leg and had been squatting on the pavement for years, calling for alms. In the evening someone would come with a barrow and take him away. He had never been known to walk. But now, on learning that the bank was about to collapse, Ganpat astonished everyone by leaping to his feet and actually running at a good speed in the direction of the bank. It soon became known that he had well over a thousand rupees in savings.

Men stood in groups at street corners, discussing the situation. There hadn't been so much excitement since India last won a Test Match. The small town in the foot-hills seldom had a crisis, never had floods or earthquakes or droughts. And so the imminent crash of the local bank set everyone talking and speculating and rushing about in a frenzy.

Some boasted of their farsightedness, congratulating themselves on having taken out their money, or on never putting any in. Others speculated on the reasons for the crash, putting it all down to Seth Govind Ram's pleasure-loving ways. The Seth had fled the state, said one. He had fled the country, said another. He had a South American passport, said a third. Others insisted that he was hiding somewhere in the town. And there was a rumour that he had hanged himself from the tamarind tree, where he had been found that morning by the sweeper-boy.

Someone who had a relative working as a clerk in the bank decided to phone him and get the facts.

'I don't know anything about it,' said the clerk, 'except that half the town is here, trying to take their money out. Everyone seems to have gone mad!'

'There's a rumour that none of you have been paid.'

'Well, all the clerks have had their salaries. We wouldn't be working otherwise. It may be that some of the part-time workers are getting paid late, but that isn't due to a shortage of money—only a few hundred rupees—it's just that the clerk who looks after their payments is on sick leave. You don't expect me to do his work, do you?' And he put the telephone down.

By afternoon the bank had gone through all its ready money, and the harassed manager was helpless. Emergency funds could only be obtained from one of the government banks, and now it was nearly closing time. He wasn't sure he could persuade the crowd outside to wait until the following morning. And Seth Govind Ram could be of no help from his luxury houseboat in Kashmir, five hundred miles away.

THE BOY WHO BROKE THE BANK

The clerks shut down their counters. But the people gathered outside on the steps of the bank, shouting: 'We want our money!' 'Give it to us today, break in!' 'Fetch Seth Govind Ram, we know he's hiding in the vaults!'

Mischief-makers, who did not have a paisa in the bank, joined the crowd. The manager stood at the door and tried to calm his angry customers. He declared that the bank had plenty of money, that they could withdraw all they wanted the following morning.

'We want it now!' chanted the people. 'Now, now, now!'

A few stones were thrown, and the manager retreated indoors, closing the iron-grilled gate.

A brick hurtled through the air and smashed into the plate-glass window which advertized the bank's assets.

Then the police arrived. They climbed the steps of the bank and, using their long sticks, pushed the crowd back until people began falling over each other. Gradually everyone dispersed, shouting that they would be back in the morning.

◆

Nathu arrived next morning to sweep the steps of the bank.

He saw the refuse and the broken glass and the stones cluttering up the steps. Raising his hands in horror, he cried: 'Goondas! Hooligans! May they suffer from a thousand ills! It was bad enough being paid irregularly—now I must suffer an increase of work!' He smote the steps with his broom, scattering the refuse.

'Good morning, Nathu,' said Sitaram, the washer-man's son, getting down from his bicycle. 'Are you ready to take up a new job from the first of next month? You'll have to, I suppose, now that the bank is closing.'

'What did you say?' said Nathu.

'Haven't you heard? The bank's gone bankrupt. You'd better hang around until the others arrive, and then start demanding your money too. You'll be lucky if you get it!' He waved cheerfully, and pedalled away on his bicycle.

Nathu went back to sweeping the steps, muttering to himself. When he had finished, he sat down on the bottom step to await the arrival of the manager. He was determined to get his pay.

'Who would have thought the bank would collapse,' he said to himself, and looked thoughtfully across the street. 'I wonder how it could have happened.'

KOKI PLAYS THE GAME

'There's a cricket match on Saturday, isn't there?' asked Koki.

'That's right,' said Ranji. 'We're playing the Public School team.'

'I might come and watch,' said Koki.

'As you like. It won't be much of a game. We'll beat them easily.'

Ranji's own cricket team was quite different from his school team. It consisted of boys big and small, long and short, from various walks of life. Even Koki, a girl, was allowed honorary membership, and had sometimes been 'twelfth man'—an extra. She knew the game well, and often bowled to Ranji in the mornings when he wanted batting practice. Only a couple of the teammates could afford to go to private schools like Ranji's; most of them went to the local government school, and two or three had stopped going to school altogether.

There was Bhartu, who delivered newspapers in the mornings; the brothers Mukesh and Rakesh, whose father kept a sweet shop; and a tailor's son, Amir Ali. There was Billy Jones, an Anglo-Indian boy; 'Lumboo', the Tall One; Sitaram, the washerman's son, and several others. And there was also Bhim, who couldn't play at all, but who made a good umpire (when his glasses weren't steamed over) and who accompanied the team wherever it went.

This Saturday they were playing on their 'home' ground,

a patch of wasteland behind a new cinema called the Apsara ('Heavenly Dancer').

The Public School boys had all arrived first, which was only natural since they lived together in the same boarding school. The members of Ranji's team came from different directions, so it was some time before they had all assembled. Even then, they were two short. But Ranji won the toss and decided to bat, hoping that the missing team members would arrive in time to take their turn at the wicket.

'If Mukesh and Rakesh aren't here in time, we won't have them in the team,' said Ranji sternly.

'Don't sack them,' said Lumboo. 'They always bring us sweets and snacks from their father's shop. We need them in the team even if they don't score any runs.'

'Well, if they turn up *without* refreshments, they'll be sacked,' said Ranji, always ready to be fair.

The two umpires had gone out to set up the stumps—Bhim, on behalf of Ranji's team, and a teacher from the Public School.

'I don't like the look of that teacher,' said Amir Ali.

'Well, we won't take any risks.'

Billy Jones and Lumboo always opened the batting. Lumboo's height helped him to deal with the fast-rising ball. He took the first ball.

The Public School's opening bowler was speedy but inaccurate. This was because he was trying to bowl too fast. His first ball went for a wide, which gave Ranji's team its first run. The second ball wasn't quite so wide, but it was still about a foot from the leg stump. Lumboo took a swipe at it and missed. The third ball pitched halfway down the wicket and kept low. It struck Lumboo on the pads.

'How's that!' shouted the bowler, wicketkeeper and slip-fielders in unison.

The Public School's umpire did not hesitate. Up went his finger. Lumboo was given out leg-before-wicket. Lumboo stood aghast. He looked down at where his feet were placed, then back at his stumps.

'I'm not in front of the wicket,' he complained to no one in particular.

'The umpire's word is law,' said the wicketkeeper.

Lumboo slowly walked back to where his teammates reclined against a pile of bricks.

'I wasn't out!' he protested.

'Never mind,' said Ranji, whose turn it was to bat. 'You'll get your chance when you come on to bowl.'

He walked to the wicket with a confident air, his bat resting on his shoulder. He took guard carefully and, tapping his bat on the ground, faced the bowler. He received a straight ball, fast, and met it on the half-volley, driving it straight back past the bowler. It sped to the boundary, amidst delighted cries from Ranji's teammates. Four runs.

The next ball was short, just outside the off stump. Ranji stepped back and square-cut it past point. Another four. There were more cheers, and this time Ranji distinctly heard a girl's voice shouting: 'Good shot, Ranji!'

He looked back to where his teammates were gathered. There was no girl among them. He turned and looked towards the opposite boundary, and there, under the giant cinema hoarding, stood Koki. She waved to him.

Ranji did not wave back. He felt acutely self-conscious. Settling down to face the bowler again, he was aware of two

LESSONS IN FUN AND FROLIC

things at once—of the bowler making faces and charging up to bowl, and of Koki standing on the boundary and waiting for him to hit another four.

This loss of concentration caused him to misjudge the next ball. Instead of playing forward, he played back.

The ball took the edge of his bat and flew straight into the wicketkeeper's gloves.

'How's that!' shouted all the fielders, appealing for a catch.

Ranji did not wait for the umpire—in this case, Bhim, to give him out. He knew he'd touched the ball. Scowling, he walked back to his team. It was all Koki's fault!

Now, there was a good partnership between Sitaram and Bhartu. Sitaram, who helped his father with the town's washing on Sundays, was in the habit of laying out clothes on a flat stone and pounding them with a stout stick—the method followed by most washermen.

He dealt with the cricket ball in much the same way—clouting it hard, and sending it to various points of the compass. He hit up 25 valuable runs before he was out, caught off a big hit. Bhartu pushed and prodded, merely keeping one end going, until he too was out to an LBW decision. Billy Jones had gone the same way, taking the ball on his pads. No one was happy with the LBW decisions.

'We must have neutral umpires,' said Amir Ali.

'But who wants to be an umpire?' said Ranji. 'We won't find anyone. We'll have to use our own team members—or let the other side provide *both* umpires!'

'Not after today,' said Lumboo.

Meanwhile, Mukesh and Rakesh had arrived, carrying paper bags full of samosas and jalebis. As a result, everyone cheered up. Wickets fell almost as rapidly as the snacks and sweets were consumed. Mukesh and Rakesh, who were the last men in, held out for several overs until Rakesh was given out—LBW! Ranji's team was all out for 87 runs—not really a match-winning score, except on a tricky wicket.

It was the Public School team's turn to bat. One of their opening batsmen was bowled by Lumboo for naught. The other batsman was twice rapped on the pads by balls from Ranji, but his loud appeals for LBW were turned down—by the Public School's umpire, naturally! Muttering to himself, Ranji hurled down a thunderbolt of a ball. It rose sharply and struck the batsman on the hand. Howling with pain, he dropped his bat and wrung his hand. Then he showed everyone a swollen finger and decided to 'retire hurt'.

'There's more than one way of getting them out,' muttered Ranji, as he passed the umpire.

The next two batsmen were good players, not as nervous as the openers. One of them got what might have been a faint tickle to an out-swinger from Lumboo, but he was given the benefit of the doubt by Bhim—who, as umpires went, was as impartial as a star. He showed no favours to his own team, no matter what the other umpire did. *It just isn't fair*, thought Ranji.

The number three and four batsmen put on 40 runs between them, and by mid-afternoon Ranji's players were feeling tired and hungry. Then three quick wickets fell to Sitaram's spinners. Three wickets remained, and 20 runs were needed by the Public School for victory.

This was when Bhartu, running to take a catch, collided with chubby Mukesh. Both of them went sprawling on the grass, and when they got up the ball was found lodged in the back of Mukesh's pants. How it got there no one could tell, but after much discussion the umpires had to agree that it qualified as a catch and the batsman was given out. But Bhartu had to leave the ground with a bleeding nose.

Ranji looked around for a replacement. There was no one in sight except Koki.

'Come and field,' said Ranji brusquely.

Koki needed no persuading. She slipped off her sandals and dashed barefoot on to the field, taking up Bhartu's position near the boundary.

The tail-end batsmen were now swinging at the ball in a desperate attempt to hit the remaining runs. A hard-hit drive sped past Koki and went for four runs. Ranji gave her a hard look. Then the two batsmen got into a muddle while trying to take a quick run, and one of them was run out.

The last man came in. The Public School was 8 runs behind. But a couple of boundaries would take care of that.

The batsmen ran two. And then one of them, over-confident and sure of victory, swung out at a slow, tempting ball from Sitaram, and the ball flew towards Koki in a long, curving arc.

Koki had to run a few yards to her left. Then she leapt like a gazelle and took the ball in both hands. Ranji's team had won, and Koki had made the winning catch.

It was her last appearance as 'twelfth man'. From that day onwards she was a regular member of the team.

THE GREAT TRAIN JOURNEY

Suraj waved to a passing train, and kept waving until only the spiralling smoke remained. He liked waving to trains. He wondered about the people in them, and about where they were going and what it would be like there. And when the train had passed, leaving behind only the hot, empty track, Suraj was lonely.

He was a little lonely now. His hands in his pockets, he wandered along the railway track, kicking at loose pebbles and sending them down the bank. Soon there were other tracks, a railway-siding, a stationary goods train.

Suraj walked the length of the goods train. The carriage doors were closed and, as there were no windows, he couldn't see inside. He looked around to see if he was observed, and then, satisfied that he was alone, began trying the doors. He was almost at the end of the train when a carriage door gave way to his thrust.

It was dark inside the carriage. Suraj stood outside in the bright sunlight, peering into the darkness, trying to recognise bulky, shapeless objects. He stepped into the carriage and felt around. The objects were crates, and through the cross-section of woodwork he felt straw. He opened the other door and the sun streamed into the compartment, driving out the musty darkness.

Suraj sat down on a packing-case, his chin cupped in his hands. The school was closed for the summer holidays, and he had been wandering about all day and still did not know what to do with himself. The carriage was bare of any sort of glamour. Passing trains fascinated him—moving trains, crowded trains, shrieking, panting trains all fascinated him—but this smelly, dark compartment filled him only with gloom and more loneliness.

He did not really look gloomy or lonely. He looked fierce at times, when he glared out at people from under his dark eyebrows, but otherwise he usually wore a contented look—and no one could guess just how deep his thoughts were!

Perhaps, if he had company, some fun could be had in the carriage. If there had been a friend with him, someone like Ranji…

He looked at the crates. He was always curious about things that were bolted or nailed down or in some way concealed from him—things like parcels and locked rooms—and carriage doors and crates!

He went from one crate to another, and soon his perseverance was rewarded. The cover of one hadn't been properly nailed down. Suraj got his fingers under the edge and prised up the lid. Absorbed in this operation, he did not notice the slight shudder that passed through the train.

He plunged his hands into the straw and pulled out an apple.

It was a dark, ruby-red apple, and it lay in the dusty palm of Suraj's hand like some gigantic precious stone, smooth and round and glowing in the sunlight. Suraj looked up, out of the doorway, and thought he saw a tree walking past the train.

He dropped the apple and stared.

There was another tree, and another, all walking past the door with increasing rapidity. Suraj stepped for ward but lost his balance and fell on his hands and knees. The floor beneath him was vibrating, the wheels were clattering on the rails, the carriage was swaying. The trees were running now, swooping past the train, and the telegraph poles joined them in the crazy race.

Crouching on his hands and knees, Suraj stared out of the open door and realized that the train was moving, moving fast, moving away from his home and puffing into the unknown. He crept cautiously to the door and looked out. The ground seemed to rush away from the wheels. He couldn't jump. Was there, he wondered, any way of stopping the train? He looked around the compartment again: only crates of apples. He wouldn't starve, that was one consolation.

He picked up the apple he had dropped and pulled a crate nearer to the doorway. Sitting down, he took a bite from the apple and stared out of the open door.

'Greetings, friend,' said a voice from behind, and Suraj spun round guiltily, his mouth full of apple.

A dirty, bearded face was looking out at him from behind a pile of crates. The mouth was open in a wide, paan-stained grin.

'Er—namaste,' said Suraj apprehensively. 'Who are you?'

The man stepped out from behind the crates and confronted the boy.

'I'll have one of those, too,' he said, pointing to the apple.

Suraj gave the man an apple, and stood his ground while the carriage rocked on the rails. The man took a step forward, lost his balance, and sat down on the floor.

'And where are you going, friend?' he asked. 'Have you a ticket?'

'No,' said Suraj. 'Have you?'

The man pulled at his beard and mused upon the question but did not answer it. He took a bite from the apple and said,

'No, I don't have a ticket. But I usually reserve this compartment for myself. This is the first time I've had company. Where are you going? Are you a hippy like me?'

'I don't know,' said Suraj. 'Where does this train go?'

The scruffy ticketless traveller looked concerned for a moment, then smiled and said, 'Where do you want to go?'

'I want to go everywhere,' said Suraj. 'I want to go to England and China and Africa and Greenland. I want to go all over the world!'

'Then you're on the right train,' said the man. 'This train goes everywhere. First it will take you to the sea, and there you will have to get on a ship if you want to go to China.'

'How do I get on a ship?' asked Suraj.

The man, who had been fumbling about in the folds and pockets of his shabby clothes, produced a packet of bidis and a box of matches, and began smoking the aromatic leaf.

'Can you cook?' he asked.

'Yes,' said Suraj untruthfully.

'Can you scrub a deck?'

'Why not?'

'Can you sail a ship?'

'I can sail anything.'

'Then you'll get to China,' said the man.

He leant back against a crate, stuck his dirty feet up on another crate, and puffed contentedly at his bidi.

Suraj finished his apple, took another from the crate, and dug his teeth into it. He took aim with the core of the old apple and tried to hit a telegraph pole, but missed it by metres; it wasn't the same as throwing a cricket ball. Then, to make the apple more interesting, he began to take big bites to see if he could devour it in three mouthfuls. But it took him four bites to finish the apple, so he started on another.

Suraj had always wanted to be in a train, a train that would take him to strange new places, over hundreds and hundreds of kilometres. And here was a train doing just that, and he wasn't quite sure if it was what he really wanted…

The train was coming to a station. The engine whistled, slowed down. The number of railway lines increased, crossed, spread out in different directions. Before the train could come to a stop, Suraj's companion came to the door and jumped to the ground.

'You'd better keep out of sight if you don't want to be caught!' he called. And waving his hand, he disappeared into the jungle across the railway tracks.

The train was at a siding. Suraj couldn't see any signs of life, but he heard voices and the sound of carriage doors being opened and closed. He suspected that the apples wouldn't stay in the compartment much longer, so he stuffed one into each pocket, and climbed on to a wooden rack in a corner.

Presently men's voices were heard in the doorway. Two labourers stepped into the compartment and began moving the crates towards the door, where they were taken over by others. Soon the compartment was empty.

Suraj waited until the men had gone away before coming down from the rack. After about five minutes the train started again. It shunted up and down, then gathered speed and went rushing across the plain.

Suraj felt a thrill of anticipation. Where would they be going now? He wondered what his parents would do when he failed to come home that night; they would think he had run away, or been kidnapped, or been involved in an accident. They would have the police out and there would be search parties. Suraj would be famous: the boy who disappeared!

The train came out of the jungle and passed fields of sugar-cane and villages of mud huts. Children shouted and waved to the train, though there was no one in it except Suraj, the guard and the engine-driver. Suraj waved back. Usually he was in a field, waving; today, he was actually on the train.

He was beginning to enjoy the ride. The train would take him to the sea. There would be ships with funnels and ships with sails, and there might even be one to take him across the ocean to some distant land. He felt a bit sorry for his mother and father—they *would* miss him... They would believe he had been lost for ever...! But one day, a fortune made, he would return home and then nobody would care any more about school reports and what he ate and why he came home late... Ranji would be waiting for him at the station, and Suraj would bring him back a present—an African lion, perhaps, or a transistor-radio... But he wished Ranji was with him now; he wished the ragged hippy was still with him. An adventure was always more fun when one had company.

He had finished both apples by the time the train showed signs of reaching another station. This time it seemed to be moving into the station itself, not just a siding. It passed a lot of signals and buildings and advertisement-boards before slowing to a halt beside a wide, familiar platform.

Suraj looked out of the door and caught sight of the board bearing the station's name. He was so astonished that he almost fell out of the compartment. He was back in his home town! After travelling forty or fifty kilometres, here he was, home again.

THE GREAT TRAIN JOURNEY

He couldn't understand it. The train hadn't turned, of that he was certain; and it hadn't been moving backwards, he was certain of that, too. He climbed out of the compartment and looked up and down the platform. Yes, the engine had changed ends! It was only the local apple train.

Suraj glowered angrily at everyone on the platform. It was as though the rest of the world had played a trick on him.

He made his way to the waiting-room and slipped into the street through the back door. He did not want a ticket-collector asking him awkward questions. It had been a free ride, and with that he comforted himself. Shrugging his shoulders, Suraj sauntered down the road to the bazaar. Some day, he thought he'd take a train and really go somewhere; and he'd buy a ticket, just to make sure of getting there.

'I'm going everywhere,' he said fiercely. 'I'm going everywhere, and no one can stop me!'

THE ROOM OF MANY COLOURS

Last week I wrote a story, and all the time I was writing it I thought it was a good story; but when it was finished and I had read it through, I found that there was something missing, that it didn't ring true. So I tore it up. I wrote a poem, about an old man sleeping in the sun, and this was true, but it was finished quickly, and once again I was left with the problem of what to write next. And I remembered my father, who taught me to write; and I thought, why not write about my father, and about the trees we planted, and about the people I knew while growing up and about what happened on the way to growing up...

And so, like Alice, I must begin at the beginning, and in the beginning there was this red insect, just like a velvet button, which I found on the front lawn of the bungalow. The grass was still wet with overnight rain.

I placed the insect on the palm of my hand and took it into the house to show my father.

'Look, Dad,' I said, 'I haven't seen an insect like this before. Where has it come from?'

'Where did you find it?' he asked.

'On the grass.'

'It must have come down from the sky,' he said. 'It must have come down with the rain.'

Later he told me how the insect really happened but I

preferred his first explanation. It was more fun to have it dropping from the sky.

I was seven at the time, and my father was thirty-seven, but, right from the beginning, he made me feel that I was old enough to talk to him about everything—insects, people, trees, steam engines, King George, comics, crocodiles, the Mahatma, the Viceroy, America, Mozambique and Timbuctoo. We took long walks together, explored old ruins, chased butterflies and waved to passing trains.

My mother had gone away when I was four, and I had very dim memories of her. Most other children had their mothers with them, and I found it a bit strange that mine couldn't stay. Whenever I asked my father why she'd gone, he'd say, 'You'll understand when you grow up.' And if I asked him *where* she had gone, he'd look troubled and say, 'I really don't know.' This was the only question of mine to which he didn't have an answer.

But I was quite happy living alone with my father; I had never known any other kind of life.

We were sitting on an old wall, looking out to sea at a couple of Arab dhows and a tram steamer, when my father said, 'Would you like to go to sea one day?'

'Where does the sea go?' I asked.

'It goes everywhere.'

'Does it go to the end of the world?'

'It goes right round the world. It's a round world.'

'It can't be.'

'It is. But it's so big, you can't see the roundness. When a fly sits on a watermelon, it can't see right round the melon, can it? The melon must seem quite flat to the fly. Well, in comparison to the world, we're much, much smaller than the tiniest of insects.'

LESSONS IN FUN AND FROLIC

'Have you been around the world?' I asked.

'No, only as far as England. That's where your grandfather was born.'

'And my grandmother?'

'She came to India from Norway when she was quite small. Norway is a cold land, with mountains and snow, and the sea cutting deep into the land. I was there as a boy. It's very beautiful, and the people are good and work hard.'

'I'd like to go there.'

'You will, one day. When you are older, I'll take you to Norway.'

'Is it better than England?'

'It's quite different.'

'Is it better than India?'

'It's quite different.'

'Is India like England?'

'No, it's different.'

'Well, what does "different" mean?'

'It means things are not the same. It means people are different. It means the weather is different. It means tree and birds and insects are different.'

'Are English crocodiles different from Indian crocodiles?'

'They don't have crocodiles in England.'

'Oh, then it must be different.'

'It would be a dull world if it was the same everywhere,' said my father.

He never lost patience with my endless questioning. If he wanted a rest, he would take out his pipe and spend a long time lighting it. If this took very long I'd find something else to do. But sometimes I'd wait patiently until the pipe was drawing, and then return to the attack.

'Will we always be in India?' I asked.

'No, we'll have to go away one day. You see, it's hard to explain, but it isn't really our country.'

'Ayah says it belongs to the king of England, and the jewels in his crown were taken from India, and that when the Indians get their jewels back the king will lose India! But first they have to get the crown from the king, but this is very difficult, she says, because the crown is always on his head. He even sleeps wearing his crown!'

Ayah was my nanny. She loved me deeply, and was always filling my head with strange and wonderful stories.

My father did not comment on Ayah's views. All he said was, 'We'll have to go away some day.'

'How long have we been here?' I asked.

'Two hundred years.'

'No, I mean us.'

'Well, you were born in India, so that's seven years for you.'

'Then can't I stay here?'

'Do you want to?'

'I want to go across the sea. But can we take Ayah with us?'

'I don't know, son. Let's walk along the beach.'

We lived in an old palace beside a lake. The palace looked like a ruin from the outside, but the rooms were cool and comfortable. We lived in one wing, and my father organized a small school in another wing. His pupils were the children of the raja and the raja's relatives. My father had started life in India as a tea planter, but he had been trained as a teacher and the idea of starting a school in a small state facing the Arabian Sea had appealed to him. The pay wasn't much, but we had a palace to live in, the latest 1938 model Hillman to drive about in, and a number of servants. In those days, of course, everyone had servants (although the servants did not have any!). Ayah was our own; but the cook, the bearer, the gardener and the bhisti were all provided by the state.

Sometimes I sat in the schoolroom with the other children (who were all much bigger than me), sometimes I remained in the house with Ayah, sometimes I followed the gardener, Dukhi, about the spacious garden.

Dukhi means 'sad', and though I never could discover if the gardener had anything to feel sad about, the name certainly suited him. He had grown to resemble the drooping weeds that he was always digging up with a tiny spade. I seldom saw him standing up. He always sat on the ground with his knees well up to his chin, and attacked the weeds from this position. He could spend all day on his haunches, moving about the garden simply by shuffling his feet along the grass.

I tried to imitate his posture, sitting down on my heels and putting my knees into my armpits, but I could never hold the position for more than five minutes.

Time had no meaning in a large garden, and Dukhi never hurried. Life, for him, was not a matter of one year succeeding another, but of five seasons—winter, spring, hot weather, monsoon and autumn—arriving and departing. His seedbeds had always to be in readiness for the coming season, and he did not look any further than the next monsoon. It was impossible to tell his age. He may have been thirty-six or eighty-six. He was either very young for his years or very old for them.

Dukhi loved bright colours, especially reds and yellows. He liked strongly scented flowers, like jasmine and honeysuckle. He couldn't understand my father's preference for the more delicately perfumed petunias and sweetpeas. But I shared Dukhi's fondness for the common bright orange marigold, which is offered in temples and is used to make garlands and nosegays. When the garden was bare of all colour, the marigold would still be there, gay and flashy, challenging the sun.

Dukhi was very fond of making nosegays, and I liked to watch him at work. A sunflower formed the centrepiece. It was surrounded by roses, marigolds and oleander, fringed with green leaves and bound together with silver thread. The perfume was overpowering. The nosegays were presented to me or my father on special occasions, that is, on a birthday or to guests of my father's who were considered important.

One day I found Dukhi making a nosegay, and said, 'No one is coming today, Dukhi. It isn't even a birthday.'

'It is a birthday, Chota Sahib,' he said. 'Little Sahib' was the title he had given me. It wasn't much of a title compared to Raja Sahib, Diwan Sahib or Burra Sahib, but it was nice to have a title at the age of seven.

'Oh,' I said. 'And is there a party, too?'

'No party.'

'What's the use of a birthday without a party? What's the use of a birthday without presents?'

'This person doesn't like presents—just flowers.'

'Who is it?' I asked, full of curiosity.

'If you want to find out, you can take these flowers to her. She lives right at the top of that far side of the palace. There are twenty-two steps to climb. Remember that, Chota Sahib, you take twenty-three steps and you will go over the edge and into the lake!'

I started climbing the stairs.

It was a spiral staircase of wrought iron, and it went round and round and up and up, and it made me quite dizzy and tired.

At the top I found myself on a small balcony, which looked out over the lake and another palace, at the crowded city and the distant harbour. I heard a voice, a rather high, musical voice, saying (in English), 'Are you a ghost?' I turned to see who had spoken but found the balcony empty. The voice had come from a dark room.

I turned to the stairway, ready to flee, but the voice said, 'Oh, don't go, there's nothing to be frightened of!'

And so I stood still, peering cautiously into the darkness of the room.

'First, tell me—are you a ghost?'

'I'm a boy,' I said.

'And I'm a girl. We can be friends. I can't come out there, so you had better come in. Come along, I'm not a ghost either—not yet, anyway!'

As there was nothing very frightening about the voice, I stepped into the room. It was dark inside, and coming in from the glare, it took me some time to make out the tiny, elderly lady seated on a cushioned gilt chair. She wore a red sari, lots of coloured bangles on her wrists and golden earrings. Her hair was streaked with white, but her skin was still quite smooth and unlined, and she had large and very beautiful eyes.

'You must be Master Bond!' she said. 'Do you know who I am?'

'You're a lady with a birthday,' I said, 'but that's all I know. Dukhi didn't tell me any more.'

'If you promise to keep it a secret, I'll tell you who I am. You see, everyone thinks I'm mad. Do you think so too?'

'I don't know.'

'Well, you must tell me if you think so,' she said with a chuckle. Her laugh was the sort of sound made by the gecko, a little wall lizard, coming from deep down in the throat. 'I have a feeling you are a truthful boy. Do you find it very difficult to tell the truth?'

'Sometimes.'

'Sometimes. Of course, there are times when I tell lies—lots of little lies—because they're such fun! But would you call me a liar? I wouldn't, if I were you, but *would* you?'

'Are you a liar?'

'I'm asking you! If I were to tell you that I was a queen—that I *am* a queen—would you believe me?'

I thought deeply about this, and then said, 'I'll try to believe you.'

'Oh, but you *must* believe me. I'm a real queen, I'm a rani! Look, I've got diamonds to prove it!' And she held out her hands and there was a ring on each finger, the stones glowing and glittering in the dim light. 'Diamonds, rubies, pearls and emeralds! Only a queen can have these!' She was most anxious that I should believe her.

'You must be a queen,' I said.

'Right!' she snapped. 'In that case, would you mind calling me "Your Highness"?'

'Your Highness,' I said.

She smiled. It was a slow, beautiful smile. Her whole face lit up.

'I could love you,' she said. 'But better still, I'll give you something to eat. Do you like chocolates?'

'Yes, Your Highness.'

'Well,' she said, taking a box from the table beside her, 'these have come all the way from England. Take two. Only two, mind, otherwise the box will finish before Thursday, and I don't want that to happen because I won't get any more till Saturday. That's when Captain MacWhirr's ship gets in, the *SS Lucy*, loaded with boxes and boxes of chocolates!'

'All for you?' I asked in considerable awe.

'Yes, of course. They have to last at least three months. I get them from England. I get only the best chocolates. I like them with pink crunchy fillings, don't you?'

'Oh, yes!' I exclaimed, full of envy.

'Never mind,' she said, 'I may give you one, now and then— it you're very nice to me! Here you are, help yourself…' She pushed the chocolate box towards me.

I took a silver-wrapped chocolate, and then just as I was thinking of taking a second, she quickly took the box away.

'No more!' she said. 'They have to last till Saturday.'

'But I took only *one*,' I said with some indignation.

'Did you?' She gave me a sharp look, decided I was telling the truth, and said graciously, 'Well, in that case you can have another.'

Watching the rani carefully, in case she snatched the box away again, I selected a second chocolate, this one with a green wrapper. I don't remember what kind of day it was outside, but I remember the bright green of the chocolate wrapper.

I thought it would be rude to eat the chocolates in front of a queen, so I put them in my pocket and said, 'I'd better go now. Ayah will be looking for me.'

'And when will you be coming to see me again?'

'I don't know,' I said.

'There's something I want you to do for me,' she said, placing one finger on my shoulder and giving me a conspiratorial look. 'Will you do it?'

'What is it, Your Highness?'

'What is it? Why do you ask? A real prince never asks where or why or whatever, he simply does what the princess asks of him. When I was a princess—before I became a queen, that is—I asked a prince to swim across the lake and fetch me a lily growing on the other bank.'

'And did he get it for you?'

'He drowned halfway across. Let that be a lesson to you. Never agree to do something without knowing what it is.'

'But I thought you said…'

'Never mind what I said. It's what I say that matters!'

'Oh, all right,' I said, fidgeting to be gone. 'What is it you want me to do?'

'Nothing.' Her tiny rosebud lips pouted and she stared sullenly at a picture on the wall. Now that my eyes had grown used to the dim light in the room, I noticed that the walls were hung with portraits of stout rajas and ranis, turbaned and bedecked in fine clothes. There were also portraits of Queen Victoria and King George V of England. And, in the centre of all this distinguished company, a large picture of Mickey Mouse.

'I'll do it if it isn't too dangerous,' I said.

'Then listen.' She took my hand and drew me towards her—what a tiny hand she had!—and whispered, 'I want a *red* rose from the palace garden. But be careful! Don't let Dukhi the gardener catch you. He'll know it's for me. He knows I love roses. And he hates me! I'll tell you why, one day. But if he catches you, he'll do something terrible.'

'To me?'

'No, to himself. That's much worse, isn't it? He'll tie himself into knots, or lie naked on a bed of thorns, or go on a long fast with nothing to eat but fruit, sweets and chicken! So you will be careful, won't you?'

'Oh, but he doesn't hate you,' I cried in protest, remembering the flowers he'd sent for her, and looking around I found that I'd been sitting on them. 'Look, he sent these flowers for your birthday!'

'Well, if he sent them for my birthday, you can take them back,' she snapped. 'But if he sent them for *me*...' and she suddenly softened and looked coy, 'then I might keep them. Thank you, my dear, it was a very sweet thought.' And she leaned forward as though to kiss me.

'It's late, I must go!' I said in alarm, and turning on my heels, ran out of the room and down the spiral staircase.

Father hadn't started lunch, or rather tiffin, as we called it then. He usually waited for me if I was late. I don't suppose he enjoyed eating alone.

For tiffin we usually had rice, mutton curry (koftas or meat balls, with plenty of gravy, was my favourite curry), fried dal and a hot lime or mango pickle. For supper, we had English food—a soup, roast pork and fried potatoes, a rich gravy made by my father, and a custard or caramel pudding. My father enjoyed cooking, but it was only in the morning that he found time for it. Breakfast was his own creation. He cooked eggs in a variety of interesting ways, and favoured some Italian recipes which he had collected during a trip to Europe, long before I was born.

In deference to the feelings of our Hindu friends, we did not eat beef, but, apart from mutton and chicken, there was a plentiful supply of other meats—partridge, venison, lobster and even porcupine!

'And where have you been?' asked my father, helping himself to rice as soon as he saw me come in.

'To the top of the old palace,' I said.

'Did you meet anyone there?'

'Yes, I met a tiny lady who told me she was a rani. She gave me chocolates.'

'As a rule, she doesn't like visitors.'

'Oh, she didn't mind me. But is she really a queen?'

'Well, she's the daughter of a maharaja. That makes her a princess. She never married. There's a story that she fell in love with a commoner, one of the palace servants, and wanted to marry him, but of course they wouldn't allow that. She became very melancholic, and started living all by herself in the old palace. They give her everything she needs, but she doesn't go out or have visitors. Everyone says she's mad.'

'How do they know?' I asked.

'Because she's different from other people, I suppose.'

'Is that being mad?'

'No. Not really, I suppose madness is not seeing things as others see them.'

'Is that very bad?'

'No,' said Father, who for once was finding it very difficult to explain something to me. 'But people who are like that—people whose minds are so different that they don't think, step by step, as we do, whose thoughts jump all over the place—such people are very difficult to live with...'

'Step by step,' I repeated. 'Step by step...'

'You aren't eating,' said my father. 'Hurry up, and you can

come with me to school today.'

I always looked forward to attending my father's classes. He did not take me to the schoolroom very often, because he wanted school to be a treat, to begin with, and then later, the routine wouldn't be so unwelcome.

Sitting there with older children, understanding only half of what they were learning, I felt important and part grown-up. And of course I did learn to read and write, although I first learnt to read upside-down, by means of standing in front of the others' desks and peering across at their books. Later, when I went to school, I had some difficulty in learning to read the right way up; and even today I sometimes read upside-down, for the sake of variety. I don't mean that I read standing on my head, simply that I held the book upside-down.

I had at my command a number of rhymes and jingles, the most interesting of these being 'Solomon Grundy'.

> Solomon Grundy,
> Born on a Monday,
> Christened on Tuesday,
> Married on Wednesday,
> Took ill on Thursday,
> Worse on Friday,
> Died on Saturday,
> Buried on Sunday:
> This is the end of
> Solomon Grundy.

Was that all that life amounted to, in the end? And were we all Solomon Grundys? These were questions that bothered me at the time. Another puzzling rhyme was the one that went:

> Hark, hark,
> The dogs do bark,
> The beggars are coming to town;
> Some in rags,
> Some in bags,
> And some in velvet gowns.

This rhyme puzzled me for a long time. There were beggars aplenty in the bazaar, and sometimes they came to the house, and some of them did wear rags and bags (and some nothing at all) and the dogs did bark at them, but the beggar in the velvet gown never came our way.

'Who's this beggar in a velvet gown?' I asked my father. 'Not a beggar at all,' he said.

'Then why call him one?'

And I went to Ayah and asked her the same question, 'Who is the beggar in the velvet gown?'

'Jesus Christ,' said Ayah.

Ayah was a fervent Christian and made me say my prayers at night, even when I was very sleepy. She had, I think, Arab and Negro blood in addition to the blood of the Koli fishing community to which her mother had belonged. Her father, a sailor on an Arab dhow, had been a convert to Christianity. Ayah was a large, buxom woman, with heavy hands and feet and a slow, swaying gait that had all the grace and majesty of a royal elephant. Elephants for all their size are nimble creatures; and Ayah, too, was nimble, sensitive and gentle with her big hands. Her face was always sweet and childlike.

Although a Christian, she clung to many of the beliefs of her parents and loved to tell me stories about mischievous spirits and evil spirits, humans who changed into animals, and snakes who had been princes in their former lives.

There was the story of the snake who married a princess. At first the princess did not wish to marry the snake, whom she had met in a forest, but the snake insisted saying, 'I'll kill you if you won't marry me,' and of course that settled the question. The snake led his bride away and took her to a great treasure. 'I was a prince in my former life,' he explained. 'This treasure is yours.' And then the snake very gallantly disappeared.

'Snakes,' declared Ayah, 'were very lucky omens if seen early in the morning.'

'But, what if the snake bites the lucky person?' I asked.

'He will be lucky all the same,' said Ayah with a logic that was all her own.

Snakes! There were a number of them living in the big garden, and my father had advised me to avoid the long grass. But I had seen snakes crossing the road (a lucky omen, according to Ayah) and they were never aggressive.

'A snake won't attack you,' said Father, 'provided you leave it alone. Of course, if you step on one it will probably bite.'

'Are all snakes poisonous?'

'Yes, but only a few are poisonous enough to kill a man. Others use their poison on rats and frogs. A good thing, too, otherwise during the rains the house would be taken over by the frogs.'

One afternoon, while Father was at school, Ayah found a snake in the bathtub. It wasn't early morning and so the snake couldn't have been a lucky one. Ayah was frightened and ran into the garden calling for help. Dukhi came running. Ayah ordered me to stay outside while they went after the snake.

And it was while I was alone in the garden—an unusual

circumstance, since Dukhi was nearly always there—that I remembered the rani's request. On an impulse, I went to the nearest rose bush and plucked the largest rose, pricking my thumb in the process.

And then, without waiting to see what had happened to the snake (it finally escaped), I started up the steps to the top of the old palace.

When I got to the top, I knocked on the door of the rani's room. Getting no reply, I walked along the balcony until I reached another doorway. There were wooden panels around the door, with elephants, camels and turbaned warriors carved into it. As the door was open, I walked boldly into the room then stood still in astonishment. The room was filled with a strange light.

There were windows going right round the room, and each small windowpane was made of a different coloured glass. The sun that came through one window flung red and green and purple colours on the figure of the little rani who stood there with her face pressed to the glass.

She spoke to me without turning from the window. 'This is my favourite room. I have all the colours here. I can see a different world through each pane of glass. Come, join me!' And she beckoned to me, her small hand fluttering like a delicate butterfly.

I went up to the rani. She was only a little taller than me, and we were able to share the same windowpane.

'See, it's a red world!' she said.

The garden below, the palace and the lake, were all tinted red. I watched the rani's world for a little while and then touched her on the arm and said, 'I have brought you a rose!'

She started away from me, and her eyes looked frightened. She would not look at the rose.

'Oh, why did you bring it?' she cried, wringing her hands. 'He'll be arrested now!'

'Who'll be arrested?'

'The prince, of course!'

'But *I* took it,' I said. 'No one saw me. Ayah and Dukhi were inside the house, catching a snake.'

'Did they catch it?' she asked, forgetting about the rose.

'I don't know. I didn't wait to see!'

'They should follow the snake, instead of catching it. It may lead them to a treasure. All snakes have treasures to guard.'

This seemed to confirm what Ayah had been telling me, and I resolved that I would follow the next snake that I met.

'Don't you like the rose, then?' I asked.

'Did you steal it?'

'Yes.'

'Good. Flowers should always be stolen. They're more fragrant then.'

◆

Because of a man called Hitler war had been declared in Europe and Britain was fighting Germany.

In my comic papers, the Germans were usually shown as blundering idiots; so I didn't see how Britain could possibly lose the war, nor why it should concern India, nor why it should he necessary for my father to join up. But I remember his showing me a newspaper headline which said:

BOMBS FALL ON BUCKINGHAM PALACE—
KING AND QUEEN SAFE

I expect that had something to do with it.

He went to Delhi for an interview with the RAF and I was left in Ayah's charge.

It was a week I remember well, because it was the first time I had been left on my own. That first night I was afraid—afraid of the dark, afraid of the emptiness of the house, afraid of the howling of the jackals outside. The loud ticking of the clock was the only reassuring sound: clocks really made themselves heard in those days! I tried concentrating on the ticking, shutting out other sounds and the menace of the dark, but it wouldn't work. I thought I heard a faint hissing near the bed, and sat up, bathed in perspiration, certain that a snake was in the room. I shouted for Ayah and she came running, switching on all the lights.

'A snake!' I cried. 'There's a snake in the room!'

'Where, baba?'

'I don't know where, but I *heard* it.'

Ayah looked under the bed, and behind the chairs and tables, but there was no snake to be found. She persuaded me that I must have heard the breeze whispering in the mosquito curtains.

But I didn't want to be left alone.

'I'm coming to you,' I said and followed her into her small room near the kitchen.

Ayah slept on a low string cot. The mattress was thin, the blanket worn and patched up; but Ayah's warm and solid body made up for the discomfort of the bed. I snuggled up to her and was soon asleep.

I had almost forgotten the rani in the old palace and was about to pay her a visit when, to my surprise, I found her in the garden. I had risen early that morning, and had gone running barefoot over the dew-drenched grass. No one was about, but

LESSONS IN FUN AND FROLIC

I startled a flock of parrots and the birds rose screeching from a banyan tree and wheeled away to some other corner of the palace grounds. I was just in time to see a mongoose scurrying across the grass with an egg in its mouth. The mongoose must have been raiding the poultry farm at the palace.

I was trying to locate the mongoose's hideout, and was on all fours in a jungle of tall cosmos plants when I heard the rustle of clothes, and turned to find the rani staring at me.

She didn't ask me what I was doing there, but simply said: 'I don't think he could have gone in there.'

'But I saw him go this way,' I said.

'Nonsense! He doesn't live in this part of the garden. He lives in the roots of the banyan tree.'

'But that's where the snake lives,' I said

'You mean the snake who was a prince. Well, that's whom I'm looking for!'

'A snake who was a prince!' I gaped at the rani.

She made a gesture of impatience with her butterfly hands, and said, 'Tut, you're only a child, you can't understand. The prince lives in the roots of the banyan tree, but he comes out early every morning. Have you seen him?'

'No. But I saw a mongoose.'

The rani became frightened. 'Oh dear, is there a mongoose in the garden? He might kill the prince!'

'How can a mongoose kill a prince?' I asked.

'You don't understand, Master Bond. Princes, when they die, are born again as snakes.'

'*All* princes?'

'No, only those who die before they can marry.'

'Did your prince die before he could marry you?'

'Yes. And he returned to this garden in the form of a beautiful snake.'

'Well,' I said, 'I hope it wasn't the snake the water carrier killed last week.'

'He killed a snake!' The rani looked horrified. She was quivering all over. 'It might have been the prince!'

'It was a brown snake,' I said.

'Oh, then it wasn't him.' She looked very relieved. 'Brown snakes are only ministers and people like that. It has to be a green snake to be a prince.'

'I haven't seen any green snakes here.'

'There's one living in the roots of the banyan tree. You won't kill it, will you?'

'Not if it's really a prince.'

'And you won't let others kill it?'

'I'll tell Ayah.'

'Good. You're on my side. But be careful of the gardener. Keep him away from the banyan tree. He's always killing snakes. I don't trust him at all.'

She came nearer and, leaning forward a little, looked into my eyes.

'Blue eyes—I trust them. But don't trust green eyes. And yellow eyes are evil.'

'I've never seen yellow eyes.'

'That's because you're pure,' she said and turned away and hurried across the lawn as though she had just remembered a very urgent appointment.

The sun was up, slanting through the branches of the banyan tree, and Ayah's voice could be heard calling me for breakfast.

'Dukhi,' I said, when I found him in the garden later that

day, 'Dukhi, don't kill the snake in the banyan tree.'

'A snake in the banyan tree!' he exclaimed, seizing his hose.

'No, no!' I said. 'I haven't seen it. But the rani says there's one. She says it was a prince in its former life, and that we shouldn't kill it.'

'Oh,' said Dukhi, smiling to himself. 'The rani says so. All right, you tell her we won't kill it.'

'Is it true that she was in love with a prince but that he died before she could marry him?'

'Something like that,' said Dukhi. 'It was a long time ago—before I came here.'

'My father says it wasn't a prince, but a commoner. Are you a commoner, Dukhi?'

'A commoner? What's that, Chota Sahib?'

'I'm not sure. Someone very poor, I suppose.'

'Then I must be a commoner,' said Dukhi.

'Were you in love with the rani?' I asked.

Dukhi was so startled that he dropped his hose and lost his balance; the first time I'd seen him lose his poise while squatting on his haunches.

'Don't say such things, Chota Sahib!'

'Why not?'

'You'll get me into trouble.'

'Then it must be true.'

Dukhi threw up his hands in mock despair and started collecting his implements.

'It's true, it's true!' I cried, dancing round him, and then I ran indoors to Ayah and said, 'Ayah, Dukhi was in love with the rani!'

Ayah gave a shriek of laughter, then looked very serious

and put her finger against my lips.

'Don't say such things,' she said. 'Dukhi is of a very low caste. People won't like it if they hear what you say. And besides, the rani told you her prince died and turned into a snake. Well, Dukhi hasn't become a snake as yet, has he?'

True, Dukhi didn't look as though he could be anything but a gardener; but I wasn't satisfied with his denials or with Ayah's attempts to still my tongue. Hadn't Dukhi sent the rani a nosegay?

When my father came home, he looked quite pleased with himself.

'What have you brought for me?' was the first question I asked.

He had brought me some new books, a dartboard and a train set; and in my excitement over examining these gifts, I forgot to ask about the result of his trip.

It was during tiffin that he told me what had happened—and what was going to happen.

'We'll be going away soon,' he said. 'I've joined the Royal Air Force. I'll have to work in Delhi.'

'Oh! Will you be in the war, Dad? Will you fly a plane?'

'No, I'm too old to be flying planes. I'll be forty years old in July. The RAF will be giving me what they call intelligence work—decoding secret messages and things like that and I don't suppose I'll be able to tell you much about it.'

This didn't sound as exciting as flying planes, but it sounded important and rather mysterious.

'Well, I hope it's interesting,' I said. 'Is Delhi a good place to live in?'

'I'm not sure. It will be very hot by the middle of April.

And you won't be able to stay with me, Ruskin—not at first, anyway, not until I can get married quarters and then, only if your mother returns... Meanwhile, you'll stay with your grandmother in Dehra.' He must have seen the disappointment in my face, because he quickly added: 'Of course, I'll come to see you often. Dehra isn't far from Delhi—only a night's train journey.'

But I was dismayed. It wasn't that I didn't want to stay with my grandmother, but I had grown so used to sharing my father's life and even watching him at work, that the thought of being separated from him was unbearable.

'Not as bad as going to boarding school,' he said. 'And that's the only alternative.'

'Not boarding school,' I said quickly, 'I'll run away from boarding school.'

'Well, you won't want to run away from your grandmother. She's very fond of you. And if you come with me to Delhi, you'll be alone all day in a stuffy little hut while I'm away at work. Sometimes I may have to go on tour—then what happens?'

'I don't mind being on my own.' And this was true. I had already grown accustomed to having my own room and my own trunk and my own bookshelf and I felt as though I was about to lose these things.

'Will Ayah come too?' I asked.

My father looked thoughtful. 'Would you like that?'

'Ayah must come,' I said firmly. 'Otherwise I'll run away.'

'I'll have to ask her,' said my father.

Ayah, it turned out, was quite ready to come with us. In fact, she was indignant that Father should have considered leaving her behind. She had brought me up since my mother went away, and she wasn't going to hand over charge to any upstart aunt or governess. She was pleased and excited at the prospect of the move, and this helped to raise my spirits.

'What is Dehra like?' I asked my father.

'It's a green place,' he said. 'It lies in a valley in the foothills of the Himalayas and it's surrounded by forests. There are lots of trees in Dehra.'

'Does Grandmother's house have trees?'

'Yes. There's a big jackfruit tree in the garden. Your grandmother planted it when I was a boy. And there's an old banyan tree, which is good to climb. And there are fruit trees, litchis, mangoes, papayas.'

'Are there any books?'

'Grandmother's books won't interest you. But I'll be bringing you books from Delhi whenever I come to see you.'

I was beginning to look forward to the move. Changing houses had always been fun. Changing towns ought to be fun, too.

A few days before we left, I went to say goodbye to the rani.

'I'm going away,' I said.

'How lovely!' said the rani. 'I wish I could go away!'

'Why don't you?'

'They won't let me. They're afraid to let me out of the palace.'

'What are they afraid of, Your Highness?'

'That I might run away. Run away, far, far away, to the land where the leopards are learning to pray.'

Gosh, I thought, she's really quite crazy... But then she was silent, and started smoking a small hookah.

She drew on the hookah, looked at me, and asked, 'Where is your mother?'

'I haven't one.'

'Everyone has a mother. Did yours die?'

'No. She went away.'

She drew on her hookah again and then said, very sweetly, 'Don't go away…'

'I must,' I said. 'It's because of the war.'

'What war? Is there a war on? You see, no one tells me anything.'

'It's between us and Hitler,' I said.

'And who is Hitler?'

'He's a German.'

'I knew a German once, Dr Schreinherr, he had beautiful hands.'

'Was he an artist?'

'He was a dentist.'

The rani got up from her couch and accompanied me out on to the balcony. When we looked down at the garden, we could see Dukhi weeding a flower bed. Both of us gazed down at him in silence, and I wondered what the rani would say if I asked her if she had ever been in love with the palace gardener. Ayah had told me it would be an insulting question, so I held my peace. But as I walked slowly down the spiral staircase, the rani's voice came after me.

'Thank him,' she said. 'Thank him for the beautiful rose.'

A CASE FOR INSPECTOR LAL

I met Inspector Keemat Lal about two years ago, while I was living in the hot, dusty town of Shahpur in the plains of northern India.

Keemat Lal had charge of the local police station. He was a heavily built man, slow and rather ponderous, and inclined to be lazy; but, like most lazy people, he was intelligent. He was also a failure. He had remained an Inspector for a number of years, and had given up all hopes of a further promotion. His luck was against him, he said. He should never have been a policeman. He had been born under the sign of Capricorn and should really have gone into the restaurant business; but now it was too late to do anything about it.

The Inspector and I had little in common. He was nearing forty, and I was twenty-five. But both of us spoke English, and in Shahpur there were very few people who did. In addition, we were both fond of beer. There were no places of entertainment in Shahpur. The searing heat, the dust that came whirling up from the east, the mosquitoes (almost as numerous as the flies), and the general monotony gave one a thirst for something more substantial than stale lemonade.

My house was on the outskirts of the town, where we were often not disturbed. On two or three evenings in the week, just as the sun was going down and making it possible for one to emerge from the khas-cooled confines of a dark, high-ceilinged bedroom, Inspector Keemat Lal would appear on the verandah steps, mopping the sweat from his face with a small towel, which he used instead of a handkerchief. My only servant, excited at the prospect of serving an inspector of police, would hurry out with glasses, a bucket of ice and several bottles of the best Indian beer.

One evening, after we had overtaken our fourth bottle, I said, 'You must have had some interesting cases in your career, Inspector.'

'Most of them were rather dull,' he said. 'At least the successful ones were. The sensational cases usually went unsolved—otherwise I might have been a superintendent by now. I suppose you are talking of murder cases. Do you remember the shooting of the Minister of the Interior? I was on that one, but it was a political murder and we never solved it.'

'Tell me about a case you solved,' I said. 'An interesting one.' When I saw him looking uncomfortable, I added, 'You don't have to worry, Inspector. I'm a very discreet person, in spite of all the beer I consume.'

'But how can you be discreet? You are a writer.'

I protested: 'Writers are usually very discreet. They always change the names of people and places.'

He gave me one of his rare smiles. 'And how would you describe me, if you were to put me into a story?'

'Oh, I'd leave you as you are. No one would believe in you, anyway.'

He laughed indulgently and poured out more beer. 'I suppose I can change names, too... I will tell you a very interesting case. The victim was an unusual person, and so was the killer. But you must promise not to write this story.'

'I promise,' I lied.

'Do you know Panauli?'

'In the hills? Yes, I have been there once or twice.'

'Good, then you will follow me without my having to be too descriptive. This happened about three years ago, shortly after I had been stationed at Panauli. Nothing much ever happened there. There were a few cases of theft and cheating, and an occasional fight during the summer. A murder took place about once every ten years. It was, therefore, quite an event when the Rani of— was found dead in her sitting-room, her head split open by an axe. I knew that I would have to solve the case if I wanted to stay in Panauli.

'The trouble was, anyone could have killed the Rani, and there were some who made no secret of their satisfaction that she was dead. She had been an unpopular woman. Her husband was dead, her children were scattered, and her money—for she had never been a very wealthy Rani—had been dwindling away. She lived alone in an old house on the outskirts of the town, ruling the locality with the stern authority of a matriarch. She had a servant, and he was the man who found the body and came to the police, dithering and tongue-tied. I arrested him at once, of course. I knew he was probably innocent, but a basic rule is to grab the first man on the scene of the crime, especially if he happens to be a servant. But we let him go after a beating. There was nothing much he could tell us, and he had a sound alibi.

'The axe with which the Rani had been killed must have been a small woodcutter's axe—so we deduced from the wound. We couldn't find the weapon. It might have been used by a man or a woman, and there were several of both sexes who had a grudge against the Rani. There were bazaar rumours that she had been supplementing her income by trafficking in young women: she had the necessary connections. There were also rumours that she possessed vast wealth, and that it was stored away in her godowns. We did not find any treasure. There were so many rumours darting about like battered shuttlecocks that I decided to stop wasting my time in trying to follow them up. Instead I restricted my enquiries to those people who had been close to the Rani—either in their personal relationships or in actual physical proximity.

'To begin with, there was Mr Kapur, a wealthy businessman from Bombay who had a house in Panauli. He was supposed to be an old admirer of the Rani's. I discovered that he had occasionally lent her money, and that, in spite of his professed friendship for her, he had charged a high rate of interest.

'Then there were her immediate neighbours—an American missionary and his wife, who had been trying to convert the Rani to Christianity; an English spinster of seventy who made no secret of the fact that she and the Rani had hated each other with great enthusiasm; a local councillor and his family, who did not get on well with their aristocratic neighbour; and a tailor, who kept his shop close by. None of these people had any powerful motive for killing the Rani—or none that I could discover. But the tailor's daughter interested me.

'Her name was Kusum. She was twelve or thirteen years old—a thin dark girl, with lovely black eyes and a swift, disarming smile. While I was making my routine enquiries in the vicinity of the Rani's house, I noticed that the girl always tried to avoid me. When I questioned her about the Rani, and about her own movements on the day of the crime, she pretended to be very vague and stupid.

'But I could see she was not stupid, and I became convinced that she knew something unusual about the Rani. She might even know something about the murder. She could have been protecting someone, and was afraid to tell me what she knew. Often, when I spoke to her of the violence of the Rani's death, I saw fear in her eyes. I began to think the girl's life might be in danger, and I had a close watch kept on her. I liked her. I liked her youth and freshness and the innocence and wonder in her eyes. I spoke to her whenever I could, kindly and paternally, and though I knew she rather liked me and found me amusing—the ups and downs of Panauli always left me panting for breath—and though I could see that she *wanted* to tell me something, she always held back at the last moment.

'Then, one afternoon while I was in the Rani's house going through her effects, I saw something glistening in a narrow crack near the doorstep. I would not have noticed it if the sun had not been pouring through the window, glinting off the little object. I stooped and picked up a piece of glass. It was part of a broken bangle.

'I turned the fragment over in my hand. There was something familiar about its colour and design. Didn't Kusum wear similar glass bangles? I went to look for the girl but she was not at her father's shop. I was told that she had gone down the hill, to gather firewood.

'I decided to take the narrow path down the hill. It went round some rocks and cactus, and then disappeared into a forest of oak trees. I found Kusum sitting at the edge of the forest, a bundle of twigs beside her.

'"You are always wandering about alone," I said. "Don't you feel afraid?"

'"It is safer when I am alone," she replied. "Nobody comes here."

'I glanced quickly at the bangles on her wrist, and noticed that their colour matched that of the broken piece. I held out the bit of broken glass and said, "I found it in the Rani's house. It must have fallen…"

'She did not wait for me to finish what I was saying. With a look of terror, she sprang up from the grass and fled into the forest.

'I was completely taken aback. I had not expected such a reaction. Of what significance was the broken bangle? I hurried after the girl, slipping on the smooth pine needles that covered the slopes. I was searching amongst the trees when I heard someone sobbing behind me. When I turned round, I saw the girl standing on a boulder, facing me with an axe in her hands.

'When Kusum saw me staring at her, she raised the axe and rushed down the slope towards me.

'I was too bewildered to be able to do anything but stare with open mouth as she rushed at me with the axe. The impetus of her run would have brought her right up against me, and the axe, coming down, would probably have crushed my skull, thick though it is. But while she was still six feet from me, the axe flew out of her hands. It sprang into the air as though it had a life of its own and came curving towards me.

'In spite of my weight, I moved swiftly aside. The axe grazed my shoulder and sank into the soft bark of the tree behind me. And Kusum dropped at my feet, weeping hysterically.

Inspector Keemat Lal paused in order to replenish his glass. He took a long pull at the beer, and the froth glistened on his moustache.

'And then what happened?' I prompted him.

'Perhaps it could only have happened in India—and to a person like me,' he said. 'This sudden compassion for the person you are supposed to destroy. Instead of being furious and outraged, instead of seizing the girl and marching her off to the police station, I stroked her head and said silly comforting things.'

'And she told you that she had killed the Rani?'

'She told me how the Rani had called her to her house and given her tea and sweets. Mr Kapur had been there. After some time he began stroking Kusum's arms and squeezing her knees. She had drawn away, but Kapur kept pawing her. The Rani was telling Kusum not to be afraid, that no harm would come to her. Kusum slipped away from the man and made a rush for the door. The Rani caught her by the shoulders and pushed her back into the room. The Rani was getting angry. Kusum saw the axe lying in a corner of the room. She seized it, raised it above her head and threatened Kapur. The man realized that he had gone too far, and, valuing his neck, backed away. But the Rani, in a great rage, sprang at the girl. And Kusum, in desperation and panic, brought the axe down across the Rani's head.'

'The Rani fell to the ground. Without waiting to see what Kapur might do, Kusum fled from the house. Her bangle must have broken when she stumbled against the door. She ran into the forest and, after concealing the axe amongst some tall ferns, lay weeping on the grass until it grew dark. But such was her nature, and such the resilience of youth, that she recovered sufficiently to be able to return home looking her normal self. And during the following days she managed to remain silent about the whole business.'

'What did you do about it?' I asked.

Keemat Lal looked me straight in my beery eye.

'Nothing,' he said. 'I did absolutely nothing. I couldn't have the girl put away in a remand home. It would have crushed her spirit.'

'And what about Kapur?'

'Oh, he had his own reasons for remaining quiet, as you may guess. No, the case was closed—or perhaps I should say the file was put in my pending tray. My promotion, too, went into the pending tray.'

'It didn't turn out very well for you,' I said.

'No. Here I am in Shahpur, and still an Inspector. But, tell me, what would you have done if you had been in my place?'

I considered his question carefully for a moment or two, then said, 'I suppose it would have depended on how much sympathy the girl evoked in me. She had killed in innocence...'

'Then you would have put your personal feelings above your duty to uphold the law?'

'Yes. But I would not have made a very good policeman.'

'Exactly.'

'Still, it's a pity that Kapur got off so easily.'

'There was no alternative if I was to let the girl go. But he didn't get off altogether. He found himself in trouble later for swindling some manufacturing concern, and went to jail for a couple of years.'

'And the girl—did you see her again?'

'Well, before I was transferred from Panauli, I saw her occasionally on the road. She was usually on her way to school. She would greet me with joined palms, and call me Uncle.'

The beer bottles were all empty, and Inspector Keemat Lal got up to leave. His final words to me were, 'I should never have been a policeman.'

OUR GREAT ESCAPE

It had been a lonely winter for a fourteen-year-old. I had spent the first few weeks of the vacation with my mother and stepfather in Dehra. Then they left for Delhi, and I was pretty much on my own. Of course, the servants were there to take care of my needs, but there was no one to keep me company. I would wander off in the mornings, taking some path up the hills, come back home for lunch, read a bit and then stroll off again till it was time for dinner. Sometimes I walked up to my grandparents' house, but it seemed so different now, with people I didn't know occupying the house.

The three-month winter break over, I was almost eager to return to my boarding school in Shimla.

It wasn't as though I had many friends at school. I needed a friend but it was not easy to find one among a horde of rowdy, pea-shooting eighth formers, who carved their names on desks and stuck chewing gum on the class teacher's chair. Had I grown up with other children, I might have developed a taste for schoolboy anarchy; but in sharing my father's loneliness after his separation from my mother, and in being bereft of any close family ties, I had turned into a premature adult.

After a month in the eighth form, I began to notice a new boy, Omar, and then only because he was a quiet, almost taciturn person who took no part in the form's feverish attempt to imitate the Marx Brothers at the circus. He showed no resentment at the prevailing anarchy, nor did he make a move to participate in it. Once he caught me looking at him, and he smiled ruefully, tolerantly. Did I sense another adult in the class? Someone who was a little older than his years?

Even before we began talking to each other, Omar and I developed an understanding of sorts, and we'd nod almost respectfully to each other when we met in the classroom corridors or the environs of the dining hall or the dormitory. We were not in the same house. The house system practised its own form of apartheid, whereby a member of one house was not expected to fraternize with someone belonging to another. Those public schools certainly knew how to clamp you into compartments. However, these barriers vanished when Omar and I found ourselves selected for the School Colts' hockey team, Omar as a full-back, I as the goalkeeper.

The taciturn Omar now spoke to me occasionally, and we combined well on the field of play. A good understanding is needed between a goalkeeper and a full-back. We were on the same wavelength. I anticipated his moves, he was familiar with mine. Years later, when I read Conrad's *The Secret Sharer*, I thought of Omar.

It wasn't until we were away from the confines of school, classroom and dining hall that our friendship flourished. The hockey team travelled to Sanawar on the next mountain range, where we were to play a couple of matches against our old rivals, the Lawrence Memorial Royal Military School. This had been my father's old school, so I was keen to explore its grounds and peep into its classrooms.

Omar and I were thrown together a good deal during the visit to Sanawar, and in our more leisurely moments, strolling undisturbed around a school where we were guests and not pupils, we exchanged life histories and other confidences. Omar, too, had lost his father—had I sensed that before?—shot in some tribal encounter on the Frontier, for he hailed from the lawless lands beyond Peshawar. A wealthy uncle was seeing to Omar's education.

We wandered into the school chapel, and there I found my father's name—A. A. Bond—on the school's roll of honour board: old boys who had lost their lives while serving during the two World Wars.

'What did his initials stand for?' asked Omar.

'Aubrey Alexander.'

'Unusual names, like yours. Why did your parents call you Rusty?'

'I am not sure.' I told him about the book I was writing. It was my first one and was called *Nine Months* (the length of the school term, not a pregnancy), and it described some of the happenings at school and lampooned a few of our teachers. I had filled three slim exercise books with this premature literary project, and I allowed Omar to go through them. He must have been my first reader and critic.

'They're very interesting,' he said, 'but you'll get into trouble if someone finds them, especially Mr Fisher.'

I have to admit it wasn't great literature. I was better at hockey and football. I made some spectacular saves, and we won our matches against Sanawar. When we returned to Shimla, we were school heroes for a couple of days and lost some of our reticence; we were even a little more forthcoming with other boys. And then Mr Fisher, my housemaster, discovered my literary opus, *Nine Months*, under my mattress, and took it away and read it (as he told me later) from cover to cover.

OUR GREAT ESCAPE

Corporal punishment then being in vogue, I was given six of the best with a springy Malacca cane, and my manuscript was torn up and deposited in Mr Fisher's wastepaper basket. All I had to show for my efforts were some purple welts on my bottom. These were proudly displayed to all who were interested, and I was a hero for another two days.

'Will you go away too when the British leave India?' Omar asked me one day.

'I don't think so,' I said. 'I don't have anyone to go back to in England, and my guardian, Mr Harrison, too seems to have no intention of going back.'

'Everyone is saying that our leaders and the British are going to divide the country. Shimla will be in India, Peshawar in Pakistan!'

'Oh, it won't happen,' I said glibly. 'How can they cut up such a big country?' But even as we chatted about the possibility, Nehru, Jinnah and Mountbatten, and all those who mattered, were preparing their instruments for major surgery.

Before their decision impinged on our lives and everyone else's, we found a little freedom of our own, in an underground tunnel that we discovered below the third flat.

It was really part of an old, disused drainage system, and when Omar and I began exploring it, we had no idea just how far it extended. After crawling along on our bellies for some twenty feet, we found ourselves in complete darkness. Omar had brought along a small pencil torch, and with its help we continued writhing forward (moving backwards would have been quite impossible) until we saw a glimmer of light at the end of the tunnel. Dusty, musty, very scruffy, we emerged at last on to a grassy knoll, a little way outside the school boundary.

It's always a great thrill to escape beyond the boundaries that adults have devised. Here we were in unknown territory. To travel without passports—that would be the ultimate in freedom!

But more passports were on their way—and more boundaries.

Lord Mountbatten, viceroy and governor-general-to-be, came for our Founder's Day and gave away the prizes. I had won a prize for something or the other, and mounted the rostrum to receive my book from this towering, handsome man in his pinstripe suit. Bishop Cotton's was then the premier school of India, often referred to as the 'Eton of the East'. Viceroys and governors had graced its functions. Many of its boys had gone on to eminence in the civil services and armed forces. There was one 'old boy' about whom they maintained a stolid silence—General Dyer, who had ordered the massacre at Amritsar and destroyed the trust that had been building up between Britain and India.

Now Mountbatten spoke of the momentous events that were happening all around us—the War had just come to an end, the United Nations held out the promise of a world living in peace and harmony, and India, an equal partner with Britain, would be among the great nations...

A few weeks later, Bengal and the Punjab provinces were bisected. Riots flared up across northern India, and there was a great exodus of people crossing the newly-drawn frontiers of Pakistan and India. Homes were destroyed, thousands lost their lives.

The common room radio and the occasional newspaper kept us abreast of events, but in our tunnel, Omar and I felt immune from all that was happening, worlds away from all the pillage, murder and revenge. And outside the tunnel, on the pine knoll below the school, there was fresh untrodden grass, sprinkled with clover and daisies; the only sounds we heard were the hammering of a woodpecker and the distant insistent call of the Himalayan Barbet. Who could touch us there?

'And when all the wars are done,' I said, 'a butterfly will still be beautiful.'

'Did you read that somewhere?'

'No, it just came into my head.'

'Already you're a writer.'

'No, I want to play hockey for India or football for Arsenal. Only winning teams!'

'You can't win forever. Better to be a writer.'

When the monsoon arrived, the tunnel was flooded, the drain choked with rubble. We were allowed out to the cinema to see Laurence Olivier's *Hamlet*, a film that did nothing to raise our spirits on a wet and gloomy afternoon; but it was our last picture that year, because communal riots suddenly broke out in Shimla's Lower Bazaar, an area that was still much as Kipling had described it—'a man who knows his way there can defy all the police of India's summer capital'—and we were confined to school indefinitely.

One morning after prayers in the chapel, the headmaster announced that the Muslim boys—those who had their homes in what was now Pakistan—would have to be evacuated, sent to their homes across the border with an armed convoy.

The tunnel no longer provided an escape for us. The bazaar was out of bounds. The flooded playing field was deserted. Omar and I sat on a damp wooden bench and talked about the future in vaguely hopeful terms, but we didn't solve any problems. Mountbatten and Nehru and Jinnah were doing all the solving.

It was soon time for Omar to leave—he left along with some fifty other boys from Lahore, Pindi and Peshawar. The rest of us—Hindus, Christians, Parsis—helped them load their luggage into the waiting trucks. A couple of boys broke down and wept. So did our departing school captain, a Pathan who had been known for his stoic and unemotional demeanour. Omar waved cheerfully to me and I waved back. We had vowed to meet again some day.

The convoy got through safely enough. There was only one casualty—the school cook, who had strayed into an off-limits area in the foothill town of Kalika and been set upon by a mob. He wasn't seen again.

Towards the end of the school year, just as we were all getting ready to leave for the school holidays, I received a letter from Omar. He told me something about his new school and how he missed my company and our games and our tunnel to freedom. I replied and gave him my home address, but I did not hear from him again.

Some seventeen or eighteen years later, I did get news of Omar, but in an entirely different context. India and Pakistan were at war, and in a bombing raid over Ambala, not far from Shimla, a Pakistani plane was shot down. Its crew died in the crash. One of them, I learnt later, was Omar.

Did he, I wonder, get a glimpse of the playing fields we knew so well as boys? Perhaps memories of his schooldays flooded back as he flew over the foothills. Perhaps he remembered the tunnel through which we were able to make our little escape to freedom.

But there are no tunnels in the sky.

THE TROUBLE WITH DJINNS

My friend Jimmy has only one arm. He lost the other when he was a young man of twenty-five. The story of how he lost his good right arm is a little difficult to believe, but I swear that it is absolutely true.

To begin with, Jimmy was (and presumably still is) a djinn. Now a djinn isn't really a human like us. A djinn is a spirit creature from another world who has assumed, for a lifetime, the physical aspect of a human being. Jimmy was a true djinn and he had the djinn's gift of being able to elongate his arm at will. Most djinns can stretch their arms to a distance of twenty or thirty feet. Jimmy could attain forty feet. His arm would move through space or up walls or along the ground like a beautiful gliding serpent. I have seen him stretched out beneath a mango tree, helping himself to ripe mangoes from the top of the tree. He loved mangoes. He was a natural glutton and it was probably his gluttony that first led him to misuse his peculiar gifts.

We were at school together at a hill station in northern India. Jimmy was particularly good at basketball. He was clever enough not to lengthen his arm too much because he did not want anyone to know that he was a djinn. In the boxing ring, he generally won his fights. His opponents never seemed to get past his amazing reach. He just kept tapping them on the nose until they retired from the ring, bloody and bewildered.

It was during the half-term examinations that I stumbled on Jimmy's secret. We had been set a particularly difficult algebra paper, but I had managed to cover a couple of sheets with correct answers and was about to forge ahead on another sheet when I noticed someone's hand on my desk. At first I thought it was the invigilator's. But when I looked up there was no one beside me.

Could it be the boy sitting directly behind? No, he was engrossed in his question paper and had his hands to himself. Meanwhile, the hand on my desk had grasped my answer sheets and was cautiously moving off. Following its descent, I found that it was attached to an arm of amazing length and pliability. This moved stealthily down the desk and slithered across the floor, shrinking all the while, until it was restored to its normal length. Its owner was of course one who had never been any good at algebra.

I had to write out my answers a second time but after the exam, I went straight up to Jimmy, told him I didn't like his game and threatened to expose him. He begged me not to let anyone know, assured me that he couldn't really help himself and offered to be of service to me whenever I wished. It was tempting to have Jimmy as my friend, for with his long reach he would obviously be useful. I agreed to overlook the matter of the pilfered papers and we became the best of pals.

It did not take me long to discover that Jimmy's gift was more of a nuisance than a constructive aid. That was because Jimmy had a second-rate mind and did not know how to make proper use of his powers. He seldom rose above the trivial. He used his long arm in the tuck shop, in the classroom, in the dormitory. And when we were allowed out to the cinema, he used it in the dark of the hall.

THE TROUBLE WITH DJINNS

Now the trouble with all djinns is that they have a weakness for women with long black hair. The longer and blacker the hair, the better for djinns. And should a djinn manage to take possession of the woman he desires, she goes into a decline and her beauty decays. Everything about her is destroyed except for the beautiful long black hair.

Jimmy was still too young to be able to take possession in this way, but he couldn't resist touching and stroking long black hair. The cinema was the best place for the indulgence of his whims. His arm would start stretching, his fingers would feel their way along the rows of seats, and his lengthening limb would slowly work its way along the aisle until it reached the back of the seat in which sat the object of his admiration. His hand would stroke the long black hair with great tenderness and if the girl felt anything and looked round, Jimmy's hand would disappear behind the seat and lie there poised like the hood of a snake, ready to strike again.

At college two or three years later, Jimmy's first real victim succumbed to his attentions. She was a lecturer in economics, not very good looking, but her hair, black and lustrous, reached almost to her knees. She usually kept it in plaits but Jimmy saw her one morning just after she had taken a head bath, and her hair lay spread out on the cot on which she was reclining. Jimmy could no longer control himself. His spirit, the very essence of his personality, entered the woman's body and the next day she was distraught, feverish and excited. She would not eat, went into a coma and in a few days dwindled to a mere skeleton. When she died, she was nothing but skin and bone but her hair had lost none of its loveliness.

I took pains to avoid Jimmy after this tragic event. I could not prove that he was the cause of the lady's sad demise but in my own heart, I was quite certain of it. For since meeting Jimmy, I had read a good deal about djinns and knew their ways.

We did not see each other for a few years. And then, holidaying in the hills last year, I found we were staying at the same hotel. I could not very well ignore him and after we had drunk a few beers together I began to feel that I had perhaps misjudged Jimmy and that he was not the irresponsible djinn I had taken him for. Perhaps the college lecturer had died of some mysterious malady that attacks only college lecturers and Jimmy had nothing at all to do with it.

We had decided to take our lunch and a few bottles of beer to a grassy knoll just below the main motor road. It was late afternoon and I had been sleeping off the effects of the beer when I woke to find Jimmy looking rather agitated.

'What's wrong?' I asked.

'Up there, under the pine trees,' he said. 'Just above the road. Don't you see them?'

'I see two girls,' I said. 'So what?'

'The one on the left. Haven't you noticed her hair?'

'Yes, it is very long and beautiful and—now look, Jimmy, you'd better get a grip on yourself!' But already his hand was out of sight, his arm snaking up the hillside and across the road.

Presently I saw the hand emerge from some bushes near the girls and then cautiously make its way to the girl with the black tresses. So absorbed was Jimmy in the pursuit of his favourite pastime that he failed to hear the blowing of a horn. Around the bend of the road came a speeding Mercedes Benz truck.

Jimmy saw the truck but there wasn't time for him to shrink his arm back to normal. It lay right across the entire width of the road and when the truck had passed over it, it writhed and twisted like a mortally wounded python.

By the time the truck driver and I could fetch a doctor, the arm (or what was left of it) had shrunk to its ordinary size. We took Jimmy to hospital where the doctors found it necessary to amputate. The truck driver, who kept insisting that the arm he ran over was at least thirty feet long, was arrested on a charge of drunken driving.

Some weeks later I asked Jimmy, 'Why are you so depressed? You still have one arm. Isn't it gifted in the same way?'

'I never tried to find out,' he said, 'and I'm not going to try now.'

He is, of course, still a djinn at heart and whenever he sees a girl with long black hair he must be terribly tempted to try out his one good arm and stroke her beautiful tresses. But he has learnt his lesson. It is better to be a human without any gifts than a djinn or a genius with one too many.

THE BLUE UMBRELLA

I

'Neelu! Neelu!' cried Binya.

She scrambled barefoot over the rocks, ran over the short summer grass, up and over the brow of the hill, all the time calling 'Neelu, Neelu!' Neelu—Blue—was the name of the blue-grey cow. The other cow, which was white, was called Gori, meaning Fair One. They were fond of wandering off on their own, down to the stream or into the pine forest, and sometimes they came back by themselves and sometimes they stayed away—almost deliberately, it seemed to Binya.

If the cows didn't come home at the right time, Binya would be sent to fetch them. Sometimes her brother, Bijju, went with her, but these days he was busy preparing for his exams and didn't have time to help with the cows.

Binya liked being on her own, and sometimes she allowed the cows to lead her into some distant valley, and then they would all be late coming home. The cows preferred having Binya with them, because she let them wander. Bijju pulled them by their tails if they went too far.

Binya belonged to the mountains, to this part of the Himalaya known as Garhwal. Dark forests and lonely hilltops held no terrors for her. It was only when she was in the market town, jostled by the crowds in the bazaar, that she felt rather nervous and lost. The town, five miles from the village, was also a pleasure resort for tourists from all over India.

Binya was probably ten. She may have been nine or even eleven, she couldn't be sure because no one in the village kept birthdays; but her mother told her she'd been born during a winter when the snow had come up to the windows, and that was just over ten years ago, wasn't it? Two years later, her father had died, but his passing had made no difference to their way of life. They had three tiny terraced fields on the side of the mountain, and they grew potatoes, onions, ginger, beans, mustard and maize: not enough to sell in the town, but enough to live on.

Like most mountain girls, Binya was quite sturdy, fair of skin, with pink cheeks and dark eyes and her black hair tied in a pigtail. She wore pretty glass bangles on her wrists, and a necklace of glass beads. From the necklace hung a leopard's claw. It was a lucky charm, and Binya always wore it. Bijju had one, too, only his was attached to a string.

Binya's full name was Binyadevi, and Bijju's real name was Vijay, but everyone called them Binya and Bijju. Binya was two years younger than her brother.

She had stopped calling for Neelu; she had heard the cowbells tinkling, and knew the cows hadn't gone far. Singing to herself, she walked over fallen pine needles into the forest glade on the spur of the hill. She heard voices, laughter, the clatter of plates and cups, and stepping through the trees, she came upon a party of picnickers.

They were holidaymakers from the plains. The women were dressed in bright saris, the men wore light summer shirts and the children had pretty new clothes. Binya, standing in the shadows between the trees, went unnoticed; for some time she watched the picnickers, admiring their clothes, listening to their unfamiliar accents and gazing rather hungrily at the sight of all their food. And then her gaze came to rest on a bright blue umbrella, a frilly thing for women, which lay open on the grass beside its owner.

Now Binya had seen umbrellas before, and her mother had a big black umbrella which nobody used anymore because the field rats had eaten holes in it, but this was the first time Binya had seen such a small, dainty, colourful umbrella and she fell in love with it. The umbrella was like a flower, a great blue flower that had sprung up on the dry brown hillside.

She moved forward a few paces so that she could see the umbrella better. As she came out of the shadows into the sunlight, the picnickers saw her.

'Hello, look who's here!' exclaimed the older of the two women. 'A little village girl!'

'Isn't she pretty?' remarked the other. 'But how torn and dirty her clothes are!' It did not seem to bother them that Binya could hear and understand everything they said about her.

'They're very poor in the hills,' said one of the men.

'Then let's give her something to eat.' And the older woman beckoned to Binya to come closer.

Hesitantly, nervously, Binya approached the group.

Normally she would have turned and fled, but the attraction was the pretty blue umbrella. It had cast a spell over her, drawing her forward almost against her will.

'What's that on her neck?' asked the younger woman.

'A necklace of sorts.'

'It's a pendant—see, there's a claw hanging from it!'

'It's a tiger's claw,' said the man beside her. (He had never seen a tiger's claw.) 'A lucky charm. These people wear them to keep away evil spirits.' He looked to Binya for confirmation, but Binya said nothing.

'Oh, I want one too!' said the woman, who was obviously his wife.

'You can't get them in shops.'

'Buy hers, then. Give her two or three rupees, she's sure to need the money.'

The man, looking slightly embarrassed but anxious to please his young wife, produced a two-rupee note and offered it to Binya, indicating that he wanted the pendant in exchange. Binya put her hand to the necklace, half afraid that the excited woman would snatch it away from her. Solemnly she shook her head.

The man then showed her a five-rupee note, but again Binya shook her head.

'How silly she is!' exclaimed the young woman.

'It may not be hers to sell,' said the man. 'But I'll try again. How much do you want—what can we give you?' And he waved his hand towards the picnic things scattered about on the grass.

Without any hesitation Binya pointed to the umbrella.

'My umbrella!' exclaimed the young woman. 'She wants my umbrella. What cheek!'

'Well, you want her pendant, don't you?'

'That's different.'

'Is it?'

The man and his wife were beginning to quarrel with each other.

'I'll ask her to go away,' said the older woman.

'We're making such fools of ourselves.'

'But I want the pendant!' cried the other, petulantly.

And then, on an impulse, she picked up the umbrella and held it out to Binya.

'Here, take the umbrella!'

Binya removed her necklace and held it out to the young woman, who immediately placed it around her own neck. Then Binya took the umbrella and held it up. It did not look so small in her hands; in fact, it was just the right size.

She had forgotten about the picnickers, who were busy examining the pendant. She turned the blue umbrella this way and that, looked through the bright blue silk at the pulsating sun, and then, still keeping it open, turned and disappeared into the forest glade.

II

Binya seldom closed the blue umbrella. Even when she had it in the house, she left it lying open in a corner of the room. Sometimes Bijju snapped it shut, complaining that it got in the way. She would open it again a little later. It wasn't beautiful when it was closed.

Whenever Binya went out—whether it was to graze the cows, or fetch water from the spring, or carry milk to the little tea shop on the Tehri road—she took the umbrella with her. That patch of sky blue silk could always be seen on the hillside.

Old Ram Bharosa (Ram the Trustworthy) kept the tea shop on the Tehri road. It was a dusty, un-metalled road. Once a day, the Tehri bus stopped near his shop and passengers got down to sip hot tea or drink a glass of curd. He kept a few bottles of Coca-Cola too, but as there was no ice, the bottles got hot in the sun and so were seldom opened. He also kept sweets and toffees, and when Binya or Bijju had a few coins to spare, they would spend them at the shop. It was only a mile from the village.

Ram Bharosa was astonished to see Binya's blue umbrella.

'What have you there, Binya?' he asked.

Binya gave the umbrella a twirl and smiled at Ram Bharosa. She was always ready with her smile, and would willingly have lent it to anyone who was feeling unhappy.

'That's a lady's umbrella,' said Ram Bharosa. 'That's only for memsahibs. Where did you get it?'

'Someone gave it to me—for my necklace.'

'You exchanged it for your lucky claw!'

Binya nodded.

'But what do you need it for? The sun isn't hot enough, and it isn't meant for the rain. It's just a pretty thing for rich ladies to play with!'

Binya nodded and smiled again. Ram Bharosa was quite right; it was just a beautiful plaything. And that was exactly why she had fallen in love with it.

'I have an idea,' said the shopkeeper. 'It's no use to you, that umbrella. Why not sell it to me? I'll give you five rupees for it.'

'It's worth fifteen,' said Binya.

'Well, then, I'll give you ten.'

Binya laughed and shook her head.

'Twelve rupees?' said Ram Bharosa, but without much hope.

Binya placed a five-paise coin on the counter.

'I came for a toffee,' she said.

Ram Bharosa pulled at his drooping whiskers, gave Binya a wry look, and placed a toffee in the palm of her hand. He watched Binya as she walked away along the dusty road. The blue umbrella held him fascinated, and he stared after it until it was out of sight.

The villagers used this road to go to the market town. Some used the bus, a few rode on mules and most people walked. Today, everyone on the road turned their heads to stare at the girl with the bright blue umbrella.

Binya sat down in the shade of a pine tree. The umbrella, still open, lay beside her. She cradled her head in her arms, and presently she dozed off. It was that kind of day, sleepily warm and summery.

And while she slept, a wind sprang up.

It came quietly, swishing gently through the trees, humming softly. Then it was joined by other random gusts, bustling over the tops of the mountains. The trees shook their heads and came to life. The wind fanned Binya's cheeks. The umbrella stirred on the grass.

The wind grew stronger, picking up dead leaves and sending them spinning and swirling through the air. It got into the umbrella and began to drag it over the grass. Suddenly it lifted the umbrella and carried it about six feet from the sleeping girl. The sound woke Binya.

She was on her feet immediately, and then she was leaping down the steep slope. But just as she was within reach of the umbrella, the wind picked it up again and carried it further downhill.

Binya set off in pursuit. The wind was in a wicked, playful mood. It would leave the umbrella alone for a few moments but as soon as Binya came near, it would pick up the umbrella again and send it bouncing, floating, dancing away from her.

The hill grew steeper. Binya knew that after twenty yards

it would fall away in a precipice. She ran faster. And the wind ran with her, ahead of her, and the blue umbrella stayed up with the wind.

A fresh gust picked it up and carried it to the very edge of the cliff. There it balanced for a few seconds, before toppling over, out of sight.

Binya ran to the edge of the cliff. Going down on her hands and knees, she peered down the cliff face. About a hundred feet below, a small stream rushed between great boulders. Hardly anything grew on the cliff face—just a few stunted bushes, and, halfway down, a wild cherry tree growing crookedly out of the rocks and hanging across the chasm. The umbrella had stuck in the cherry tree.

Binya didn't hesitate. She may have been timid with strangers, but she was at home on a hillside. She stuck her bare leg over the edge of the cliff and began climbing down. She kept her face to the hillside, feeling her way with her feet, only changing her handhold when she knew her feet were secure. Sometimes she held on to the thorny bilberry bushes, but she did not trust the other plants, which came away very easily.

Loose stones rattled down the cliff. Once on their way, the stones did not stop until they reached the bottom of the hill; and they took other stones with them, so that there was soon a cascade of stones, and Binya had to be very careful not to start a landslide.

As agile as a mountain goat, she did not take more than five minutes to reach the crooked cherry tree. But the most difficult task remained—she had to crawl along the trunk of the tree, which stood out at right angles from the cliff. Only by doing this could she reach the trapped umbrella.

Binya felt no fear when climbing trees. She was proud of the fact that she could climb them as well as Bijju. Gripping the rough cherry bark with her toes, and using her knees as leverage, she crawled along the trunk of the projecting tree until she was almost within reach of the umbrella. She noticed with dismay that the blue cloth was torn in a couple of places.

She looked down, and it was only then that she felt afraid. She was right over the chasm, balanced precariously about eighty feet above the boulder-strewn stream. Looking down, she felt quite dizzy. Her hands shook, and the tree shook too. If she slipped now, there was only one direction in which she could fall—down, down, into the depths of that dark and shadowy ravine.

There was only one thing to do; concentrate on the patch of blue just a couple of feet away from her. She did not look down or up, but straight ahead, and willing herself forward, she managed to reach the umbrella.

She could not crawl back with it in her hands. So, after dislodging it from the forked branch in which it had stuck, she let it fall, still open, into the ravine below.

Cushioned by the wind, the umbrella floated serenely downwards, landing in a thicket of nettles.

Binya crawled back along the trunk of the cherry tree. Twenty minutes later, she emerged from the nettle clump, her precious umbrella held aloft. She had nettle stings all over her legs, but she was hardly aware of the smarting. She was as immune to nettles as Bijju was to bees.

III

About four years previously, Bijju had knocked a hive out of an oak tree, and had been badly stung on the face and legs. It had been a painful experience. But now, if a bee stung him, he felt nothing at all: he had been immunized for life!

He was on his way home from school. It was two o'clock and he hadn't eaten since six in the morning. Fortunately, the kingora bushes—the bilberries—were in fruit, and already Bijju's lips were stained purple with the juice of the wild, sour fruit.

He didn't have any money to spend at Ram Bharosa's shop, but he stopped there anyway to look at the sweets in their glass jars.

'And what will you have today?' asked Ram Bharosa.

'No money,' said Bijju.

'You can pay me later.'

Bijju shook his head. Some of his friends had taken sweets on credit, and at the end of the month they had found they'd eaten more sweets than they could possibly pay for! As a result, they'd had to hand over to Ram Bharosa some of their most treasured possessions—such as a curved knife for cutting grass or a small hand-axe or a jar for pickles or a pair of earrings—and these had become the shopkeeper's possessions and were kept by him or sold in his shop.

Ram Bharosa had set his heart on having Binya's blue umbrella, and so naturally he was anxious to give credit to either of the children, but so far neither had fallen into the trap.

Bijju moved on, his mouth full of Kingora berries. Halfway home, he saw Binya with the cows. It was late evening, and the sun had gone down, but Binya still had the umbrella open. The two small rents had been stitched up by her mother.

Bijju gave his sister a handful of berries. She handed him the umbrella while she ate the berries.

'You can have the umbrella until we get home,' she said. It

was her way of rewarding Bijju for bringing her the wild fruit.

Calling 'Neelu! Gori!' Binya and Bijju set out for home, followed at some distance by the cows.

It was dark before they reached the village, but Bijju still had the umbrella open.

◆

Most of the people in the village were a little envious of Binya's blue umbrella. No one else had ever possessed one like it. The schoolmaster's wife thought it was quite wrong for a poor cultivator's daughter to have such a fine umbrella while she, a second-class BA, had to make do with an ordinary black one. Her husband offered to have their old umbrella dyed blue; she gave him a scornful look, and loved him a little less than before. The pujari, who looked after the temple, announced that he would buy a multi-coloured umbrella the next time he was in the town. A few days later he returned looking annoyed and grumbling that they weren't available except in Delhi. Most people consoled themselves by saying that Binya's pretty umbrella wouldn't keep out the rain, if it rained heavily; that it would shrivel in the sun, if the sun was fierce; that it would collapse in a wind, if the wind was strong; that it would attract lightning, if lightning fell near it; and that it would prove unlucky, if there was any ill luck going about. Secretly, everyone admired it.

Unlike the adults, the children didn't have to pretend. They were full of praise for the umbrella. It was so light, so pretty, so bright a blue! And it was just the right size for Binya. They knew that if they said nice things about the umbrella, Binya would smile and give it to them to hold for a little while—just a very little while!

Soon it was the time of the monsoon. Big black clouds kept piling up, and thunder rolled over the hills.

Binya sat on the hillside all afternoon, waiting for the rain. As soon as the first big drop of rain came down, she raised the umbrella over her head. More drops, big ones, came pattering down. She could see them through the umbrella silk, as they broke against the cloth.

And then there was a cloudburst, and it was like standing under a waterfall. The umbrella wasn't really a rain umbrella, but it held up bravely. Only Binya's feet got wet. Rods of rain fell around her in a curtain of shivered glass.

Everywhere on the hillside people were scurrying for shelter. Some made for a charcoal burner's hut, others for a mule-shed, or Ram Bharosa's shop. Binya was the only one who didn't run. This was what she'd been waiting for—rain on her umbrella—and she wasn't in a hurry to go home. She didn't mind getting her feet wet. The cows didn't mind getting wet either.

Presently she found Bijju sheltering in a cave. He would have enjoyed getting wet, but he had his schoolbooks with him and he couldn't afford to let them get spoilt. When he saw Binya, he came out of the cave and shared the umbrella. He was a head taller than his sister, so he had to hold the umbrella for her, while she held his books.

The cows had been left far behind.

'Neelu, Neelu!' called Binya.

'Gori!' called Bijju.

When their mother saw them sauntering home through the driving rain, she called out: 'Binya! Bijju! Hurry up, and bring the cows in! What are you doing out there in the rain?'

'Just testing the umbrella,' said Bijju.

IV

The rains set in, and the sun only made brief appearances. The hills turned a lush green. Ferns sprang up on walls and tree trunks. Giant lilies reared up like leopards from the tall grass. A white mist coiled and uncoiled as it floated up from the valley. It was a beautiful season, except for the leeches.

Every day, Binya came home with a couple of leeches fastened to the flesh of her bare legs. They fell off by themselves just as soon as they'd had their thimbleful of blood, but you didn't know they were on you until they fell off, and then, later, the skin became very sore and itchy. Some of the older people still believed that to be bled by leeches was a remedy for various ailments. Whenever Ram Bharosa had a headache, he applied a leech to his throbbing temple.

Three days of incessant rain had flooded out a number of small animals who lived in holes in the ground. Binya's mother suddenly found the roof full of field rats. She had to drive them out; they ate too much of her stored-up wheat flour and rice. Bijju liked lifting up large rocks to disturb the scorpions who were sleeping beneath. And snakes came out to bask in the sun.

Binya had just crossed the small stream at the bottom of the hill when she saw something gliding out of the bushes and coming towards her. It was a long black snake. A clatter of loose stones frightened it. Seeing the girl in its way, it rose up, hissing, prepared to strike. The forked tongue darted out, the venomous head lunged at Binya.

Binya's umbrella was open as usual. She thrust it forward, between herself and the snake, and the snake's hard snout thudded twice against the strong silk of the umbrella. The reptile then turned and slithered away over the wet rocks, disappearing into a clump of ferns.

Binya forgot about the cows and ran all the way home to tell her mother how she had been saved by the umbrella. Bijju had to put away his books and go out to fetch the cows. He carried a stout stick, in case he met with any snakes.

◆

First the summer sun, and now the endless rain, meant that the umbrella was beginning to fade a little. From a bright blue it had changed to a light blue. But it was still a pretty thing, and tougher than it looked, and Ram Bharosa still desired it. He did not want to sell it; he wanted to own it. He was probably the richest man in the area—so why shouldn't he have a blue umbrella? Not a day passed without his getting a glimpse of Binya and the umbrella; and the more he saw the umbrella, the more he wanted it.

The schools closed during the monsoon, but this didn't mean that Bijju could sit at home doing nothing. Neelu and Gori were providing more milk than was required at home, so Binya's mother was able to sell a kilo of milk every day: half a kilo to the schoolmaster, and half a kilo (at reduced rate) to the temple pujari. Bijju had to deliver the milk every morning.

Ram Bharosa had asked Bijju to work in his shop during the holidays, but Bijju didn't have time—he had to help his mother with the ploughing and the transplanting of the rice seedlings. So Ram Bharosa employed a boy from the next village, a boy called Rajaram. He did all the washing-up, and ran various errands. He went to the same school as Bijju, but the two boys were not friends.

One day, as Binya passed the shop, twirling her blue umbrella, Rajaram noticed that his employer gave a deep sigh and began muttering to himself.

'What's the matter, Babuji?' asked the boy.

'Oh, nothing,' said Ram Bharosa. 'It's just a sickness that has come upon me. And it's all due to that girl Binya and her wretched umbrella.'

'Why, what has she done to you?'

'Refused to sell me her umbrella! There's pride for you. And I offered her ten rupees.'

'Perhaps, if you gave her twelve...'

'But it isn't new any longer. It isn't worth eight rupees now. All the same, I'd like to have it.'

'You wouldn't make a profit on it,' said Rajaram.

'It's not the profit I'm after, wretch! It's the thing itself. It's the beauty of it!'

'And what would you do with it, Babuji? You don't visit anyone—you're seldom out of your shop. Of what use would it be to you?'

'Of what use is a poppy in a cornfield? Of what use is a rainbow? Of what use are you, numbskull? Wretch! I, too, have a soul. I want the umbrella, because...because I want its beauty to be mine!'

Rajaram put the kettle on to boil, began dusting the counter, all the time muttering: 'I'm as useful as an umbrella,' and then, after a short period of intense thought, said: 'What will you give me, Babuji, if I get the umbrella for you?'

'What do you mean?' asked the old man.

'You know what I mean. What will you give me?'

'You mean to steal it, don't you, you wretch? What a

delightful child you are! I'm glad you're not my son or my enemy. But look, everyone will know it has been stolen, and then how will I be able to show off with it?'

'You will have to gaze upon it in secret,' said Rajaram with a chuckle. 'Or take it into Tehri, and have it coloured red! That's your problem. But tell me, Babuji, do you want it badly enough to pay me three rupees for stealing it without being seen?'

Ram Bharosa gave the boy a long, sad look. 'You're a sharp boy,' he said. 'You'll come to a bad end. I'll give you two rupees.'

'Three,' said the boy.

'Two,' said the old man.

'You don't really want it, I can see that,' said the boy.

'Wretch!' said the old man. 'Evil one! Darkener of my doorstep! Fetch me the umbrella, and I'll give you three rupees.'

V

Binya was in the forest glade where she had first seen the umbrella. No one came there for picnics during the monsoon. The grass was always wet and the pine needles were slippery underfoot. The tall trees shut out the light, and poisonous-looking mushrooms, orange and purple, sprang up everywhere. But it was a good place for porcupines, who seemed to like the mushrooms, and Binya was searching for porcupine quills.

The hill people didn't think much of porcupine quills, but far away in southern India, the quills were valued as charms and sold at a rupee each. So Ram Bharosa paid a tenth of a rupee for each quill brought to him, and he in turn sold the quills at a profit to a trader from the plains.

Binya had already found five quills, and she knew there'd be more in the long grass. For once, she'd put her umbrella down. She had to put it aside if she was to search the ground thoroughly.

It was Rajaram's chance.

He'd been following Binya for some time, concealing himself behind trees and rocks, creeping closer whenever she became absorbed in her search. He was anxious that she should not see him and be able to recognize him later.

He waited until Binya had wandered some distance from the umbrella. Then, running forward at a crouch, he seized the open umbrella and dashed off with it.

But Rajaram had very big feet. Binya heard his heavy footsteps and turned just in time to see him as he disappeared between the trees. She cried out, dropped the porcupine quills, and gave chase.

Binya was swift and sure-footed, but Rajaram had a long stride. All the same, he made the mistake of running downhill. A long-legged person is much faster going uphill than down. Binya reached the edge of the forest glade in time to see the thief scrambling down the path to the stream. He had closed the umbrella so that it would not hinder his flight.

Binya was beginning to gain on the boy. He kept to the path, while she simply slid and leapt down the steep hillside. Near the bottom of the hill the path began to straighten out, and it was here that the long-legged boy began to forge ahead again.

Bijju was coming home from another direction. He had a bundle of sticks which he'd collected for the kitchen fire. As he reached the path, he saw Binya rushing down the hill as though all the mountain spirits in Garhwal were after her.

'What's wrong?' he called. 'Why are you running?'

Binya paused only to point at the fleeing Rajaram.

'My umbrella!' she cried. 'He has stolen it!'

Bijju dropped his bundle of sticks, and ran after his sister. When he reached her side, he said, 'I'll soon catch him!' and went sprinting away over the lush green grass. He was fresh, and he was soon well ahead of Binya and gaining on the thief.

Rajaram was crossing the shallow stream when Bijju caught up with him. Rajaram was the taller boy, but Bijju was much stronger. He flung himself at the thief, caught him by the legs, and brought him down in the water. Rajaram got to his feet and tried to drag himself away, but Bijju still had him by a leg. Rajaram overbalanced and came down with a great splash. He had let the umbrella fall. It began to float away on the current. Just then Binya arrived, flushed and breathless, and went dashing into the stream after the umbrella.

Meanwhile, a tremendous fight was taking place. Locked in fierce combat, the two boys swayed together on a rock, tumbled on to the sand, rolled over and over the pebbled bank until they were again thrashing about in the shallows of the stream. The magpies, bulbuls and other birds were disturbed, and flew away with cries of alarm.

Covered with mud, gasping and spluttering, the boys groped for each other in the water. After five minutes of frenzied struggle, Bijju emerged victorious.

Rajaram lay flat on his back on the sand, exhausted, while Bijju sat astride him, pinning him down with his arms and legs.

'Let me get up!' gasped Rajaram. 'Let me go—I don't want your useless umbrella!'

'Then why did you take it?' demanded Bijju. 'Come on—tell me why!'

'It was that skinflint Ram Bharosa,' said Rajaram.

'He told me to get it for him. He said if I didn't fetch it, I'd lose my job.'

◆

By early October, the rains were coming to an end. The leeches disappeared. The ferns turned yellow, and the sunlight on the green hills was mellow and golden, like the limes on the small tree in front of Binya's home. Bijju's days were happy ones as he came home from school, munching on roasted corn. Binya's umbrella had turned a pale milky blue, and was patched in several places, but it was still the prettiest umbrella in the village, and she still carried it with her wherever she went.

The cold, cruel winter wasn't far off, but somehow October seems longer than other months, because it is a kind month: the grass is good to be upon, the breeze is warm and gentle and pine-scented. That October, everyone seemed contented— everyone, that is, except Ram Bharosa.

The old man had by now given up all hope of ever possessing Binya's umbrella. He wished he had never set eyes on it. Because of the umbrella, he had suffered the tortures of greed, the despair of loneliness. Because of the umbrella, people had stopped coming to his shop!

Ever since it had become known that Ram Bharosa had tried to have the umbrella stolen, the village people had turned against him. They stopped trusting the old man; instead of buying their soap and tea and matches from his shop, they preferred to walk an extra mile to the shops near the Tehri bus stand. Who would have dealings with a man who had sold his soul for an umbrella? The children taunted him, twisted his name around. From 'Ram the Trustworthy' he became 'Trusty Umbrella Thief'.

The old man sat alone in his empty shop, listening to the eternal hissing of his kettle and wondering if anyone would ever again step in for a glass of tea. Ram Bharosa had lost his own appetite, and ate and drank very little. There was no money coming in. He had his savings in a bank in Tehri, but it was a terrible thing to have to dip into them! To save money, he had dismissed the blundering Rajaram. So he was left without any company. The roof leaked and the wind got in through the corrugated tin sheets, but Ram Bharosa didn't care.

Bijju and Binya passed his shop almost every day. Bijju went by with a loud but tuneless whistle. He was one of the world's whistlers; cares rested lightly on his shoulders. But, strangely enough, Binya crept quietly past the shop, looking the other way, almost as though she was in some way responsible for the misery of Ram Bharosa.

She kept reasoning with herself, telling herself that the umbrella was her very own, and that she couldn't help it if others were jealous of it. But had she loved the umbrella too much? Had it mattered more to her than people mattered? She couldn't help feeling that, in a small way, she was the cause of the sad look on Ram Bharosa's face ('His face is a yard long,' said Bijju) and the ruinous condition of his shop. It was all due to his own greed, no doubt, but she didn't want him to feel too bad about what he'd done, because it made her feel bad about herself; and so she closed the umbrella whenever she came near the shop, opening it again only when she was out of sight.

One day towards the end of October, when she had ten paise in her pocket, she entered the shop and asked the old man for a toffee.

She was Ram Bharosa's first customer in almost two weeks.

He looked suspiciously at the girl. Had she come to taunt him, to flaunt the umbrella in his face? She had placed her coin on the counter. Perhaps it was a bad coin. Ram Bharosa picked it up and bit it; he held it up to the light; he rang it on the ground. It was a good coin. He gave Binya the toffee.

Binya had already left the shop when Ram Bharosa saw the closed umbrella lying on his counter. There it was, the blue umbrella he had always wanted, within his grasp at last! He had only to hide it at the back of his shop, and no one would know that he had it, no one could prove that Binya had left it behind.

He stretched out his trembling, bony hand, and took the umbrella by the handle. He pressed it open. He stood beneath it, in the dark shadows of his shop, where no sun or rain could ever touch it.

'But I'm never in the sun or in the rain,' he said aloud. 'Of what use is an umbrella to me?'

And he hurried outside and ran after Binya.

'Binya, Binya!' he shouted. 'Binya, you've left your umbrella behind!'

He wasn't used to running, but he caught up with her, held out the umbrella, saying, 'You forgot it—the umbrella!'

In that moment it belonged to both of them.

But Binya didn't take the umbrella. She shook her head and said, 'You keep it. I don't need it anymore.'

'But it's such a pretty umbrella!' protested Ram Bharosa. 'It's the best umbrella in the village.'

'I know,' said Binya. 'But an umbrella isn't everything.'

And she left the old man holding the umbrella, and went tripping down the road, and there was nothing between her and the bright blue sky.

VI

Well, now that Ram Bharosa has the blue umbrella—a gift from Binya, as he tells everyone—he is sometimes persuaded to go out into the sun or the rain, and as a result he looks much healthier. Sometimes he uses the umbrella to chase away pigs or goats. It is always left open outside the shop, and anyone who wants to borrow it may do so; and so in a way it has become everyone's umbrella. It is faded and patchy, but it is still the best umbrella in the village.

People are visiting Ram Bharosa's shop again. Whenever Bijju or Binya stop for a cup of tea, he gives them a little extra milk or sugar. They like their tea sweet and milky.

A few nights ago, a bear visited Ram Bharosa's shop. There had been snow on the higher ranges of the Himalaya, and the bear had been finding it difficult to obtain food; so it had come lower down, to see what it could pick up near the village. That night it scrambled on to the tin roof of Ram Bharosa's shop, and made off with a huge pumpkin which had been ripening on the roof. But in climbing off the roof, the bear had lost a claw.

Next morning Ram Bharosa found the claw just outside the door of his shop. He picked it up and put it in his pocket. A bear's claw was a lucky find.

A day later, when he went into the market town, he took the claw with him, and left it with a silversmith, giving the craftsman certain instructions. The silversmith made a locket for the claw, then he gave it a thin silver chain. When Ram Bharosa came again, he paid the silversmith ten rupees for his work.

The days were growing shorter, and Binya had to be home a little earlier every evening. There was a hungry leopard at large, and she couldn't leave the cows out after dark.

She was hurrying past Ram Bharosa's shop when the old man called out to her.

'Binya, spare a minute! I want to show you something.'

Binya stepped into the shop.

'What do you think of it?' asked Ram Bharosa, showing her the silver pendant with the claw.

'It's so beautiful,' said Binya, just touching the claw and the silver chain.

'It's a bear's claw,' said Ram Bharosa. 'That's even luckier than a leopard's claw. Would you like to have it?'

'I have no money,' said Binya.

'That doesn't matter. You gave me the umbrella, I give you the claw! Come, let's see what it looks like on you.'

He placed the pendant on Binya, and indeed it looked very beautiful on her.

Ram Bharosa says he will never forget the smile she gave him when she left the shop.

She was halfway home when she realized she had left the cows behind.

'Neelu, Neelu!' she called. 'Oh, Gori!'

There was a faint tinkle of bells as the cows came slowly down the mountain path.

In the distance she could hear her mother and Bijju calling for her.

She began to sing. They heard her singing, and knew she was safe and near.

She walked home through the darkening glade, singing of the stars, and the trees stood still and listened to her, and the mountains were glad.

SITA AND THE RIVER

The Island in the River

In the middle of the river, the river that began in the mountains of the Himalayas and ended in the Bay of Bengal, there was a small island. The river swept round the island, sometimes clawing at its banks but never going right over it. The river was still deep and swift at this point, because the foothills were only forty miles distant. More than twenty years had passed since the river had flooded the island, and at that time no one had lived there. But ten years ago a small family had came to live on the island, and now a small hut stood on it, mud-walled hut with a sloping thatched roof. The hut had been built into a huge rock. Only three of its walls were mud, the fourth was rock.

A few goats grazed on the short grass and the prickly leaves of the thistle. Some hens followed them about. There was a melon patch and a vegetable patch and a small field of marigolds. The marigolds were sometimes made into garlands, and the garlands were sold during weddings or festivals in the nearby town.

In the middle of the islands stood a peepul tree. It was the only tree on this tongue of land. But peepul trees will grow anywhere—through the walls of old temples, through gravestones, even from rooftops. It is usually the buildings, and not the trees, that give way!

Even during the great flood, which had occurred twenty years back, the peepul tree had stood firm.

It was an old tree, much older than the old man on the island, who was only seventy. The peepul was about three hundred. It also provided shelter for the birds who sometimes visited it from the mainland.

Three hundred years ago, the land on which the peepul tree stood had been part of the mainland; but the river had changed its course, and that bit of land with the tree on it had become an island. The tree had lived alone for many years. Now it gave shade and shelter to a small family, who were grateful for its presence.

The people of India love peepul trees, especially during the hot summer months when the heart-shaped leaves catch the least breath of air and flutter eagerly, fanning those who sit beneath.

A sacred tree, the peepul, the abode of spirits, good and bad.

'Do not yawn when you are sitting beneath the tree,' Grandmother would warn Sita, her ten-year-old granddaughter. 'And if you must yawn always snap your fingers in front of your mouth. If you forget to do that, a demon might jump down your throat!'

'And then what will happen?' asked Sita.

'He will probably ruin your digestion,' said Grandfather, who didn't take demons very seriously.

The peepul had beautiful leaves, and Grandmother likened it to the body of the mighty Lord Krishna—broad at the shoulders, then tapering down to a very slim waist.

The tree attracted birds and insects from across the river. On some nights it was full of fireflies.

SITA AND THE RIVER

Whenever Grandmother saw the fireflies, she told her favourite story.

'When we first came here,' she said, 'we were greatly troubled by mosquitoes. One night your grandfather rolled himself up in his sheet so that they couldn't get at him. After a while he peeped out of his bedsheet to make sure they were gone. He saw a firefly and said, "You clever mosquito! You could not see in the dark, so you got a lantern!"'

Grandfather was mending a fishing-net. He had fished in the river for ten years, and he was a good fisherman. He knew where to find the slim silver chilwa and the big, beautiful mahseer and the singhara with its long whiskers; he knew where the river was deep and where it was shallow; he knew which baits to use—when to use worms and when to use gram. He had taught his son to fish, but his son had gone to work in a factory in a city, nearly a hundred miles away. He had no grandson; but he had a granddaughter, Sita, and she could do all the things a boy could do, and sometimes she could do them better. She had lost her mother when she was two or three. Grandmother had taught her all that a girl should know—cooking, sewing, grinding spices, cleaning the house, feeding the birds—and Grandfather had taught her other things like taking a small boat across the river, cleaning a fish, repairing a net, or catching a snake by the tail! And some things she had learnt by herself—like climbing the peepul tree, or leaping from rock to rock in shallow water, or swimming in an inlet where the water was calm.

Neither grandparent could read or write, and as a result Sita couldn't read or write.

There was a school in one of the villages across the river, but Sita had never seen it. She had never been further than

LESSONS IN FUN AND FROLIC

Shahganj, the small market town near the river. She had never seen a city. She had never been on a train. The river cut her off from many things; but she could not miss what she had never known, and besides, she was much too busy.

While Grandfather mended his net, Sita was inside the hut, pressing her grandmother's forehead which was hot with fever. Grandmother had been ill for three days and could not eat. She had been ill before, but she had never been so bad. Grandfather had brought her some sweet oranges from Shahganj, and she could suck the juice from the oranges, but she couldn't take anything else.

She was younger than Grandfather, but, because she was sick, she looked much older. She had never been very strong. She coughed a lot, and sometimes she had difficulty in breathing.

When Sita noticed that Grandmother was sleeping, she left the bedside and tiptoed out of the room on her bare feet.

Outside, she found the sky dark with monsoon clouds. It had rained all night, and, in a few hours, it would rain again. The monsoon rains had come early, at the end of June. Now it was the end of July, and already the river was swollen. Its rushing sound seemed nearer and more menacing than usual.

Sita went to her grandfather and sat down beside him.

'When you are hungry, tell me,' she said, 'and I will make the bread.'

'Is your Grandmother asleep?'

'Yes. But she will wake soon. The pain is deep.'

The old man stared out across the river, at the dark green of the forest, at the leaden sky, and said, 'If she is not better by morning, I will take her to the hospital in Shahganj. They will know how to make her well. You may be on your own for two or three days. You have been on your own before.'

Sita nodded gravely—she had been alone before; but not in the middle of the rains, with the river so high. But she knew that someone must stay behind. She wanted Grandmother to get well, and she knew that only Grandfather could take the small boat across the river when the current was so strong.

Sita was not afraid of being left alone, but she did not like the look of the river. That morning, when she had been fetching water, she had noticed that the lever suddenly disappeared.

'Grandfather, if the river rises higher, what will I do?'
'You must keep to the high ground.'
'And if the water reaches the high ground?'
'Then go into the hut, and take the hens with you.'
'And if the water comes into the hut?'
'Then climb into the peepul tree. It is a strong tree. It will not fall. And the water cannot rise higher than the tree.'
'And the goats, Grandfather?'
'I will be taking them with me. I may have to sell them, to pay for good food and medicines for your Grandmother. As for the hens, you can put them on the roof if the water enters the hut. But do not worry too much'—and he patted Sita's head—'the water will not rise so high. Has it ever done so? I will be back soon, remember that.'
'And won't Grandmother come back?'
'Yes—but they may keep her in the hospital for some time.'

The Sound of the River

That evening it began to rain again. Big pellets of rain, scarring the surface of the river. But it was warm rain, and Sita could move about in it. She was not afraid of getting wet, she rather liked it. In the previous month, when the first monsoon shower had arrived, washing the dusty leaves of the tree and bringing up the good smell of the earth, she had exulted in it, had run about shouting for joy. She was used to it now, even a little tired of the rain, but she did not mind getting wet. It was steamy indoors, and her thin dress would soon dry in the heat from the kitchen fire.

She walked about barefooted, barelegged. She was very sure on her feet; her toes had grown accustomed to gripping all kinds of rocks, slippery or sharp. And though thin, she was surprisingly strong.

Black hair, streaming across her face. Black eyes. Slim brown arms. A scar on her thigh: when she was small, visiting her mother's village, a hyaena had entered the house where she was sleeping, fastened on to her leg and tried to drag her away; but her screams had roused the villagers, and the hyaena had run off.

She moved about in the pouring rain, chasing the hens into a shelter behind the hut. A harmless brown snake, flooded out of its hole, was moving across the open ground. Sita took a stick, picked the snake up with it, and dropped it behind a cluster of rocks. She had no quarrel with snakes. They kept down the rats and the frogs. She wondered how the rats had first come to the island—probably in someone's boat or in a sack of grain.

She disliked the huge black scorpions who left their waterlogged dwellings and tried to take shelter in the hut. It was so easy to step on one, and the sting could be very painful. She had been bitten by a scorpion the previous monsoon, and for a day and a night she had known fever and great pain. Sita had never killed living creatures, but now, whenever she found a scorpion, she crushed it with a rock!

When, finally, she went indoors, she was hungry. She ate some parched gram and warmed up some goat's milk.

Grandmother woke once, and asked for water, and Grandfather held the brass tumbler to her lips.

It rained all night.

The roof was leaking, and a small puddle formed on the floor. Grandfather kept the kerosene-lamps alight. They did not need the light but somehow it made them feel safer.

The sound of the river had always been with them, although they seldom noticed it; but that night they noticed a change in its sound. There was something like a moan, like a wind in the tops of tall trees, and a swift hiss as the water swept round the rocks and carried away pebbles. And sometimes there was a rumble, as loose earth fell into the water. Sita could not sleep.

She had a rag doll, made with Grandmother's help out of bits of old clothing. She kept it by her side every night. The doll was someone to talk to, when the nights were long and sleep elusive. Her grandparents were often ready to talk; but sometimes Sita wanted to have secrets, and, though there were no special secrets in her life, she made up a few because it was fun to have them. And if you have secrets, you must have a friend to share them with. Since there were no other children on the island, Sita shared her secrets with the rag doll, whose name was Mumta.

Grandfather and Grandmother were asleep, though the sound of Grandmother's laboured breathing was almost as persistent as the sound of the river.

'Mumta,' whispered Sita in the dark, starting one of her private conversations.

'Do you think Grandmother will get well again?'

Mumta always answered Sita's questions, even though the answers were really Sita's answers.

'She is very old,' said Mumta.

'Do you think the river will reach the hut?' asked Sita.

'If it keeps raining like this, and the river keeps rising, it will reach the hut.'

'I am afraid of the river, Mumta. Aren't you afraid?'

'Don't be afraid. The river has always been good to us.'

'What will we do if it comes into the hut?'

'We will climb on the roof.'

'And if it reaches the roof?'

'We will climb the peepul tree. The river has never gone higher than the peepul tree.'

As soon as the first light showed through the little skylight, Sita got up and went outside. It wasn't raining hard, it was drizzling, but it was the sort of drizzle that could continue for days, and it probably meant that heavy rain was falling in the hills where the river began.

Sita went down to the water's edge. She couldn't find her favourite rock, the one on which she often sat dangling her feet in the water, watching the little chilwa fish swim by. It was still there, no doubt, but the river had gone over it.

She stood on the sand, and she could feel the water oozing and bubbling beneath her feet.

The river was no longer green and blue and flecked with white; it was a muddy colour.

She went back to the hut. Grandfather was up now. He was getting his boat ready.

Sita milked the goat, thinking that perhaps it was the last

time she would be milking it; but she did not care for the goat in the same way that she cared for Mumta.

The sun was just coming up when Grandfather pushed off in the boat. Grandmother lay in the prow. She was staring hard at Sita, trying to speak, but the words would not come. She raised her hand in a blessing.

Sita bent and touched her Grandmother's feet, and then Grandfather pushed off. The little boat—with its two old people and three goats—rode swiftly on the river, edging its way towards the opposite bank. The current was very swift, and the boat would be carried about half a mile downstream before Grandfather would be able to get it to dry land.

It bobbed about on the water, getting smaller and smaller, until it was just a speck on the broad river.

And suddenly Sita was alone.

There was a wind, whipping the raindrops against her face; and there was the water, rushing past the island; and there was the distant shore, blurred by rain; and there was the small hut; and there was the tree.

Sita got busy. The hens had to be fed. They weren't concerned about anything except food. Sita threw them handfuls of coarse grain, potato-peels and peanut shells.

Then she took the broom and swept out the hut; lit the charcoal-burner, warmed some milk, and thought, 'Tomorrow there will be no milk...' She began peeling onions. Soon her eyes started smarting, and, pausing for a few moments and glancing round the quiet room, she became aware again that she was alone. Grandfather's hookah pipe stood by itself in one corner. It was a beautiful old hookah, which had belonged to Sita's great-grandfather. The bowl was made out of a coconut encased in silver. The long winding stem was at least four feet long. It was their most treasured possession. Grandmother's sturdy shisham-wood walking stick stood in another corner.

Sita looked around for Mumta, found the doll beneath the light wooden charpoy, and placed her within sight and hearing.

Thunder rolled down from the hills. Boom—boom—boom...

'The gods of the mountains are angry,' said Sita. 'Do you think they are angry with me?'

'Why should they be angry with you?' asked Mumta.

'They don't need a reason for being angry. They are angry with everything, and we are in the middle of everything. We are so small—do you think they know we are here?'

'Who knows what the gods think?'

'But I made you,' said Sita, 'and I know you are here.'

'And will you save me if the river rises?'

'Yes, of course. I won't go anywhere without you, Mumta.'

The Water Rises

Sita couldn't stay indoors for long. She went out, taking Mumta with her, and stared out across the river, to the safe land on the other side. But was it really safe there? The river looked much wider now. It had crept over its banks and spread far across the flat plain. Far away, people were driving their cattle through waterlogged, flooded fields, carrying their belongings in bundles on their heads or shoulders, leaving their homes, making for high land. It wasn't safe anywhere.

Sita wondered what had happened to Grandfather and Grandmother. If they had reached the shore safely, Grandfather would have to engage a bullock-cart or a pony-drawn carriage to get Grandmother to the district hospital, five or six miles away. Shahganj had a market, a court, a jail, a cinema and a hospital.

She wondered if she would ever see Grandmother again. She had done her best to look after the old lady, remembering the times when Grandmother had looked after her, had gently touched her fevered brow, and had told her stories—stories about the gods—about the young Krishna, friend of birds and animals, so full of mischief, always causing confusion among the other gods. He made Lord Indra angry by shifting a mountain without permission. Indra was the God of the clouds, who made the thunder and lightning, and when he was angry he sent down a deluge such as this one.

The island looked much smaller now. Some of its mud banks had dissolved quickly, sinking into the river. But in the middle of the island there was rocky ground, and the rocks would never crumble, they could only be submerged.

Sita climbed into the tree to get a better view of the flood. She had climbed the tree many times, and it took her only a few seconds to reach the higher branches. She put her hand to her eyes as a shield from the rain, and gazed upstream.

There was water everywhere. The world had become one vast river. Even the trees on the forested side of the river looked as though they had grown from the water, like mangroves. The sky was banked with massive, moisture-laden clouds. Thunder rolled down from the hills, and the river seemed to take it up with a hollow booming sound.

Something was floating down the river, something big and bloated. It was closer now, and Sita could make out its bulk—a drowned bullock, being carried downstream.

So the water had already flooded the villages further upstream. Or perhaps the bullock had strayed too close to the rising river.

Sita's worst fears were confirmed when, a little later, she saw planks of wood, small trees and bushes, and then a wooden bedstead, floating past the island.

As she climbed down from the tree, it began to rain more heavily. She ran indoors, shooing the hens before her. They flew into the hut and huddled under Grandmother's cot. Sita thought it would be best to keep them together now.

There were three hens and a cockbird. The river did not bother them. They were interested only in food, and Sita kept them content by throwing them a handful of onion-skins.

She would have liked to close the door and shut out the swish of the rain and the boom of the river; but then she would have no way of knowing how fast the water rose.

She took Mumta in her arms and began praying for the rain to stop and the river to fall. She prayed to Lord Indra, and, just in case he was busy elsewhere, she prayed to other gods too. She prayed for the safety of her grandparents and for her own safety. She put herself last—but only after an effort!

Finally Sita decided to make herself a meal. So she chopped up some onions, fried them, then added turmeric and red chilli powder, salt and water, and stirred until she had everything sizzling; and then she added a cup of lentils and covered the pot.

Doing this took her about ten minutes. It would take about half an hour for the dish to cook.

When she looked outside, she saw pools of water among the rocks. She couldn't tell if it was rainwater or overflow from the river.

She had an idea.

A big tin trunk stood in a corner of the room. In it Grandmother kept an old single-thread sewing-machine. It had belonged once to an English lady, had found its way to a Shahganj junkyard, and had been rescued by Grandfather who had paid fifteen rupees for it. It was just over a hundred years old, but it could still be used.

The trunk also contained an old sword. This had originally belonged to Sita's great-grandfather, who had used it to help defend his village against marauding Rohilla soldiers more than a century ago. Sita could tell that it had been used to fight with, because there were several small dents in the steel blade.

But there was no time for Sita to start admiring family heirlooms. She decided to stuff the trunk with everything useful or valuable. There was a chance that it wouldn't be carried away by the water.

Grandfather's hookah went into the trunk. Grandmother's walking stick went in, too. So did a number of small tins containing the spices used in cooking—nutmeg, caraway seeds, cinnamon, corrainder, pepper—also a big tin of flour and another of molasses. Even if she had to spend several hours in the tree, there would be something to eat when she came down again.

A clean white cotton dhoti of Grandfather's, and Grandmother's only spare sari also went into the trunk. Never mind if they got stained with curry powder! Never mind if they got the smell of salted fish—some of that went in, too.

Sita was so busy packing the trunk that she paid no attention to the lick of cold water at her heels. She locked the trunk, dropped the key into a crack in the rock wall, and turned to give her attention to the food. It was only then that she discovered that she was walking about on a watery floor.

She stood still, horrified by what she saw. The water was oozing over the doorsill, pushing its way into the room.

In her fright, Sita forgot about her meal and everything else. Darting out of the hut, she ran splashing through ankle-deep water toward the safety of the peepul tree. If the tree hadn't been there, such a well-known landmark, she might have floundered into deep water, into the river.

She climbed swiftly into the strong arms of the tree, made herself comfortable on a familiar branch, and pushed the wet hair away from her eyes.

The Tree

She was glad she had hurried. The hut was now surrounded by water. Only the higher parts of the island could still be seen—a few rocks, the big rock into which the hut was built, a hillock on which some brambles and thorn-apples grew.

The hens hadn't bothered to leave the hut. Instead, they were perched on the wooden bedstead.

'Will the river rise still higher?' wondered Sita. She had never seen it like this before. With a deep, muffled roar it swirled around her, stretching away in all directions.

The most unusual things went by on the water—an aluminium kettle, a cane chair, a tin of tooth powder, an empty cigarette packet, a wooden slipper, a plastic doll...

A doll!

With a sinking feeling, Sita remembered Mumta.

Poor Mumta, she had been left behind in the hut. Sita, in her hurry, had forgotten her only companion.

She climbed down from the tree and ran splashing through the water towards the hut. Already the current was pulling at her legs. When she reached the hut, she found it full of water. The hens had gone—and so had Mumta.

Sita struggled back to the tree. She was only just in time, for the waters were higher now, the island fast disappearing.

She crouched miserably in the fork of the tree, watching her world disappear. She had always loved the river. Why was it threatening her now? She remembered the doll, and she thought, *If I can be so careless with someone I have made, how can I expect the gods to notice me?*

Something went floating past the tree. Sita caught a glimpse of a stiff, upraised arm and long hair streaming behind on the water. The body of a drowned woman. It was soon gone, but it made Sita feel very small and lonely, at the mercy of great and cruel forces. She began to shiver and then to cry.

She stopped crying when she saw an empty kerosene tin, with one of the hens perched on top. The tin came bobbing along on the water and sailed slowly past the tree. The hen looked a bit ruffled but seemed secure on its perch.

A little later Sita saw the remaining hens fly up to the rock ledge to huddle there in a small recess.

The water was still rising. All that remained of the island was the big rock behind the hut, and the top of the hut, and the peepul tree.

She climbed a little higher, into the crook of a branch. A jungle crow settled in the branches above her. Sita saw the nest, the crow's nest, an untidy platform of twigs wedged in the fork of a branch.

In the nest were four speckled eggs. The crow sat on

them and cawed disconsolately. But though the bird sounded miserable its presence brought some cheer to Sita. At least she was not alone. Better to have a crow for company than no one at all.

Other things came floating out of the hut—a large pumpkin; a red turban belonging to Grandfather, unwinding in the water like a long snake; and then—Mumta!

The doll, being filled with straw and wood shavings moved quite swiftly on the water, too swiftly for Sita to do anything about rescuing it. Sita wanted to call out, to urge her friend to make for the tree; but she knew that Mumta could not swim—the doll could only float, travel with the river, and perhaps be washed ashore many miles downstream.

The trees shook in the wind and the rain. The crow cawed and flew up, circled the tree a few times, then returned to the nest. Sita clung to the branch.

The tree trembled throughout its tall frame. To Sita it felt like an earthquake tremor; she felt the shudder of the tree in her own bones.

The river swirled all around her now. It was almost up to the roof of the hut. Soon the mud walls would crumble and vanish. Except for the big rock and some trees very far away, there was only water to be seen. Water, and grey weeping sky.

In the distance, a boat with several people in it moved sluggishly away from the ruins of a flooded village. Someone looked out across the flooded river and said, 'See, there is a tree right in the middle of the river! How could it have got there? Isn't someone moving the tree?'

But the others thought he was imagining things it was only a tree carried down by the flood, they said. In worrying about their own distress, they had forgotten about the island in the middle of the river.

The river was very angry now, rampaging down from the hills and thundering across the plain, bringing with it dead animals, uprooted trees, household goods and huge fishes choked to death by the swirling mud.

The peepul tree groaned. Its long, winding roots still clung tenaciously to the earth from which it had sprung many, many years ago. But the earth was softening, the stones were being washed away. The roots of the tree were rapidly losing their hold.

The crow must have known that something was wrong because it kept flying up and circling the tree, reluctant to settle in it, yet unwilling to fly away. As long as the nest was there, the crow would remain too.

Sita's wet cotton dress clung to her thin body. The rain streamed down from her long black hair. It poured from every leaf of the tree. The crow, too, was drenched and groggy.

The tree groaned and moved again.

There was a flurry of leaves, then a surge of mud from below. To Sita it seemed as though the river was rising to meet the sky. The tree tilted swinging Sita from side to side. Her feet were in the water but she clung tenaciously to her branch.

And then, she found the tree moving, moving with the river, rocking her about, dragging its roots along the ground as it set out on the first and last journey of its life.

And as the tree moved out on the river and the little island was lost in the swirling waters, Sita forgot her fear and her loneliness. The tree was taking her with it. She was not alone. It was as though one of the gods had remembered her after all.

Taken with the Flood

The branches swung Sita about, but she did not lose her grip. The tree was her friend. It had known her all these years, and now it held her in its old and dying arms as though it were determined to keep her from the river.

The crow kept flying around the moving tree. The bird was in a great rage. Its nest was still up there—but not for long! The tree lurched and twisted, and the nest fell into the water. Sita saw the eggs sink.

The crow swooped low over the water but there was nothing it could do. In a few moments the nest had disappeared.

The bird followed the tree for some time; then, flapping its wings, it rose high into the air and flew across the river until it was out of sight.

Sita was alone once more. But there was no time for feeling lonely. Everything was in motion—up and down and sideways and forwards.

She saw a turtle swimming past—a great big river turtle, the kind that feeds on decaying flesh. Sita turned her face away. In the distance she saw a flooded village and people in flat-bottomed boats; but they were very far.

Because of its great size, the tree did not move very swiftly on the river. Sometimes, when it reached shallow water, it stopped, its roots catching in the rocks; but not for long: the river's momentum soon swept it on.

At one place, where there was a bend in the river, the tree struck a sandbank and was still. It would not move again.

Sita felt very tired. Her arms were aching and she had to cling tightly to her branch to avoid slipping into the water. The rain blurred her vision. She wondered if she should brave the current and try swimming to safety. But she did not want to leave the tree. It was all that was left to her now, and she felt safe in its branches.

Then, above the sound of the river, she heard someone calling. The voice was faint and seemed very far but, looking upriver through the curtain of rain, Sita was able to make out a small boat coming towards her.

There was a boy in the boat. He seemed quite at home in the turbulent river, and he was smiling at Sita as he guided his boat towards the tree. He held on to one of the branches to steady himself, and gave his free hand to Sita.

She grasped the outstretched hand and slipped into the boat beside the boy. He placed his bare foot against the trunk of the tree and pushed away.

The little boat moved swiftly down the river. Sita looked back and saw the big tree lying on its side on the sandbank, while the river swirled round it and pulled at its branches, carrying away its beautiful slender leaves.

And then the tree grew smaller and was left far behind. A new journey had begun.

The Boy in the Boat

She lay stretched out in the boat, too tired to talk, too tired to move. The boy looked at her but he did not say anything, he just kept smiling. He leaned on his two small oars, stroking smoothly, rhythmically, trying to keep from going into the middle of the river. He wasn't strong enough to get the boat right out of the swift current; but he kept trying.

A small boat on a big river—a river that had broken its bounds and reached across the plains in every direction—the boat moved swiftly on the wild brown water, and the girl's home and the boy's home were both left far behind.

The boy wore only a loincloth. He was a slim, wiry boy, with a hard flat belly. He had high cheekbones, strong white teeth. He was a little darker than Sita.

He did not speak until they reached a broader, smoother stretch of river, and then, resting on his oars and allowing the boat to drift a little, he said, 'You live on the island. I have seen you sometimes, from my boat. But where are the others?'

'My grandmother was sick,' said Sita. 'Grandfather took her to the hospital in Shahganj.'

'When did they leave?'

'Early this morning.'

Early that morning—and already Sita felt as though it had been many mornings ago!

'Where are you from?' she asked.

'I am from a village near the foothills. About six miles from your home. I was in my boat, trying to get across the river with the news that our village was badly flooded. The current was too strong. I was swept down and past your island. We cannot fight the river when it is like this, we must go where it takes us.'

'You must be tired,' said Sita. 'Give me the oars.'

'No. There is not much to do now. The river has gone wherever it wanted to go—it will not drive us before it any more.'

He brought in one oar, and with his free hand felt under the seat, where there was a small basket. He produced two mangoes, and gave one to Sita.

'I was supposed to sell these in Shahganj,' he said. 'My

father is very strict. Even if I return home safely, he will ask me what I got for the mangoes!'

'And what will you tell him?'

'I will say they are at the bottom of the river!'

They bit deep into the ripe fleshy mangoes, using their teeth to tear the skin away. The sweet juice trickled down their skins. The good smell—like the smell of the leaves of the cosmos flower when crushed between the palms—helped to revive Sita. The flavour of the fruit was heavenly—truly the nectar of the gods!

Sita hadn't tasted a mango for over a year. For a few moments she forgot about everything else. All that mattered was the sweet, dizzy flavour of the mango.

The boat drifted, but slowly now, for as they went further downstream, the river gradually lost its power and fury. It was late afternoon when the rain stopped; but the clouds did not break up.

'My father has many buffaloes,' said the boy, 'but several have been lost in the flood.'

'Do you go to school?' asked Sita.

'Yes, I am supposed to go to school. I don't always go, at least, not when the weather is fine! There is a school near our village. I don't think you go to school?'

'No. There is too much work at home.'

'Can you read and write?'

'Only a little…'

'Then you should go to a school.'

'It is too far away.'

'True. But you should know how to read and write. Otherwise you will be stuck on your island for the rest of your life—that is, if your island is still there!'

'But I like the island,' protested Sita.

'Because you are with people you love,' said the boy. 'But your grandparents, they are old, they will die some day—and then you will be alone, and will you like the island then?'

Sita did not answer. She was trying to think of what life would be like without her grandparents. It would be an empty island, that was true. She would be imprisoned by the river.

'I can help you,' said the boy. 'When we get back—if we get back—I will come to see you sometimes, and I will teach you to read and write. All right?'

'Yes,' said Sita, nodding thoughtfully. 'When we get back...' The boy smiled.

'My name is Krishan,' he said.

Towards evening the river changed colour. The sun, low in the sky, broke through a rift in the clouds, and the river changed slowly from grey to gold, from gold to a deep orange, and then, as the sun went down, all these colours were drowned in the river, and the river took the colour of the night.

The moon was almost at the full, and they could see a belt of forest along the line of the river.

'I will try to reach the trees,' said Krishan.

He pulled for the trees, and after ten minutes of strenuous rowing reached a bend in the river and was able to escape the pull of the main current.

Soon they were in a forest, rowing between tall trees, sal and shisham.

The boat moved slowly as Krishan took it in and out of the trees, while the moonlight made a crooked silver path over the water.

'We will tie the boat to a tree,' he said. 'Then we can rest.

Tomorrow, we will have to find out a way out of the forest.'

He produced a length of rope from the bottom of the boat, tied one end to the boat's stern, and threw the other end over a stout branch which hung only a few feet above the water. The boat came to rest against the trunk of the tree.

It was a tall, sturdy tree, the Indian mahogany. It was a safe place, for there was no rush of water in the forest; and the trees grew close together, making the earth firm and unyielding.

But those who lived in the forest were on the move. The animals had been flooded out of their holes, caves and lairs, and were looking for shelter and high ground.

Sita and Krishan had just finished tying the boat to the tree when they saw a huge python gliding over the water towards them.

'Do you think it will try to get into the boat?' asked Sita.

'I don't think so,' said Krishan, although he took the precaution of holding an oar ready to fend off the snake.

But the python went past them, its head above water, its great length trailing behind, until it was lost in the shadows.

Krishan had more mangoes in the basket, and he and Sita sucked hungrily at them while they sat in the boat.

A big sambhur-stag came threshing through the water. He did not have to swim: he was so tall that his head and shoulders remained well above the water. His antlers were big and beautiful.

'There will be other animals,' said Sita. 'Should we climb onto the tree?'

'We are quite safe in the boat,' said Krishan. 'The animals will not be dangerous tonight. They will not even hunt each other, they are only interested in reaching dry land. For once, the deer are safe from the tiger and the leopard. You lie down and sleep, I will keep watch.'

Sita stretched herself out in the boat and closed her eyes. She was very tired, and the sound of the water lapping against the sides of the boat soon lulled her to sleep.

She woke once, when a strange bird called overhead. She raised herself on one elbow; but Krishan was awake, sitting beside her, his legs drawn up and his chin resting on his knees. He was gazing out across the water. He looked blue in the moonlight, the colour of the young Lord Krishna, and for a few moments Sita was confused and wondered if the boy was actually Krishna; but when she thought about it, she decided that it wasn't possible, he was just a village boy and she had seen hundreds like him—well, not exactly like him; he was a little different...

And when she slept again, she dreamt that the boy and Krishna were one, and that she was sitting beside him on a great white bird, which flew over the mountains, over the snow peaks of the Himalayas, into the cloud-land of the gods. And there was a great rumbling sound, as though the gods were angry about the whole thing, and she woke up to this terrible sound and looked about her, and there in the moonlit glade, up to his belly in water, stood a young elephant, his trunk raised as he trumpeted his predicament to the forest—for he was a young elephant, and he was lost, and was looking for his mother.

He trumpeted again, then lowered his head and listened. And presently, from far away, came the shrill trumpeting of another elephant. It must have been the young one's mother, because he gave several excited trumpet calls, and then went stamping and churning through the floodwater towards a gap in the trees. The boat rocked in the waves made by his passing.

'It is all right,' said Krishan. 'You can go to sleep again.' 'I don't think I will sleep now,' said Sita.

'Then I will play my flute for you and the time will pass quickly.'

He produced a flute from under the seat, and putting it to his lips he began to play. And the sweetest music that Sita had ever heard came pouring from the little flute, and it seemed to fill the forest with its beautiful sound. And the music carried her away again, into the land of dreams, and they were riding on the bird once more, Sita and the blue God, and they were passing through cloud and mist, until suddenly the sun shot through the clouds. And at that moment Sita opened her eyes and saw the sky through the branches of the mahogany tree, the shiny green leaves making a bold pattern against the blinding blue of an open sky.

The forest was drenched with sunshine. Clouds were gathering again, but for an hour or two there would be hot sun on a steamy river.

Krishan was fast asleep in the bottom of the boat. His flute lay in the palm of his half-open hand. The sun came slating across his bare brown legs. A leaf had fallen on his face, but it had not woken him, it lay on his cheek as though it had grown there.

Sita did not move about, as she did not want to wake the boy. Instead she looked around her, and she thought the water level had fallen in the night, but she couldn't be sure.

Krishan woke at last. He yawned, stretched his limbs, and sat up beside Sita.

'I am hungry,' he said.

'So am I,' said Sita.

'The last mangoes,' he said, emptying the basket of its last two mangoes.

After they had finished the fruit, they sucked the big seeds until they were quite dry. The discarded seeds floated well on the water. Sita had always preferred them to paper boats.

'We had better move on,' said Krishan.

He rowed the boat through the trees, and then for about an hour they were passing through the flooded forest, under the dripping branches of rain-washed trees. Sometimes they had to use the oars to push away vines and creepers. Sometimes submerged bushes hampered them. But they were out of the forest before ten o' clock.

The water was no longer very deep, and they were soon gliding over flooded fields. In the distance they saw a village standing on high ground. In the old days, people had built their villages on hilltops as a better defence against bandits and the soldiers of invading armies. This was an old village; and, though its inhabitants had long ago exchanged their swords for pruning forks, the hill on which it stood gave it protection from the floodwaters.

A Bullock-Cart Ride

The people of the village were at first reluctant to help Sita and Krishan.

'They are strangers,' said an old woman. 'They are not our people.'

'They are of low caste,' said another. 'They cannot remain with us.'

'Nonsense!' said a tall, turbaned farmer, twirling his long

white moustache. 'They are children, not robbers. They will come into my house.'

The people of the village—long-limbed, sturdy men and women of the Jat caste—were generous by nature, and once the elderly farmer had given them the lead they were friendly and helpful.

Sita was anxious to get to her grandparents; and the farmer, who had business to transact at a village fair some twenty miles distant, offered to take Sita and Krishan with him.

The fair was being held at a place called Karauli, and at Karauli there was a railway station, and a train went to Shahganj.

It was a journey that Sita would always remember. The bullock-cart was so slow on the waterlogged roads that there was plenty of time in which to see things, to notice one another, to talk, to think, to dream.

Krishan couldn't sit still in the cart. He was used to the swift, gliding movements of his boat (which he had had to leave behind in the village), and every now and then he would jump off the cart and walk beside it, often ankle-deep in water.

There were four of them in the cart. Sita and Krishan, Hukam Singh, the Jat farmer; and his son, Phambiri, a mountain of a man who was going to take part in the wrestling matches at the fair.

Hukam Singh, who drove the bullocks, liked to talk. He had been a soldier in the British Indian Army during the First World War, and had been with his regiment to Italy and Mesopotamia.

'There is nothing to compare with soldiering,' he said, 'except, of course, farming. If you can't be a farmer, be a soldier. Are you listening, boy? Which will you be—farmer or soldier?'

'Neither,' said Krishan. 'I shall be an engineer!'

Hukam Singh's long moustaches seemed to almost bristle with indignation.

'An engineer! What next! What does your father do, boy?'

'He keeps buffaloes.'

'Ah! And his son would be an engineer?... Well, well, the world isn't what it used to be! No one knows his rightful place any more. Men sent their children to schools, and what is the result? Engineers! And who will look after the buffaloes, while you are engineering?'

'I will sell the buffaloes,' said Krishan, adding rather cheekily: 'Perhaps you will buy one of them, Subedar Sahib!'

He took the cheek out of his remark by adding 'Subedar-Sahib', the rank of a non-commissioned officer in the old Army. Hukam Singh, who had never reached this rank, was naturally flattered.

'Fortunately, Phambiri hasn't been to school! He'll be a farmer, and a fine one too.'

Phambiri simply grunted, which could have meant anything. He hadn't studied further than class six, which was just as well, as he was a man of muscle, not brain.

Phambiri loved putting his strength to some practical and useful purpose. Whenever the cartwheels got stuck in the mud, he would get off, remove his shirt, and put his shoulder to the side of the cart, while his muscles bulged and the sweat glistened on his broad back.

'Phambiri is the strongest man in our district,' said Hukum Singh proudly. 'And clever, too! It takes quick thinking to win a wrestling match.'

'I have never seen one,' said Sita.

'Then stay with us tomorrow morning, and you will see Phambiri wrestle. He has been challenged by the Karauli champion. It will be a great fight!'

'We must see Phambiri win,' said Krishan.

'Will there be time?' asked Sita.

'Why not? The train for Shahganj won't come in till evening. The fair goes on all day, and the wrestling bouts will take place in the morning.'

'Yes, you must see me win!' exclaimed Phambiri, thumping himself on the chest as he climbed back on to the cart after freeing the wheels. 'No one can defeat me!'

'How can you be so certain?' asked Krishan.

'He *has* to be certain,' said Hukam Singh. 'I have taught him to be certain! You can't win anything if you are uncertain... Isn't that right, Phambiri? You *know* you are going to win!'

'I know,' said Phambiri, with a grunt of confidence.

'Well, someone has to lose,' said Krishan.

'Very true,' said Hukam Singh smugly. 'After all, what would we do without losers? But for Phambiri, it is win, win, all the time!'

'And *if* he loses?' persisted Krishan.

'Then he will just forget that it happened, and will go on to win his next fight!'

Krishan found Hukam Singh's logic almost unanswerable, but Sita, who had been puzzled by the argument, now saw everything very clearly and said, 'Perhaps he hasn't won any fights as yet. Did he lose the last one?'

'Hush!' said Hukam Singh, looking alarmed. 'You must not let him remember. You do not remember losing a fight, do you, my son?'

'I have never lost a fight,' said Phambiri with great simplicity and confidence.

'How strange,' said Sita. 'If you lose, how can you win?'

'Only a soldier can explain that,' said Hukam Singh. 'For a man who fights, there is no such thing as defeat. You fought against the river, did you not?'

'I went with the river,' said Sita. 'I went where it took me.'

'Yes, and you would have gone to the bottom if the boy had not come along to help you. He fought the river, didn't he?'

'Yes, he fought the river,' said Sita.

'You helped me to fight it,' said Krishan.

'So you both fought,' said the old man with a nod of satisfaction. 'You did not go with the river. You did not leave everything to the gods.'

'The gods were with us,' said Sita.

And so they talked, while the bullock-cart trundled along the muddy village roads. Both bullocks were white, and were decked out for the fair with coloured beaded necklaces and bells hanging from their necks. They were patient, docile beasts. But the cartwheels, which were badly in need of oiling, protested loudly, creaking and groaning as though all the demons in the world had been trapped within them.

Sita noticed a number of birds in the paddy fields. There were black and white curlews, and cranes with pink coat-tails. A good monsoon means plenty of birds. But Hukam Singh was not happy about the cranes.

'They do great damage in the wheat fields,' he said. Lighting up a small hand-held hookah pipe, he puffed at it and became philosophical again: 'Life is one long struggle for the farmer. When he has overcome the drought, survived the flood, hunted off the pig, killed the crane, and reaped the crop, then comes that bloodsucking ghoul, the moneylender. There is no escaping him! Is your father in debt to a moneylender, boy?'

'No,' said Krishan.

'That is because he doesn't have daughters who must be married! I have two. As they resemble Phambiri, they will need generous dowries.'

In spite of his grumbling, Hukam Singh seemed fairly content with his lot. He'd had a good maize crop, and the front of his cart was piled high with corn. He would sell the crop at the fair, along with some cucumbers, eggplants and melons.

The bad road had slowed them down so much that when darkness came they were still far from Karauli. In India there is hardly any twilight. Within a short time of the sun's going down, the stars were out.

'Six miles to go,' said Hukam Singh. 'In the dark our wheels may get stuck again. Let us spend the night here. If it rains, we can pull an old tarpaulin over the cart.'

Krishan made a fire in the charcoal burner which Hukam Singh had brought along, and they had a simple meal, roasting the corn over the fire and flavouring it with salt and spices and a squeeze of lemon. There was some milk, but not enough for everyone because Phambiri drank three tumblers by himself.

'If I win tomorrow,' he said, 'I will give all of you a feast!'

They settled down to sleep in the bullock-cart, and Phambiri and his father were soon snoring. Krishan lay awake, his arms crossed behind his head, staring up at the stars. Sita was very tired but she couldn't sleep. She was worrying about her grandparents, and wondering when she would see them again.

The night was full of sounds. The loud snoring that came

from Phambiri and his father seemed to be taken up by invisible sleepers all around them, and Sita, becoming alarmed, turned to Krishan and asked, 'What is that strange noise?'

He smiled in the darkness, and she could see his white teeth and the glint of laughter in his eyes.

'Only the spirits of lost demons,' he said, and then laughed. 'Can't you recognize the music of the frogs?'

And that was what they heard—a sound more hideous than the wail of demons, a rising crescendo of noise—*wurrk, wurrk, wurrk*—coming from the flooded ditches on either side of the road. All the frogs in the jungle seemed to have gathered at that one spot, and each one appeared to have something to say for himself. The speeches continued for about an hour. Then the meeting broke up, and silence returned to the forest.

A jackal slunk across the road. A puff of wind brushed through the trees. The bullocks, freed from the cart, were asleep beside it. The men's snores were softer now. Krishan slept, a half smile on his face. Only Sita lay awake, worried and waiting for the dawn.

At the Fair

Already, at nine o' clock, the fairground was crowded. Cattle were being sold or auctioned. Stalls had opened, selling everything from pins to ploughs. Foodstuffs were on sale—hot food, spicy food, sweets and ices. A merry-go-round, badly oiled, was squeaking and groaning, while a loudspeaker blared popular film music across the grounds.

While Phambiri was preparing for his wrestling match, Hukam Singh was busy haggling over the price of pumpkins.

Sita and Krishan wandered on their own among the stalls, gazing at toys and kites and bangles and clothing, at brightly coloured, syrupy sweets. Some of the rural people had transistor-radios dangling by straps from their shoulders, the radio music competing with the loudspeaker. Occasionally a buffalo bellowed, drowning all other sounds.

Various people were engaged in roadside professions. There was the fortune-teller. He had slips of paper, each of them covered with writing, which he kept in little trays along with some grain. He had a tame sparrow. When you gave the fortune-teller your money, he allowed the little bird to hop in and out among the trays until it stopped at one and started pecking at the grain. From this tray the fortune-teller took the slip of paper and presented it to his client. The writing told you what to expect over the next few months or years.

A harassed, middle aged man, who was surrounded by six noisy sons and daughters, was looking a little concerned, because his slip of paper said: 'Do not lose hope. You will have a child soon.'

Some distance away sat a barber, and near him a professional ear-cleaner. Several children clustered around a peepshow, which was built into an old gramophone cabinet. While one man wound up the gramophone and placed a well-worn record on the turntable, his partner pushed coloured pictures through a slide-viewer.

A young man walked energetically up and down the fairground, beating a drum and announcing the day's attractions. The wrestling bouts were about to start. The main attraction was going to be the fight between Phambiri, described as a man 'whose thighs had the thickness of an elephant's trunk', and the local champion, Sher Dil ('Tiger's Heart')—a wild-looking man, with hairy chest and beetling brow. He was heavier than Phambiri but not so tall. Sita and Krishan joined Hukam Singh at one corner of the akhara, the wrestling-pit. Hukam Singh was massaging his son's famous thighs.

A gong sounded and Sher Dil entered the ring, slapping himself on the chest and grunting like a wild boar. Phambiri advanced slowly to meet him.

They came to grips immediately, and stood swaying from side to side, two giants pitting their strength against each other. The sweat glistened on their well-oiled bodies.

Sher Dil got his arms round Phambiri's waist and tried to lift him off his feet; but Phambiri had twined one powerful leg around his opponent's thigh, and they both came down together with a loud squelch, churning up the soft mud of the wrestling-pit. But neither wrestler had been pinned down.

Soon they were so covered with mud that it was difficult to distinguish one from the other. There was a flurry of arms and legs. The crowd was cheering, and Sita and Krishan were cheering too, but the wrestlers were too absorbed in their struggle to be aware of their supporters. Each sought to turn the other on to his back. That was all that mattered. There was no count.

For a few moments Sher Dil had Phambiri almost helpless, but Phambiri wriggled out of a crushing grip and, using his legs once again, sent Sher Dil rocketing across the akhara. But Sher Dil landed on his belly, and even with Phambiri on top of him, it wasn't victory.

Nothing happened for several minutes, and the crowd became restless and shouted for more action. Phambiri thought of twisting his opponent's ear; but he realized that he might get disqualified for doing that, so he restrained himself. He relaxed his grip slightly, and this gave Sher Dil a chance to heave himself up and sent Phambiri spinning across the akhara. Phambiri was still in a sitting position when the other took a flying leap at him. But Phambiri dived forward, taking his opponent between the legs, and then rising, flung him backwards with a resounding thud. Sher Dil was helpless, and Phambiri sat on his opponent's chest to remove all doubts as to who was the winner. Only when the applause of the spectators told him that he had won did he rise and leave the ring.

Accompanied by his proud father, Phambiri accepted the prize money, thirty rupees, and then went in search of a tap. After he had washed the oil and mud from his body, he put on fresh clothes. Then, putting his arms around Krishan and Sita, he said, 'You have brought me luck, both of you. Now let us celebrate!' And he led the way to the sweet shops.

They ate syrupy rasgullas (made from milk and sugar) and almond-filled fudge, and little pies filled with minced meat, and washed everything down with a fizzy orange drink.

'Now I will buy each of you a small present,' said Phambiri.

He bought a bright blue sports shirt for Krishan. He bought a new hookah bowl for his father. And he took Sita to a stall where dolls were sold, and asked her to choose one.

There were all kinds of dolls—cheap plastic dolls, and beautiful dolls made by hand, dressed in the traditional costumes of different regions of the country. Sita was immediately reminded of Mumta, her own rag doll, who had been made at home with Grandmother's help. And she remembered Grandmother, and Grandmother's sewing machine, and the home that had been swept away, and the tears started to roll down her eyes.

The dolls seemed to smile at Sita. The shopkeeper held them up one by one, and they appeared to dance, to twirl their wide skirts, to stamp their jingling feet on the counter. Each doll had its own special appeal to Sita. Each one wanted her love.

'Which one will you have?' asked Phambiri. 'Choose the prettiest, never mind the price!'

But Sita could say nothing, she could only shake her head. No doll, no matter how beautiful, could replace Mumta. She would never keep a doll again. That part of her life was over.

So instead of a doll Phambiri bought her coloured glass bangles which slipped easily over Sita's thin wrists. And then he took them into a temporary cinema, a large shed made of corrugated tin sheets.

Krishan had been in a cinema before—the towns were full of cinemas—but for Sita it was another new experience. Many things that were common enough for other boys and girls were strange and new for a girl who had spent nearly all her life on a small island in the middle of a big river.

As they found seats, a curtain rolled up and a white sheet came into view. A babble of talk dwindled into silence. Sita became aware of a whirring noise somewhere not far behind her; but, before she could turn her head to see what it was, the sheet became a rectangle of light and colour. It came to life. People moved and spoke. A story unfolded.

But, long afterwards, all that Sita could remember of her first film was a jumble of images and incidents. A train in danger: the audience murmuring with anxiety: a bridge over a river (but a smaller than hers): the bridge being blown to pieces: the engine plunging into the river: people struggling in the water: a woman rescued by a man who immediately embraced her: the lights coming on again, and the audience rising slowly and drifting out of the theatre, looking quite unconcerned and even satisfied. All those people struggling in the water were now quite safe, back in the little black box in the projection room.

Catching the Train

And now a real engine, a steam engine belching smoke and fire, was on its way to Sita.

She stood with Krishan on the station platform along with over a hundred other people waiting for the Shahganj train.

The platform was littered with the familiar bedrolls (or holdalls) without which few people in India ever travel. On these rolls sat women, children, great-aunts and great-uncles, grandfathers, grandmothers and grandchildren, while the more active adults hovered at the edge of the platform, ready to leap onto the train as soon as it arrived and reserve a space for the family. In India, people do not travel alone if they can help it. The whole family must be taken along—especially if the reason for the journey is a marriage, a pilgrimage, or simply a visit to friends or relations.

Moving among the piles of bedding and luggage were coolies, vendors of magazines, sweetmeats, tea and betel-leaf preparations. The cries of the vendors mingled with the general clamour of the station and the shunting of a steam engine in the yards.

But there came the train!

The signal was down. The crowd surged forward, swamping an assistant stationmaster. Krishan took Sita by the hand and led her forward. If they were too slow, they would not get a place on the crowded train. In front of them was a tall, burly, bearded Sikh from Punjab. Krishan decided it would be a wise move to stand behind him and move forward at the same time.

Krishan stayed closed to the Sikh who forged a way through the throng. The Sikh reached an open doorway and was through. Krishan and Sita were through! They found somewhere to sit, and were then able to look down at the platform, into the whirlpool, and enjoy themselves a little. The vendors had abandoned the people on the platform and had started selling their wares at the windows. Hukam Singh, after buying their tickets, had given Krishan and Sita a rupee to spend on the way. Krishan bought a freshly split coconut, and Sita bought a comb for her disarranged hair. She had never bothered with her hair before.

They saw a worried man rushing along the platform searching for his family; but they were already in the compartment, having beaten him to it, and eagerly helped him in at the door. A whistle shrilled, and they were off! A couple of vendors made last-minute transactions, then jumped from the slow-moving train. One man did this expertly with a tray of teacups balanced on one hand.

The train gathered speed.

'What will happen to all those people still on the platform?' asked Sita anxiously. 'Will they all be left behind?'

She put her head out of the window and looked back at the receding platform. It was strangely empty. Only the vendors and the coolies and the stray dogs and the dishevelled railway staff were in evidence. A miracle had happened. No one—absolutely no one—had been left behind!

Then the train was rushing through the night, the engine throwing out bright sparks that danced away like fireflies.

Sometimes the train had to slow down, as floodwater had weakened the embankments. Sometimes it stopped at brightly lit stations.

When the train started again and moved on into the dark countryside, Sita would stare through the glass of the window, at the bright lights of a town or the quiet glow of village lamps. She thought of Phambiri and Hukam Singh, and wondered if she would ever see them again. Already they were like people in a fairy tale, met briefly on the road and never seen again.

There was no room in the compartment in which to lie down; but Sita soon fell asleep, her head resting against Krishan's shoulder.

A Meeting and a Parting

Sita did not know where to look for Grandfather. For an hour, she and Krishan wandered through the Shahganj bazaar, growing hungrier all the time. They had no money left, and they were hot and thirsty.

Outside the bazaar, near a small temple, they saw a tree in which several small boys were helping themselves to the sour, purple fruit.

It did not take Krishan long to join the boys in the tree. They did not object to his joining them. It wasn't their tree, anyway.

Sita stood beneath the tree, while Krishan threw the jamuns down to her. They soon had a small pile of the fruit. They were on the road again, their faces stained with purple juice.

They were asking the way to the Shahganj hospital when Sita caught a glimpse of her grandfather on the road.

At first the old man did not recognize her. He was walking stiffly down the road, looking straight ahead, and would have walked right past the dusty, dishevelled girl, had she not charged straight at his thin, shaky legs and clasped him round the waist.

'Sita!' he cried, when he had recovered his wind and his balance. 'Why are you here? How did you get off the island? I have been very worried—it has been bad, these last two days...'

'Is Grandmother all right?' asked Sita.

But even as she spoke, she knew that Grandmother was no longer with them. The dazed look in the old man's eyes told her as much. She wanted to cry—not for Grandmother, who could suffer no more, but for Grandfather, who looked so helpless and bewildered; she did not want him to be unhappy. She forced back her tears, and took his gnarled and trembling hand; and, with Krishan walking beside her, led the old man down the crowded street.

She knew, then, that it would be on her shoulder that Grandfather would lean on in the years to come.

They decided to remain in Shahganj for a couple of days, staying at a dharamsala—a wayside rest-house—until the floodwaters subsided. Grandfather still had two of the goats—it had not been necessary to sell more than one—but he did not want to take the risk of rowing a crowded boat across to the island. The river was still fast and dangerous.

But Krishan could not stay with Sita any longer.

'I must go now,' he said. 'My father and mother will be very worried, and they will not know where to look for me. In a day or two the water will go down, and you will be able to go back to your home.'

'Perhaps the island has gone forever,' said Sita.

'It will be there,' said Krishan. 'It is a rocky island. Bad for crops, but good for a house!'

'Will you come?' asked Sita.

What she really wanted to say was, 'Will you come to see me?' but she was too shy to say it; and besides, she wasn't sure if Krishan would want to see her again.

'I will come,' said Krishan. 'That is, if my father gets me another boat!'

As he turned to go, he gave her his flute.

'Keep it for me,' he said. 'I will come for it one day.'

When he saw her hesitate, he smiled and said, 'It is a good flute!'

The Return

There was more rain, but the worst was over, and when Grandfather and Sita returned to the island, the river was no longer in spate.

Grandfather could hardly believe his eyes when he saw that the tree had disappeared—the tree that had seemed as permanent as the island, as much a part of his life as the river itself had been. He marvelled at Sita's escape.

'It was the tree that saved you,' he said.

'And the boy,' said Sita.

'Yes, and the boy.'

She thought about Krishan and wondered if she would ever see him again. Would he, like Phambiri and Hukam Singh, be one of those people who arrived as though out of a fairy tale and then disappeared silently and mysteriously? She did not know it then, but some of the moving forces of our lives are

LESSONS IN FUN AND FROLIC

meant to touch us briefly and go their way...

And because Grandmother was no longer with them, life on the island was quite different. The evenings were sad and lonely.

But there was a lot of work to be done, and Sita did not have much time to think of Grandmother or Krishan or the world she had glimpsed during her journey.

For three nights they slept under a crude shelter made out of gunny-bags. During the day Sita helped Grandfather rebuild the mud hut. Once again, they used the big rock for support.

The trunk which Sita had packed so carefully had not been swept off the island, but the water had got into it, and the food and clothing had been spoilt. But Grandfather's hookah had been saved, and, in the evenings after work was done and they had eaten their light meal which Sita prepared, he would smoke with a little of his old contentment, and tell Sita about other floods which he had experienced as a boy. And he would tell her about the wrestling matches he had won, and the kites he had flown, for he remembered a time when grown men flew kites, and great battles were fought, the kites swooping and swerving in the sky, tangling with each other until the string of one was cut.

Kite-flying was then the sport of kings, Grandfather remembered how the Raja himself would come down to the riverbank and join in this noble pastime. There was time in those days to spend an hour with a gay, dancing strip of paper. Now everyone hurried, in a heat of hope, and delicate things like kites and daydreams were trampled underfoot.

Grandfather remembered the 'Dragon Kite' that he had built—a great kite with a face painted on it, the eyes made of small mirrors, the tail like a long crawling serpent. A large crowd assembled to watch its launching. At the first attempt it refused to leave the ground. And then the wind came from the right direction, and the Dragon Kite soared into the sky, wriggling its way higher and higher, with the sun still glinting in its eyes. And it went very high, it pulled fiercely on the twine determined to be free, to break loose, to live a life of its own. And eventually it did.

The twine snapped, the kite leapt away toward the sun, sailed on heavenward until it was lost to view. It was never found again, and Grandfather wondered if he had made too vivid, too living a thing of the great kite. He did not make another like it.

It was like her doll, thought Sita.

Mumta had been a real person, not a doll, and now Sita could not make another like her.

Sita planted a mango seed in the same spot where the peepul tree had stood. It would be many years before it grew into a big tree, but Sita liked to imagine sitting in the branches one day, picking the mangoes straight from the tree and feasting on them all day.

Grandfather was more particular about making a vegetable garden, putting down peas, carrots, gram and mustard.

One day, when most of the hard work had been done and the new hut was ready, Sita took the flute which had been given to her by Krishan, and walked down to the water's edge and tried to play it. But all she could produce was a few broken notes, and even the goats paid no attention to her music.

Sometimes Sita thought she saw a boat coming down the river, and she would run to meet it; but usually there was no boat, or, if there was, it belonged to a stranger or to another fisherman. And so she stopped looking out for boats.

Slowly, the rains came to an end. The floodwaters had receded, and in the villages people were beginning to till the land again and sow crops for the winter months. There were more cattle fairs and wrestling matches. The days were warm and sultry. The water in the river was no longer muddy, and one evening Grandfather brought home a huge mahseer fish, and Sita made it into a delicious curry.

Deep River

Grandfather sat outside the hut, smoking his hookah. Sita was at the far end of the island, spreading clothes on the rocks to dry. One of the goats had followed her. It was the friendlier of the two and often followed Sita about the island. She had made it a necklace of coloured beads.

She sat down on a smooth rock, and, as she did so, she noticed a small bright object in the sand near her feet. She picked it up. It was a little wooden toy—a coloured peacock, Lord Krishna's favourite bird—it must have come down on the river and been swept ashore on the island. Some of the paint had been rubbed off; but for Sita, who had no toys, it was a great find.

There was a soft footfall behind her. She looked round, and there was Krishan, barefooted, standing over her and smiling.

'I thought you wouldn't come,' said Sita.

'There was much work in my village. Did you keep my flute?' 'Yes, but I cannot play it properly.'

'I will teach you,' said Krishan.

He sat down beside her, and they cooled their feet in the

water, which was clear now, taking in the blue of the sky. You could see the sand and the pebbles of the river-bed.

'Sometimes the river is angry and sometimes it is kind,' said Sita. 'We are part of the river,' said Krishan.

◆

It was a good river, deep and strong, beginning in the mountains and ending in the sea.

Along its banks, for hundreds of miles, lived millions of people, and Sita was only one small girl among them, and no one had ever heard of her, no one knew her—except for the old man, and the boy, and the water that was blue and white and wonderful.

THE STORY OF MADHU

I met little Madhu several years ago, when I lived alone in an obscure town near the Himalayan foothills. I was in my late twenties then, and my outlook on life was still quite romantic; the cynicism that was to come with the thirties had not yet set in.

I preferred the solitude of the small district town to the kind of social life I might have found in the cities; and in my books, my writing and the surrounding hills, there was enough for my pleasure and occupation.

On summer mornings I would often sit beneath an old mango tree, with a notebook or a sketch pad on my knees. The house which I had rented (for a very nominal sum) stood on the outskirts of the town; and a large tank and a few poor houses could be seen from the garden wall. A narrow public pathway passed under the low wall.

One morning, while I sat beneath the mango tree, I saw a young girl of about nine, wearing torn clothes, darting about on the pathway and along the high banks of the tank.

Sometimes she stopped to look at me; and, when I showed that I noticed her, she felt encouraged and gave me a shy, fleeting smile. The next day I discovered her leaning over the garden wall, following my actions as I paced up and down on the grass.

In a few days an acquaintance had been formed. I began to take the girl's presence for granted, and even to look for her;

and she, in turn, would linger about on the pathway until she saw me come out of the house.

One day, as she passed the gate, I called her to me. 'What is your name?' I asked. 'And where do you live?'

'Madhu,' she said, brushing back her long untidy black hair and smiling at me from large black eyes. She pointed across the road: 'I live with my grandmother.'

'Is she very old?' I asked.

Madhu nodded confidingly and whispered: 'A hundred years...'

'We will never be that old,' I said. She was very slight and frail, like a flower growing in a rock, vulnerable to wind and rain.

I discovered later that the old lady was not her grandmother but a childless woman who had found the baby girl on the banks of the tank. Madhu's real parentage was unknown; but the wizened old woman had, out of compassion, brought up the child as her own.

My gate once entered, Madhu included the garden in her circle of activities. She was there every morning, chasing butterflies, stalking squirrels and mynahs, her voice brimming with laughter, her slight figure flitting about between the trees.

Sometimes, but not often, I gave her a toy or a new dress; and one day she put aside her shyness and brought me a present of a nosegay, made up of marigolds and wild blue cotton flowers.

'For you,' she said, and put the flowers in my lap.

'They are very beautiful,' I said, picking out the brightest marigold and putting it in her hair. 'But they are not as beautiful as you.'

Over a year passed before I began to take more than a mildly patronizing interest in Madhu.

LESSONS IN FUN AND FROLIC

It occurred to me after some time that she should be taught to read and write, and I asked a local teacher to give her lessons in the garden for an hour every day. She clapped her hands with pleasure at the prospect of what was to be for her a fascinating new game.

In a few weeks Madhu was surprising us with her capacity for absorbing knowledge. She always came to me to repeat the lessons of the day, and pestered me with questions on a variety of subjects. How big was the world? And were the stars really like our world? Or were they the sons and daughters of the sun and the moon?

My interest in Madhu deepened, and my life, so empty till then, became imbued with a new purpose. As she sat on the grass beside me, reading aloud, or listening to me with a look of complete trust and belief, all the love that had been lying dormant in me during my years of self-exile surfaced in a sudden surge of tenderness.

Three years glided away imperceptibly, and at the age of thirteen Madhu was on the verge of blossoming into a woman. I began to feel a certain responsibility towards her.

It was dangerous, I knew, to allow a child so pretty to live almost alone and unprotected, and to run unrestrained about the grounds. And in a censorious society she would be made to suffer if she spent too much time in my company.

She could see no need for any separation; but I decided to send her to a mission school in the next district, where I could visit her from time to time.

'But why?' said Madhu. 'I can learn more from you, and from the teacher who comes. I am so happy here.'

'You will meet other girls and make many friends,' I told

THE STORY OF MADHU

her. 'I will come to see you. And, when you come home, we will be even happier. It is good that you should go.'

It was the middle of June, a hot and oppressive month in the Siwaliks. Madhu had expressed her readiness to go to school, and when, one evening, I did not see her as usual in the garden, I thought nothing of it; but the next day I was informed that she had fever and could not leave the house.

Illness was something Madhu had not known before, and for this reason I felt afraid. I hurried down the path which led to the old woman's cottage. It seemed strange that I had never once entered it during my long friendship with Madhu.

It was a humble mud hut, the ceiling just high enough to enable me to stand upright, the room dark but clean. Madhu was lying on a string cot exhausted by fever, her eyes closed, her long hair unkempt, one small hand hanging over the side.

It struck me then how little, during all this time, I had thought of her physical comforts. There was no chair; I knelt down, and took her hand in mine. I knew, from the fierce heat of her body, that she was seriously ill.

She recognized my touch, and a smile passed across her face before she opened her eyes. She held on to my hand, then laid it across her cheek.

I looked round the little room in which she had grown up. It had scarcely an article of furniture apart from two string cots, on one of which the old woman sat and watched us, her white, wizened head nodding like a puppet's.

In a corner lay Madhu's little treasures. I recognized among them the presents which during the past four years I had given her. She had kept everything. On her dark arm she still wore a small piece of ribbon which I had playfully tied there about a year ago. She had given her heart, even before she was conscious of possessing one, to a stranger unworthy of the gift.

As the evening drew on, a gust of wind blew open the door of the dark room, and a gleam of sunshine streamed in, lighting up a portion of the wall. It was the time when every evening she would join me under the mango tree. She had been quiet for almost an hour, and now a slight pressure of her hand drew my eyes back to her face.

'What will we do now?' she said. 'When will you send me to school?'

'Not for a long time. First you must get well and strong. That is all that matters.' She didn't seem to hear me. I think she knew she was dying, but she did not resent its happening.

'Who will read to you under the tree?' she went on. 'Who will look after you?' she asked, with the solicitude of a grown woman.

'You will, Madhu. You are grown up now. There will be no one else to look after me.'

The old woman was standing at my shoulder. A hundred years—and little Madhu was slipping away. The woman took Madhu's hand from mine, and laid it gently down. I sat by the cot a little longer, and then I rose to go, all the loneliness in the world pressing upon my heart.

MISS BABCOCK'S BIG TOE

If two people are thrown together for a long time, they can become either close friends or sworn enemies. Thus, it was with Tata and me when we both went down with mumps and had to spend a fortnight together in the school hospital. It wasn't really a hospital—just a five-bed ward in a small cottage on the approach road to our prep-school in Chhota Shimla. It was supervised by a retired nurse, an elderly matron called Miss Babcock, who was all but stone deaf.

Miss Babcock was an able nurse, but she was a fidgety, fussy person, always dashing about from ward to dispensary and to her own room, as a result the boys called her Miss Shuttlecock. As she couldn't hear us, she didn't mind. But her hearing difficulty did create something of a problem, both for her and for her patients. If someone in the ward felt ill late at night, he had to shout or ring a bell, and she heard neither. So, someone had to get up and fetch her.

Miss Babcock devised an ingenious method of waking her in an emergency. She tied a long piece of string to the foot of the sick person's bed; then took the other end of the string to her own room, where, upon retiring for the night, she tied it to her big toe.

A vigorous pull on the string from the sick person, and Miss Babcock would be wide awake!

Now, what could be more tempting to a small boy than—

such a device? The string was tied to the foot of Tata's bed, and he was a restless fellow, always wanting water, always complaining of aches and pains. And sometimes, out of plain mischief, he would give several tugs on that string until Miss Babcock arrived with a pill or a glass of water.

'You'll have my toe off by morning,' she complained. 'You don't have to pull quite so hard.'

And what was worse, when Tata did fall asleep, he snored to high heaven and nothing could wake him! I had to lie awake most of the night, listening to his rhythmic snoring. It was like a trumpet tuning up or a bullfrog calling to its mates.

Fortunately, a couple of nights later, we were joined in the ward by Bimal, a friend and fellow 'feather', who had also contracted mumps. One night of Tata's snoring, and Bimal resolved to do something about it.

'Wait until he's fast asleep,' said Bimal, 'and then we'll carry his bed outside and leave him in the veranda.' We did more than that. As Tata commenced his nightly imitation of all the wind instruments in the London Philharmonic Orchestra, we lifted up his bed as gently as possible and carried it out into the garden, putting it down beneath the nearest pine tree.

'It's healthier outside,' said Bimal, justifying our action. 'All this fresh air should cure him.' Leaving Tata to serenade the stars, we returned to the ward expecting to enjoy a good night's sleep. So did Miss Babcock.

However, we couldn't sleep long. We were woken by Miss Babcock running around the ward screaming, 'Where's Tata? Where's Tata?' She ran outside, and we followed dutifully, barefoot, in our pyjamas.

The bed stood where we had put it down, but of Tata,

there was no sign. Instead, there was a large black-faced langur at the foot of the bed, baring its teeth in a grin of disfavour.

'Tata's gone,' gasped Miss Babcock.

'He must be a sleepwalker.' said Bimal.

'Maybe the leopard took him,' I said. Just then there was a commotion in the shrubbery at the end of the garden and shouting, 'Help, help!' Tata emerged from the bushes, followed by several lithe, long-tailed langurs, merrily giving chase. Apparently, he'd woken up at the crack of dawn to find his bed surrounded by a gang of inquisitive simians. They had meant no harm, but Tata had panicked, and made a dash for life and liberty, running into the forest instead of into the cottage. We got Tata and his bed back into the ward, and Miss Babcock took his temperature and gave him a dose of salts. Oddly enough, in all the excitement no one asked how Tata and his bed had travelled in the night.

And strangely, he did not snore the following night; so perhaps the pine-scented night air really helped. Needless to say, we all soon recovered from the mumps, and Miss Babcock's big toe received a well-deserved rest.

THE ZIGZAG WALK

Uncle Ken always maintained that the best way to succeed in life was to zigzag. 'If you keep going off in new directions,' he declared, 'you will meet new career opportunities!'

Well, opportunities certainly came Uncle Ken's way, but he was not a success in the sense that Dale Carnegie or Deepak Chopra would have defined a successful man...

In a long life devoted to 'muddling through' with the help of the family, Uncle Ken's many projects had included a chicken farm (rather like the one operated by Ukridge in Wodehouse's *Love Among the Chickens*) and a mineral water bottling project. For this latter enterprise, he bought a thousand old soda-water bottles and filled them with sulphur water from the springs, five miles from Dehra. It was good stuff, taken in small quantities, but drunk one bottle at a time it proved corrosive—'sulphur and brimstone' as one irate customer described it—and angry buyers demonstrated in front of the house, throwing empty bottles over the wall into Grandmother's garden.

Grandmother was furious—more with Uncle Ken than with the demonstrators—and made him give everyone's money back.

'You have to be healthy and strong to take sulphur water,' he explained later.

'I thought it was supposed to make you healthy and strong,' I said.

Grandfather remarked that it did not compare with plain

soda water, which he took with his whisky. 'Why don't you just bottle soda water?' he said, 'there's a much bigger demand for it.'

But Uncle Ken believed that he had to be original in all things.

'The secret to success is to zigzag,' he said.

'You certainly zigzagged round the garden when your customers were throwing their bottles back at you,' said Grandmother.

Uncle Ken also invented the zigzag walk.

The only way you could really come to know a place well was to walk in a truly haphazard way. To make a zigzag walk you take the first turning to the left, the first to the right, then the first to the left and so on. It can be quite fascinating provided you are in no hurry to reach your destination. The trouble was that Uncle Ken used this zigzag method even when he had a train to catch.

When Grandmother asked him to go to the station to meet Aunt Mabel and her children, who were arriving from Lucknow, he zigzagged through the town, taking in the botanical gardens in the west and the limestone factories to the east, finally reaching the station by way of the goods yard, in order, as he said, 'to take them by surprise'.

Nobody was surprised, least of all Aunt Mabel who had taken a tonga and reached the house while Uncle Ken was still sitting on the station platform, waiting for the next train to come in. I was sent to fetch him.

'Let's zigzag home again,' he said.

'Only on one condition, we eat chaat every fifteen minutes,' I said.

So we went home by way of all the most winding bazaars,

and in north Indian towns they do tend to zigzag, stopping at numerous chaat and halwai shops, until Uncle Ken had finished his money. We got home very late and were scolded by everyone; but as Uncle Ken told me, we were pioneers and had to expect to be misunderstood and even maligned. Posterity would recognize the true value of zigzagging.

'The zigzag way,' he said, 'is the diagonal between heart and reason.'

In our more troubled times, had he taken to preaching on the subject, he might have acquired a large following of dropouts. But Uncle Ken was the original dropout. He would not have tolerated others.

Had he been a space traveller, he would have gone from star to star, zigzagging across the Milky Way.

Uncle Ken would not have succeeded in getting anywhere very fast, but I think he did succeed in getting at least one convert (myself) to see his point: 'When you zigzag, you are not choosing what to see in this world but you are giving the world a chance to see you!'

FOUR BOYS ON A GLACIER

On a day that promised rain we bundled ourselves into the bus that was to take us to Kapkote (where people lost their caps and coats, punned Anil), the starting-point of our Himalayan trek. I was seventeen at the time, and Anil and Somi were sixteen. Each of us carried a haversack, and we had also brought along a good-sized bedding-roll which, apart from blankets, contained bags of rice and flour, thoughtfully provided by Anil's mother. We had no idea how we would carry the bedding-roll once we started walking, but we didn't worry too much about details.

We were soon in the hills of Kumaon, on a winding road that took us up and up, until we saw the valley and our small town spread out beneath us, the river a silver ribbon across the plain. We took a sharp bend, the valley disappeared, and the mountains towered above us.

At Kapkote, we had refreshments and the shopkeeper told us we could spend the night in one of his rooms. The surroundings were pleasant, the hills wooded with deodars, the lower slopes planted with fresh green paddy. At night there was a wind moaning in the trees and it found its way through the cracks in the windows and eventually through our blankets.

Next morning we washed our faces at a small stream near the shop and filled our water bottles for the day's march. A boy from the nearby village approached us, and asked where we were going.

'To the glacier,' said Somi.

'I'll come with you', said the boy. 'I know the way'

'You're too small,' said Anil. 'We need someone who can carry our bedding-roll.'

'I'm small but I'm strong,' said the boy, who certainly looked sturdy. He had pink cheeks and a well-knit body.

'See!' he said, and, picking up a rock the size of a football, he heaved it across the stream.

'I think he can come with us,' I said.

And then, we were walking—at first above the little Sarayu river, then climbing higher along the rough mule track, always within sound of the water, which we glimpsed now and then, swift, green and bubbling.

We were at the forest rest-house by six in the evening, after covering fifteen miles. Anil found the watchman asleep in a patch of fading sunlight and roused him. The watchman, who hadn't been bothered by visitors for weeks, grumbled at our intrusion but opened a room for us. He also produced some potatoes from his store, and these were roasted for dinner.

Just as we were about to get into our beds we heard a thud on the corrugated tin roof, and then the sound of someone—or something—scrambling about on the roof. Anil, Somi and I were alarmed; but Bisnu, who was already under the blankets, merely yawned, and turned over on his side.

'It's only a bear,' he said. 'Didn't you see the pumpkins on the roof? Bears love pumpkins.'

For half an hour we had to listen to the bear as it clambered about on the roof, feasting on the watchman's ripe pumpkins. At last there was silence. Anil and I crawled out of our blankets and went to the window. And through the frosted glass we saw a black Himalayan bear ambling across the slope in front of the house.

Our next rest-house lay in a narrow valley, on the banks of the rushing Pindar River, which twisted its way through the mountains. We walked on, past terraced fields and small stone houses, until there were no more fields or houses, only forest and sun and silence.

It was different from the silence of a room or an empty street.

And then, the silence broke into sound—the sound of the river.

Far down in the valley, the Pindar tumbled over itself in its impatience to reach the plains. We began to run; slipped and stumbled, but continued running.

The rest-house stood on a ledge just above the river, and the sound of the water rushing down the mountain-defile could be heard at all times. The sound of the birds, which we had grown used to, was drowned by the sound of the water, but the birds themselves could be seen, many-coloured, standing out splendidly against the dark green forest foliage—the red crowned jay, the paradise flycatcher, the purple whistling thrush and others we could not recognise.

Higher up the mountain, above some terraced land where oats and barley were grown, stood a small cluster of huts. This, we were told by the watchman, was the last village on the way to the glacier. It was, in fact, one of the last villages in India, because if we crossed the difficult passes beyond the glacier, we would find ourselves in Tibet.

Anil asked the watchman about the Abominable Snowman. The Nepalese believe in the existence of the Snowman, and our watchman was Nepalese.

'Yes, I have seen the yeti,' he told us. 'A great shaggy, flat-footed creature. In the winter, when it snows heavily, he passes the bungalow at night. I have seen his tracks the next morning.'

'Does he come this way in the summer?' asked Somi, anxiously.

'No,' said the watchman. 'But sometimes I have seen the *lidini*. You have to be careful of her.'

'And who is the *lidini?*' asked Anil.

'She is the snow-woman, and far more dangerous. She has the same height as the yeti—about seven feet when her back is straight—and her hair is much longer. Also she has very long teeth. Her feet face inwards, but she can run very fast, especially downhill. If you see a lidini, and she chases you, always run in an uphill direction. She tires quickly because of her crooked feet. But when running downhill she has no trouble at all, and you want to be very fast to escape her!'

'Well, we are quite fast,' said Anil with a nervous laugh. 'But its just a fairy-story, I don't believe a word of it.'

The watchman was most offended, and refused to tell us anything more about snowmen and snow-women. But he helped Bisnu make a fire, and presented us with a black, sticky sweet, which we ate with relish.

It was a fine, sunny morning when we set out to cover the last seven miles to the glacier. We had expected a stiff climb, but the rest-house was 11,000 feet above sea-level, and the rest of the climb was fairly gradual.

Suddenly, abruptly, there were no more trees. As the bungalow dropped out of sight, the trees and bushes gave way to short grass and little pink and blue alpine flowers. The snow peaks were close now, ringing us in on every side. We passed white waterfalls, cascading hundreds of feet down precipitous rock faces, thundering into the little river. A great white eagle hovered over us.

The hill fell away, and there, confronting us, was a great white field of snow and ice, cradled between two shining peaks. We were speechless for several minutes. Then we proceeded cautiously on to the snow, supporting each other on the slippery surface. We could not go far, because we were quite unequipped for any high-altitude climbing. But it was a satisfying feeling to know that we were the only young men from our town who had walked so far and so high.

The sun was reflected sharply from the snow and we felt surprisingly warm. It was delicious to feel the sun crawling over our bodies, sinking deep into our bones. Meanwhile, almost imperceptibly, clouds had covered some of the peaks, and white mist drifted down the mountain slopes. It was time to return: we would barely make it to the bungalow before it grew dark.

We took our time returning to Kapkote; stopped by the Sarayu River; bathed with the village boys we had seen on the way up; collected strawberries and ferns and wild flowers; and finally said goodbye to Bisnu.

Anil wanted to take Bisnu along with us, but the boy's parents refused to let him go, saying that he was too young for the life of a city.

'Never mind,' said Somi. 'We'll go on another trek next year, and we'll take you with us, Bisnu.'

This promise pleased Bisnu, and he saw us off at the bus-stop, shouldering our bedding-roll to the end. Then he climbed a pine tree to have a better view of us leaving. We saw him waving to us from the tree as the bus went round the bend from Kapkote, and then the hills were left behind and the plains stretched out below.

THE LEOPARD

I first saw the leopard when I was crossing the small stream at the bottom of the hill.

The ravine was so deep that for most of the day it remained in shadow. This encouraged many birds and animals to emerge from cover during the daylight hours. Few people ever passed that way: only milkmen and charcoal burners from the surrounding villages. As a result, the ravine had become a little haven for wildlife, one of the few natural sanctuaries left near Mussoorie, a hill station in northern India.

Below my cottage was a forest of oak and maple and Himalayan rhododendron. A narrow path twisted its way down through the trees, over an open ridge where red sorrel grew wild, and then steeply down through a tangle of wild raspberries, creeping vines and slender bamboo. At the bottom of the hill the path led on to a grassy verge, surrounded by wild dog roses. (It is surprising how closely the flora of the lower Himalayas, between 5,000 and 8,000 feet, resembles that of the English countryside.)

The stream ran close by the verge, tumbling over smooth pebbles, over rocks worn yellow with age, on its way to the plains and to the little Song River and finally to the sacred Ganga River.

When I first discovered the stream, it was early April and the wild roses were flowering—small white blossoms lying in clusters.

I walked down to the stream almost every day after two or three hours of writing. I had lived in cities too long and had returned to the hills to renew myself, both physically and mentally. Once you have lived with mountains for any length of time you belong to them, and must return again and again.

Nearly every morning, and sometimes during the day, I heard the cry of the barking deer. And in the evening, walking through the forest, I disturbed parties of pheasants. The birds went gliding down the ravine on open, motionless wings. I saw pine martens and a handsome red fox, and I recognized the footprints of a bear.

As I had not come to take anything from the forest, the birds and animals soon grew accustomed to my presence; or possibly they recognized my footsteps. After some time, my approach did not disturb them.

The langoors in the oak and rhododendron trees, who would at first go leaping through the branches at my approach, now watched me with some curiosity as they munched the tender green shoots of the oak. The young ones scuffled and wrestled like boys while their parents groomed each other's coats, stretching themselves out on the sunlit hillside.

But one evening, as I passed, I heard them chattering in the trees, and I knew I was not the cause of their excitement. As I crossed the stream and began climbing the hill, the grunting and chattering increased, as though the langoors were trying to warn me of some hidden danger. A shower of pebbles came rattling down the steep hillside, and I looked up to see a sinewy, orange-gold leopard poised on a rock about twenty feet above me.

He was not looking towards me but had his head thrust

attentively forward, in the direction of the ravine. Yet he must have sensed my presence, because, he slowly turned his head and looked down at me.

He seemed a little puzzled at my presence there; and when, to give myself courage, I clapped my hands sharply, the leopard sprang away into the thickets, making absolutely no sound as he melted into the shadows.

I had disturbed the animal in his quest for food. But a little after I heard the quickening cry of a barking deer as it fled through the forest. The hunt was still on.

The leopard, like other members of the cat family, is nearing extinction in India, and I was surprised to find one so close to Mussoorie. Probably the deforestation that had been taking place in the surrounding hills had driven the deer into this green valley; and the leopard, naturally, had followed.

It was some weeks before I saw the leopard again, although I was often made aware of its presence. A dry, rasping cough sometimes gave it away. At times I felt almost certain that I was being followed.

Once, when I was late getting home, and the brief twilight gave way to a dark moonless night, I was startled by a family of porcupines running about in a clearing. I looked around nervously and saw two bright eyes staring at me from a thicket. I stood still, my heart banging away against my ribs. Then the eyes danced away and I realized that they were only fireflies.

In May and June, when the hills are brown and dry, it is always cool and green near the stream, where ferns and maidenhair and long grasses continue to thrive.

Downstream I found a small pool where I could bathe, and a cave with water dripping from the roof, the water spangled gold and silver in the shafts of sunlight that pushed through the slits in the cave roof.

'He maketh me to lie down in green pastures; he leadeth me beside the still waters.' Perhaps David had discovered a similar paradise when he wrote those words; perhaps I, too, would write good words. The hill station's summer visitors had not discovered this haven of wild and green things. I was beginning to feel that the place belonged to me, that dominion was mine.

The stream had at least one other regular visitor, a spotted forktail, and though it did not fly away at my approach, it became restless if I stayed too long, and then she would move from boulder to boulder uttering a long complaining cry.

I spent an afternoon trying to discover the bird's nest, which I was certain contained young ones, because I had seen the forktail carrying grubs in her bill. The problem was that when the bird flew upstream, I had difficulty in following her rapidly enough as the rocks were sharp and slippery.

Eventually I decorated myself with bracken fronds and, after slowly making my way upstream, hid myself in the hollow stump of a tree at a spot where the forktail often disappeared. I had no intention of robbing the bird. I was simply curious to see its home.

By crouching down, I was able to command a view of a small stretch of the stream and the side of the ravine; but I had done little to deceive the forktail, who continued to object strongly to my presence so near her home.

I summoned up my reserves of patience and sat perfectly still for about ten minutes. The forktail quietened down. Out of sight, out of mind. But where had she gone? Probably into the walls of the ravine where, I felt sure, she was guarding her nest.

I decided to take her by surprise and stood up suddenly, in time to see not the forktail on her doorstep but the leopard bounding away with a grunt of surprise! Two urgent springs, and he had crossed the stream and plunged into the forest.

I was as astonished as the leopard, and forgot all about the forktail and her nest. Had the leopard been following me again?

I decided against this possibility. Only man-eaters follow humans and, as far as I knew, there had never been a man-eater in the vicinity of Mussoorie.

During the monsoon the stream became a rushing torrent; bushes and small trees were swept away, and the friendly murmur of the water became a threatening boom. I did not visit the place too often as there were leeches in the long grass.

One day I found the remains of a barking deer, which had only been partly eaten. I wondered why the leopard had not hidden the rest of his meal, and decided that it must have been disturbed while eating.

Then, climbing the hill, I met a party of hunters resting beneath the oaks. They asked me if I had seen a leopard. I said I had not. They said they knew there was a leopard in the forest.

Leopard skins, they told me, were selling in Delhi at over a thousand rupees each. Of course there was a ban on the export of skins, but they gave me to understand that there were ways and means… I thanked them for their information and walked on, feeling uneasy and disturbed.

The hunters had seen the carcass of the deer, and they had seen the leopard's pug marks, and they kept coming to the forest. Almost every evening I heard their guns banging away; for they were ready to fire at almost anything.

'There's a leopard about,' they always told me.

'You should carry a gun.'

'I don't have one,' I said.

There were fewer birds to be seen, and even the langoors had moved on. The red fox did not show itself; and the pine martens, who had become quite bold, now dashed into hiding at my approach. The smell of one human is like the smell of any other.

And then the rains were over and it was October. I could lie in the sun, on sweet-smelling grass, and gaze up through a pattern of oak leaves into a blinding blue heaven. And I would praise God for leaves and grass and the smell of things—the smell of mint and bruised clover—and the touch of things—the touch of grass and air and sky, the touch of the sky's blueness.

I thought no more of the men. My attitude towards them was similar to that of the denizens of the forest. These were men, unpredictable, and to be avoided if possible.

On the other side of the ravine rose Pari Tibba, Hill of the Fairies; a bleak, scrub-covered hill where no one lived.

It was said that in the previous century Englishmen had tried building their houses on the hill, but the area had always attracted lightning, due to either the hill's location or due to its mineral deposits; after several houses had been struck by lighting, the settlers had moved on to the next hill, where the town now stands.

To the hillmen it is Pari Tibba, haunted by the spirits of a pair of ill-fated lovers who perished there in a storm; to others it is known as Burnt Hill, because of its scarred and stunted trees.

One day, after crossing the stream, I climbed Pari Tibba—a stiff undertaking, because there was no path to the top and I had to scramble up a precipitous rock face with the help of rocks and roots that were apt to come loose in my groping hand.

But at the top was a plateau with a few pine trees, their upper branches catching the wind and humming softly. There I found the ruins of what must have been the houses of the first settlers—just a few piles of rubble, now overgrown with weeds, sorrel, dandelions and nettles.

As I walked though the roofless ruins, I was struck by the silence that surrounded me, the absence of birds and animals, the sense of complete desolation.

The silence was so absolute that it seemed to be ringing in my ears. But there was something else of which I was becoming increasingly aware: the strong feline odour of one of the cat family. I paused and looked about. I was alone. There was no movement of dry leaf or loose stone.

The ruins were for the most part open to the sky. Their rotting rafters had collapsed, jamming together to form a low passage like the entrance to a mine; and this dark cavern seemed to lead down into the ground. The smell was stronger when I approached this spot, so I stopped again and waited there, wondering if I had discovered the lair of the leopard, wondering if the animal was now at rest after a night's hunt.

Perhaps he was crouching there in the dark, watching me, recognizing me, knowing me as the man who walked alone in the forest without a weapon.

I like to think that he was there, that he knew me, and that he acknowledged my visit in the friendliest way: by ignoring me altogether.

Perhaps I had made him confident—too confident, too careless, too trusting of the human in his midst. I did not venture any further; I was not out of my mind. I did not seek physical contact, or even another glimpse of that beautiful sinewy body, springing from rock to rock. It was his trust I wanted, and I think he gave it to me.

But did the leopard, trusting one man, make the mistake of bestowing his trust on others? Did I, by casting out all fear—my own fear, and the leopard's protective fear—leave him defenceless? Because the next day, coming up the path from the stream, shouting and beating drums, were the hunters. They had a long bamboo pole across their shoulders; and slung from the pole, feet up, head down, was the lifeless body of the leopard, shot in the neck and in the head.

'We told you there was a leopard!' they shouted, in great good humour. 'Isn't he a fine specimen?'

'Yes,' I said. 'He was a beautiful leopard.'

I walked home through the silent forest. It was very silent, almost as though the birds and animals knew that their trust had been violated.

I remembered the lines of a poem by D.H. Lawrence; and, as I climbed the steep and lonely path to my home, the words beat out their rhythm in my mind: 'There was room in the world for a mountain lion and me.'

MY FAILED OMELETTES
AND OTHER DISASTERS

In nearly fifty years of writing for a living, I have never succeeded in writing a bestseller. And now I know why. I can't cook.

Had I been able to do so, I could have turned out a few of those sumptuous-looking cookery books that brighten up the bookstore windows before being snapped up by folk who can't cook either.

As it is, if I were forced to write a cook book, it would probably be called *Fifty Different Ways of Boiling An Egg and Other Disasters*.

I used to think that boiling an egg would be a simple undertaking. But when I came to live at 7,000 feet in the Himalayan foothills, I found that just getting the water to boil was something of an achievement. I don't know if it's the altitude or the density of the water, but it just won't come to a boil in time for breakfast. As a result, my eggs are only half-boiled. 'Never mind,' I tell everyone, 'half-boiled eggs are more nutritious than full-boiled eggs.'

'Why boil them at all?' asks my five-year-old grandson, Gautam, who is my Mr Dick, always offering good advice. 'Raw eggs are probably healthier.'

'Just you wait and see,' I told him. 'I'll make you a cheese omelette you'll never forget.' And I did. It was a bit messy, as I was over-generous with the tomatoes, but I thought it tasted rather good. Gautam, however, pushed his plate away, saying, 'You forgot to put in the egg.'

101 Failed Omelettes might well be the title of my bestseller.

I love watching other people cook—a habit that I acquired at a young age, when I would watch my Granny at work in the kitchen, turning out delicious curries, koftas and custards. I would try helping her, but she soon put a stop to my feeble contributions. On one occasion she asked me to add a cup of spices to a large curry dish she was preparing, and absent-mindedly I added a cup of sugar. The result—a very sweet curry! Another invention of mine.

I was better at remembering Granny's kitchen proverbs. Here are some of them:

'There is skill in all things, even in making porridge.'

'Dry bread at home is better then curried prawns abroad.'

'Eating and drinking should not keep men from thinking.'

'Better a small fish than an empty dish.'

And her favourite maxim, with which she reprimanded me whenever I showed signs of gluttony: 'Don't let your tongue cut your throat.'

And as for making porridge, it's certainly no simple matter. I made one or two attempts, but it always came out lumpy.

'What's this?' asked Gautam suspiciously, when I offered him some.

'Porridge!' I said enthusiastically. 'It's eaten by those brave Scottish Highlanders who were always fighting the English!'

'And did they win?' he asked.

'Well—er—not usually. But they were outnumbered!'

He looked doubtfully at the porridge. 'Some other time,' he said.

So why not take the advice of Thoreau and try to simplify life? Simplify, simplify! Or simply sandwiches...

These shouldn't be too difficult, I decided. After all, they are basically bread and butter. But have you tried cutting bread into thin slices? Don't. It's highly dangerous. If you're a pianist, you could be putting your career at great risk.

You must get your bread ready sliced. Butter it generously. Now add your fillings. Cheese, tomato, lettuce, cucumber, whatever. Gosh, I was really going places! Slap another slice of buttered bread over this mouth-watering assemblage. Now cut in two. Result: Everything spills out at the sides and on to the tablecloth.

'Now look what you've gone and done,' says Gautam, in his best Oliver Hardy manner.

'Never mind,' I tell him. 'Practice makes perfect!'

And one of these days you're going to find *Bond's Book of Better Sandwiches* up there on the bestseller lists.

THE SCHOOL AMONG THE PINES

1

A leopard, lithe and sinewy, drank at the mountain stream, and then lay down on the grass to bask in the late February sunshine. Its tail twitched occasionally and the animal appeared to be sleeping. At the sound of distant voices it raised its head to listen, then stood up and leapt lightly over the boulders in the stream, disappearing among the trees on the opposite bank.

A minute or two later, three children came walking down the forest path. They were a girl and two boys, and they were singing in their local dialect an old song they had learnt from their grandparents.

> Five more miles to go!
> We climb through rain and snow.
> A river to cross...
> A mountain to pass...
> Now we've four more miles to go!

Their school satchels looked new, their clothes had been washed and pressed. Their loud and cheerful singing startled a Spotted Forktail. The bird left its favourite rock in the stream and flew down the dark ravine.

'Well, we have only three more miles to go,' said the bigger boy, Prakash, who had been this way hundreds of times. 'But first we have to cross the stream.'

He was a sturdy twelve-year-old with eyes like raspberries and a mop of bushy hair that refused to settle down on his head. The girl and her small brother were taking this path for the first time.

'I'm feeling tired, Bina,' said the little boy.

Bina smiled at him, and Prakash said, 'Don't worry, Sonu, you'll get used to the walk. There's plenty of time.' He glanced at the old watch he'd been given by his grandfather. It needed constant winding. 'We can rest here for five or six minutes.'

They sat down on a smooth boulder and watched the clear water of the shallow stream tumbling downhill. Bina examined the old watch on Prakash's wrist. The glass was badly scratched and she could barely make out the figures on the dial. 'Are you sure it still gives the right time?' she asked.

'Well, it loses five minutes every day, so I put it ten minutes forward at night. That means by morning it's quite accurate! Even our teacher, Mr Mani, asks me for the time. If he doesn't ask, I tell him! The clock in our classroom keeps stopping.'

They removed their shoes and let the cold mountain water run over their feet. Bina was the same age as Prakash. She had pink cheeks, soft brown eyes, and hair that was just beginning to lose its natural curls. Hers was a gentle face, but a determined little chin showed that she could be a strong person. Sonu, her younger brother, was ten. He was a thin boy who had been sickly as a child but was now beginning to fill out. Although he did not look very athletic, he could run like the wind.

Bina had been going to school in her own village of Koli, on the other side of the mountain. But it had been a primary school, finishing at Class Five. Now, in order to study in the

Sixth, she would have to walk several miles every day to Nauti, where there was a high school going up to the Eighth. It had been decided that Sonu would also shift to the new school, to give Bina company. Prakash, their neighbour in Koli, was already a pupil at the Nauti school. His mischievous nature, which sometimes got him into trouble, had resulted in his having to repeat a year.

But this didn't seem to bother him. 'What's the hurry?' he had told his indignant parents. 'You're not sending me to a foreign land when I finish school. And our cows aren't running away, are they?'

'You would prefer to look after the cows, wouldn't you?' asked Bina, as they got up to continue their walk.

'Oh, school's all right. Wait till you see old Mr Mani. He always gets our names mixed up, as well as the subjects he's supposed to be teaching. At our last lesson, instead of maths, he gave us a geography lesson!'

'More fun than maths,' said Bina.

'Yes, but there's a new teacher this year. She's very young, they say, just out of college. I wonder what she'll be like.'

Bina walked faster and Sonu had some trouble keeping up with them. She was excited about the new school and the prospect of different surroundings. She had seldom been outside her own village, with its small school and single ration shop. The day's routine never varied—helping her mother in the fields or with household tasks like fetching water from the spring or cutting grass and fodder for the cattle. Her father, who was a soldier, was away for nine months in the year and Sonu was still too small for the heavier tasks.

As they neared Nauti village, they were joined by other children coming from different directions. Even where there were no major roads, the mountains were full of little lanes and short cuts. Like a game of snakes and ladders, these narrow paths zigzagged around the hills and villages, cutting through fields and crossing narrow ravines until they came together to form a fairly busy road along which mules, cattle and goats joined the throng.

Nauti was a fairly large village, and from here a broader but dustier road started for Tehri. There was a small bus, several trucks and (for part of the way) a road-roller. The road hadn't been completed because the heavy diesel roller couldn't take the steep climb to Nauti. It stood on the roadside half way up the road from Tehri.

Prakash knew almost everyone in the area, and exchanged greetings and gossip with other children as well as with muleteers, bus drivers, milkmen and labourers working on the road. He loved telling everyone the time, even if they weren't interested.

'It's nine o'clock,' he would announce, glancing at his wrist. 'Isn't your bus leaving today?'

'Off with you!' the bus driver would respond, 'I'll leave when I'm ready.'

As the children approached Nauti, the small flat school buildings came into view on the outskirts of the village, fringed with a line of long-leaved pines. A small crowd had assembled on the playing field. Something unusual seemed to have happened. Prakash ran forward to see what it was all about. Bina and Sonu stood aside, waiting in a patch of sunlight near the boundary wall.

Prakash soon came running back to them. He was bubbling over with excitement.

'It's Mr Mani!' he gasped. 'He's disappeared! People are saying a leopard must have carried him off!'

2

Mr Mani wasn't really old. He was about fifty-five and was expected to retire soon. But for the children, adults over forty seemed ancient! And Mr Mani had always been a bit absent-minded, even as a young man.

He had gone out for his early morning walk, saying he'd be back by eight o'clock, in time to have his breakfast and be ready for class. He wasn't married, but his sister and her husband stayed with him. When it was past nine o'clock his sister presumed he'd stopped at a neighbour's house for breakfast (he loved tucking into other people's breakfast) and that he had gone on to school from there. But when the school bell rang at ten o'clock, and everyone but Mr Mani was present, questions were asked and guesses were made.

No one had seen him return from his walk and enquiries made in the village showed that he had not stopped at anyone's house. For Mr Mani to disappear was puzzling; for him to disappear without his breakfast was extraordinary.

Then a milkman returning from the next village said he had seen a leopard sitting on a rock on the outskirts of the pine forest. There had been talk of a cattle-killer in the valley, of leopards and other animals being displaced by the construction of a dam. But as yet no one had heard of a leopard attacking a man. Could Mr Mani have been its first victim? Someone found a strip of red cloth entangled in a blackberry bush and went running through the village showing it to everyone. Mr Mani had been known to wear red pyjamas. Surely, he had been seized and eaten! But where were his remains? And why had he been in his pyjamas?

Meanwhile, Bina and Sonu and the rest of the children had followed their teachers into the school playground. Feeling a little lost, Bina looked around for Prakash. She found herself facing a dark slender young woman wearing spectacles, who must have been in her early twenties—just a little too old to be another student. She had a kind expressive face and she seemed a little concerned by all that had been happening.

Bina noticed that she had lovely hands; it was obvious that the new teacher hadn't milked cows or worked in the fields!

'You must be new here,' said the teacher, smiling at Bina. 'And is this your little brother?'

'Yes, we've come from Koli village. We were at school there.'

'It's a long walk from Koli. You didn't see any leopards, did you? Well, I'm new too. Are you in the Sixth class?'

'Sonu is in the Third. I'm in the Sixth.'

'Then I'm your new teacher. My name is Tania Ramola. Come along, let's see if we can settle down in our classroom.'

Mr Mani turned up at twelve o'clock, wondering what all the fuss was about. No, he snapped, he had not been attacked by a leopard; and yes, he had lost his pyjamas and would someone kindly return them to him?

'How did you lose your pyjamas, sir?' asked Prakash.

'They were blown off the washing line!' snapped Mr Mani.

After much questioning, Mr Mani admitted that he had gone further than he had intended, and that he had lost his way coming back. He had been a bit upset because the new teacher, a slip of a girl, had been given charge of the Sixth, while he was still with the Fifth, along with that troublesome boy Prakash, who kept on reminding him of the time! The headmaster had explained that as Mr Mani was due to retire at the end of the year, the school did not wish to burden him with a senior class. But Mr Mani looked upon the whole thing as a plot to get rid of him. He glowered at Miss Ramola whenever he passed her. And when she smiled back at him, he looked the other way!

Mr Mani had been getting even more absent-minded of late—putting on his shoes without his socks, wearing his homespun waistcoat inside out, mixing up people's names and, of course, eating other people's lunches and dinners. His sister had made a special mutton broth (*pai*) for the postmaster, who was down with flu and had asked Mr Mani to take it over in a thermos. When the postmaster opened the thermos, he found only a few drops of broth at the bottom—Mr Mani had drunk the rest somewhere along the way.

When sometimes Mr Mani spoke of his coming retirement, it was to describe his plans for the small field he owned just behind the house. Right now, it was full of potatoes, which did not require much looking after; but he had plans for growing dahlias, roses, French beans, and other fruits and flowers.

The next time he visited Tehri, he promised himself, he would buy some dahlia bulbs and rose cuttings. The monsoon season would be a good time to put them down. And meanwhile, his potatoes were still flourishing.

3

Bina enjoyed her first day at the new school. She felt at ease with Miss Ramola, as did most of the boys and girls in her class. Tania Ramola had been to distant towns such as Delhi and Lucknow—places they had only read about—and it was said that she had a brother who was a pilot and flew planes all over the world. Perhaps he'd fly over Nauti some day!

Most of the children had, of course, seen planes flying overhead, but none of them had seen a ship, and only a few had been on a train. Tehri mountain was far from the railway and hundreds of miles from the sea. But they all knew about the big dam that was being built at Tehri, just forty miles away.

Bina, Sonu and Prakash had company for part of the way home, but gradually the other children went off in different directions. Once they had crossed the stream, they were on their own again.

It was a steep climb all the way back to their village. Prakash had a supply of peanuts which he shared with Bina and Sonu, and at a small spring they quenched their thirst.

When they were less than a mile from home, they met a postman who had finished his round of the villages in the area and was now returning to Nauti.

'Don't waste time along the way,' he told them. 'Try to get home before dark.'

'What's the hurry?' asked Prakash, glancing at his watch. 'It's only five o'clock.'

'There's a leopard around. I saw it this morning, not far from the stream. No one is sure how it got here. So don't take any chances. Get home early.'

'So there really is a leopard,' said Sonu.

They took his advice and walked faster, and Sonu forgot to complain about his aching feet.

They were home well before sunset.

There was a smell of cooking in the air and they were hungry.

'Cabbage and roti,' said Prakash gloomily. 'But I could eat anything today.' He stopped outside his small slate-roofed house, and Bina and Sonu waved him goodbye, then carried on across a couple of ploughed fields until they reached their small stone house.

'Stuffed tomatoes,' said Sonu, sniffing just outside the front door.

'And lemon pickle,' said Bina, who had helped cut, sun and salt the lemons a month previously.

Their mother was lighting the kitchen stove. They greeted her with great hugs and demands for an immediate dinner. She was a good cook who could make even the simplest of dishes taste delicious. Her favourite saying was, 'Homemade *pai* is better than chicken soup in Delhi,' and Bina and Sonu had to agree.

Electricity had yet to reach their village, and they took their meal by the light of a kerosene lamp. After the meal, Sonu settled down to do a little homework, while Bina stepped outside to look at the stars.

Across the fields, someone was playing a flute. *It must be Prakash*, thought Bina. *He always breaks off on the high notes.* But the flute music was simple and appealing, and she began singing softly to herself in the dark.

4

Mr Mani was having trouble with the porcupines. They had been getting into his garden at night and digging up and eating his potatoes. From his bedroom window—left open, now that the mild-April weather had arrived—he could listen to them enjoying the vegetables he had worked hard to grow. Scrunch, scrunch! *Katar, katar*, as their sharp teeth sliced through the largest and juiciest of potatoes. For Mr Mani it was as though they were biting through his own flesh. And the sound of them digging industriously as they rooted up those healthy, leafy plants, made him tremble with rage and indignation. The unfairness of it all!

Yes, Mr Mani hated porcupines. He prayed for their destruction, their removal from the face of the earth. But, as his friends were quick to point out, 'Bhagwan protected porcupines too,' and in any case you could never see the creatures or catch them, they were completely nocturnal.

Mr Mani got out of bed every night, torch in one hand, a stout stick in the other, but as soon as he stepped into the garden the crunching and digging stopped and he was greeted by the most infuriating of silences. He would grope around in the dark, swinging wildly with the stick, but not a single porcupine was to be seen or heard. As soon as he was back in bed—the sounds would start all over again. Scrunch, scrunch, *katar, katar*...

Mr Mani came to his class tired and dishevelled, with rings beneath his eyes and a permanent frown on his face. It took some time for his pupils to discover the reason for his misery, but when they did, they felt sorry for their teacher and took to discussing ways and means of saving his potatoes from the porcupines.

It was Prakash who came up with the idea of a moat or waterditch. 'Porcupines don't like water,' he said knowledgeably.

'How do you know?' asked one of his friends.

'Throw water on one and see how it runs! They don't like getting their quills wet.'

There was no one who could disprove Prakash's theory, and the class fell in with the idea of building a moat, especially as it meant getting most of the day off.

'Anything to make Mr Mani happy,' said the headmaster, and the rest of the school watched with envy as the pupils of

Class Five, armed with spades and shovels collected from all parts of the village, took up their positions around Mr Mani's potato field and began digging a ditch.

By evening the moat was ready, but it was still dry and the porcupines got in again that night and had a great feast.

'At this rate,' said Mr Mani gloomily 'there won't be any potatoes left to save.'

But next day Prakash and the other boys and girls managed to divert the water from a stream that flowed past the village. They had the satisfaction of watching it flow gently into the ditch. Everyone went home in a good mood. By nightfall, the ditch had overflowed, the potato field was flooded, and Mr Mani found himself trapped inside his house. But Prakash and his friends had won the day. The porcupines stayed away that night!

A month had passed, and wild violets, daisies and buttercups now sprinkled the hill slopes, and on her way to school Bina gathered enough to make a little posy. The bunch of flowers fitted easily into an old ink well. Miss Ramola was delighted to find this little display in the middle of her desk.

'Who put these here?' she asked in surprise.

Bina kept quiet, and the rest of the class smiled secretively. After that, they took turns bringing flowers for the classroom.

On her long walks to school and home again, Bina became aware that April was the month of new leaves. The oak leaves were bright green above and silver beneath, and when they rippled in the breeze they were like clouds of silvery green. The path was strewn with old leaves, dry and crackly. Sonu loved kicking them around.

Clouds of white butterflies floated across the stream. Sonu

was chasing a butterfly when he stumbled over something dark and repulsive. He went sprawling on the grass. When he got to his feet, he looked down at the remains of a small animal.

'Bina! Prakash! Come quickly!' he shouted.

It was part of a sheep, killed some days earlier by a much larger animal.

'Only a leopard could have done this,' said Prakash.

'Let's get away, then,' said Sonu. 'It might still be around!'

'No, there's nothing left to eat. The leopard will be hunting elsewhere by now. Perhaps it's moved on to the next valley.'

'Still, I'm frightened,' said Sonu. 'There may be more leopards!'

Bina took him by the hand. 'Leopards don't attack humans!' she said.

'They will, if they get a taste for people!' insisted Prakash.

'Well, this one hasn't attacked any people as yet,' said Bina, although she couldn't be sure. Hadn't there been rumours of a leopard attacking some workers near the dam? But she did not want Sonu to feel afraid, so she did not mention the story. All she said was, 'It has probably come here because of all the activity near the dam.'

All the same, they hurried home. And for a few days, whenever they reached the stream, they crossed over very quickly, unwilling to linger too long at that lovely spot.

5

A few days later, a school party was on its way to Tehri to see the new dam that was being built.

Miss Ramola had arranged to take her class, and Mr Mani, not wishing to be left out, insisted on taking his class as well. That meant there were about fifty boys and girls taking part in the outing. The little bus could only take thirty. A friendly truck driver agreed to take some children if they were prepared to sit on sacks of potatoes. And Prakash persuaded the owner of the diesel roller to turn it round and head it back to Tehri—with him and a couple of friends up on the driving seat.

Prakash's small group set off at sunrise, as they had to walk some distance in order to reach the stranded road roller. The bus left at 9 a.m. with Miss Ramola and her class, and Mr Mani and some of his pupils. The truck was to follow later.

It was Bina's first visit to a large town and her first bus ride.

The sharp curves along the winding, downhill road made several children feel sick. The bus driver seemed to be in a tearing hurry. He took them along at rolling, rollicking speed, which made Bina feel quite giddy. She rested her head on her arms and refused to look out of the window. Hairpin bends and cliff edges, pine forests and snowcapped peaks, all swept past her, but she felt too ill to want to look at anything. It was just as well—those sudden drops, hundreds of feet to the valley below, were quite frightening. Bina began to wish that she hadn't come—or that she had joined Prakash on the road roller instead!

Miss Ramola and Mr Mani didn't seem to notice the lurching and groaning of the old bus. They had made this journey many times. They were busy arguing about the advantages and disadvantages of large dams—an argument that was to continue on and off for much of the day; sometimes in Hindi, sometimes in English, sometimes in the local dialect!

Meanwhile, Prakash and his friends had reached the roller. The driver hadn't turned up, but they managed to reverse it and get it going in the direction of Tehri. They were soon overtaken by both the bus and the truck but kept moving along at a steady chug. Prakash spotted Bina at the window of the bus and waved cheerfully. She responded feebly.

Bina felt better when the road levelled out near Tehri. As they crossed an old bridge over the wide river, they were startled by a loud bang which made the bus shudder. A cloud of dust rose above the town.

'They're blasting the mountain,' said Miss Ramola.

'End of a mountain,' said Mr Mani mournfully.

While they were drinking cups of tea at the bus stop, waiting for the potato truck and the road roller, Miss Ramola and Mr Mani continued their argument about the dam. Miss Ramola maintained that it would bring electric power and water for irrigation to large areas of the country, including the surrounding area. Mr Mani declared that it was a menace, as it was situated in an earthquake zone. There would be a terrible disaster if the dam burst! Bina found it all very confusing. *And what about the animals in the area*, she wondered. *What would happen to them?*

The argument was becoming quite heated when the potato truck arrived. There was no sign of the road roller, so it was decided that Mr Mani should wait for Prakash and his friends while Miss Ramola's group went ahead.

Some eight or nine miles before Tehri the road roller had broken down, and Prakash and his friends were forced to walk. They had not gone far, however, when a mule train came along—five or six mules that had been delivering sacks of grain in Nauti. A boy rode on the first mule, but the others had no loads.

'Can you give us a ride to Tehri?' called Prakash.

'Make yourselves comfortable,' said the boy.

There were no saddles, only gunny sacks strapped on to the mules with rope. They had a rough but jolly ride down to the Tehri bus stop. None of them had ever ridden mules; but they had saved at least an hour on the road.

Looking around the bus stop for the rest of the party, they could find no one from their school. And Mr Mani, who should have been waiting for them, had vanished.

6

Tania Ramola and her group had taken the steep road to the hill above Tehri. Half an hour's climbing brought them to a little plateau which overlooked the town, the river and the dam site.

The earthworks for the dam were only just coming up, but a wide tunnel had been bored through the mountain to divert the river into another channel. Down below, the old town was still spread out across the valley and from a distance it looked quite charming and picturesque.

'Will the whole town be swallowed up by the waters of the dam?' asked Bina.

'Yes, all of it,' said Miss Ramola. 'The clock tower and the old palace. The long bazaar, and the temples, the schools and the jail, and hundreds of houses, for many miles up the valley. All those people will have to go—thousands of them! Of course, they'll be resettled elsewhere.'

'But the town's been here for hundreds of years,' said Bina. 'They were quite happy without the dam, weren't they?'

'I suppose they were. But the dam isn't just for them—it's for the millions who live further downstream, across the plains.'

'And it doesn't matter what happens to this place?'

'The local people will be given new homes, somewhere else.' Miss Ramola found herself on the defensive and decided to change the subject. 'Everyone must be hungry. It's time we had our lunch.'

Bina kept quiet. She didn't think the local people would want to go away. And it was a good thing, she mused, that there was only a small stream and not a big river running past her village. To be uprooted like this—a town and hundreds of villages—and put down somewhere on the hot, dusty plains—seemed to her unbearable.

'Well, I'm glad I don't live in Tehri,' she said.

She did not know it, but all the animals and most of the birds had already left the area. The leopard had been among them.

They walked through the colourful, crowded bazaar, where fruit sellers did business beside silversmiths, and pavement vendors sold everything from umbrellas to glass bangles. Sparrows attacked sacks of grain, monkeys made off with bananas, and stray cows and dogs rummaged in refuse bins, but nobody took any notice. Music blared from radios. Buses blew their horns. Sonu bought a whistle to add to the general din, but Miss Ramola told him to put it away. Bina had kept ten rupees aside, and now she used it to buy a cotton head scarf for her mother.

As they were about to enter a small restaurant for a meal, they were joined by Prakash and his companions; but of Mr Mani there was still no sign.

'He must have met one of his relatives,' said Prakash. 'He has relatives everywhere.'

After a simple meal of rice and lentils, they walked the length of the bazaar without seeing Mr Mani. At last, when they were about to give up the search, they saw him emerge from a bylane, a large sack slung over his shoulder.

'Sir, where have you been?' asked Prakash. 'We have been looking for you everywhere.'

On Mr Mani's face was a look of triumph.

'Help me with this bag,' he said breathlessly.

'You've bought more potatoes, sir,' said Prakash.

'Not potatoes, boy. Dahlia bulbs!'

7

It was dark by the time they were all back in Nauti. Mr Mani had refused to be separated from his sack of dahlia bulbs, and had been forced to sit in the back of the truck with Prakash and most of the boys.

Bina did not feel so ill on the return journey. Going uphill was definitely better than going downhill! But by the time the bus reached Nauti it was too late for most of the children to walk back to the more distant villages. The boys were put up in different homes, while the girls were given beds in the school verandah.

The night was warm and still. Large moths fluttered around the single bulb that lit the verandah. Counting moths, Sonu soon fell asleep. But Bina stayed awake for some time, listening to the sounds of the night. A nightjar went *tonk-tonk* in the bushes, and somewhere in the forest an owl hooted softly. The sharp call of a barking deer travelled up the valley, from the direction of the stream. Jackals kept howling. It seemed that there were more of them than ever before.

Bina was not the only one to hear the barking deer. The leopard, stretched full length on a rocky ledge, heard it too. The leopard raised its head and then got up slowly. The deer was its natural prey. But there weren't many left, and that was why the leopard, robbed of its forest by the dam, had taken to attacking dogs and cattle near the villages.

As the cry of the barking deer sounded nearer, the leopard left its lookout point and moved swiftly through the shadows towards the stream.

8

In early June the hills were dry and dusty, and forest fires broke out, destroying shrubs and trees, killing birds and small animals. The resin in the pines made these trees burn more fiercely, and the wind would take sparks from the trees and carry them into the dry grass and leaves, so that new fires would spring up before the old ones had died out. Fortunately, Bina's village was not in the pine belt; the fires did not reach it. But Nauti was surrounded by a fire that raged for three days, and the children had to stay away from school.

And then, towards the end of June, the monsoon rains arrived and there was an end to forest fires. The monsoon lasts three months and the lower Himalayas would be drenched in rain, mist and cloud for the next three months.

The first rain arrived while Bina, Prakash and Sonu were returning home from school. Those first few drops on the dusty path made them cry out with excitement. Then the rain grew heavier and a wonderful aroma rose from the earth.

'The best smell in the world!' exclaimed Bina.

Everything suddenly came to life. The grass, the crops, the trees, the birds. Even the leaves of the trees glistened and looked new.

That first wet weekend, Bina and Sonu helped their mother plant beans, maize and cucumbers. Sometimes, when the rain was very heavy, they had to run indoors. Otherwise they worked in the rain, the soft mud clinging to their bare legs.

Prakash now owned a black dog with one ear up and one ear down. The dog ran around getting in everyone's way, barking at cows, goats, hens and humans, without frightening any of them. Prakash said it was a very clever dog, but no one else seemed to think so. Prakash also said it would protect the village from the leopard, but others said the dog would be the first to be taken—he'd run straight into the jaws of Mr Spots!

In Nauti, Tania Ramola was trying to find a dry spot in the quarters she'd been given. It was an old building and the roof was leaking in several places. Mugs and buckets were scattered about the floor in order to catch the drip.

Mr Mani had dug up all his potatoes and presented them to the friends and neighbours who had given him lunches and dinners. He was having the time of his life, planting dahlia bulbs all over his garden.

'I'll have a field of many-coloured dahlias!' he announced. 'Just wait till the end of August!'

'Watch out for those porcupines,' warned his sister. 'They eat dahlia bulbs too!'

Mr Mani made an inspection tour of his moat, no longer in flood, and found everything in good order. Prakash had done his job well.

Now, when the children crossed the stream, they found that the water level had risen by about a foot. Small cascades had turned into waterfalls. Ferns had sprung up on the banks. Frogs chanted.

Prakash and his dog dashed across the stream. Bina and Sonu followed more cautiously. The current was much stronger now and the water was almost up to their knees. Once they had crossed the stream, they hurried along the path, anxious not to be caught in a sudden downpour.

By the time they reached school, each of them had two or three leeches clinging to their legs. They had to use salt to remove them. The leeches were the most troublesome part of the rainy season. Even the leopard did not like them. It could not lie in the long grass without getting leeches on its paws and face.

One day, when Bina, Prakash and Sonu were about to cross the stream they heard a low rumble, which grew louder every second. Looking up at the opposite hill, they saw several trees shudder, tilt outwards and begin to fall. Earth and rocks bulged out from the mountain, then came crashing down into the ravine.

'Landslide!' shouted Sonu.

'It's carried away the path,' said Bina. 'Don't go any further.'

There was a tremendous roar as more rocks, trees and bushes fell away and crashed down the hillside.

Prakash's dog, who had gone ahead, came running back, tail between his legs.

They remained rooted to the spot until the rocks had stopped falling and the dust had settled. Birds circled the area, calling wildly. A frightened barking deer ran past them.

'We can't go to school now,' said Prakash. 'There's no way around.'

They turned and trudged home through the gathering mist.

In Koli, Prakash's parents had heard the roar of the landslide. They were setting out in search of the children when they saw them emerge from the mist, waving cheerfully.

9

They had to miss school for another three days, and Bina was afraid they might not be able to take their final exams. Although Prakash was not really troubled at the thought of missing exams, he did not like feeling helpless just because their path had been swept away. So he explored the hillside until he found a goat track going around the mountain. It joined up with another path near Nauti. This made their walk longer by a mile, but Bina did not mind. It was much cooler now that the rains were in full swing.

The only trouble with the new route was that it passed close to the leopard's lair. The animal had made this area its own since being forced to leave the dam area.

One day Prakash's dog ran ahead of them, barking furiously. Then he ran back, whimpering.

'He's always running away from something,' observed Sonu. But a minute later he understood the reason for the dog's fear.

They rounded a bend and Sonu saw the leopard standing in their way. They were struck dumb—too terrified to run. It was a strong, sinewy creature. A low growl rose from its throat. It seemed ready to spring.

They stood perfectly still, afraid to move or say a word. And the leopard must have been equally surprised. It stared at them for a few seconds, then bounded across the path and into the oak forest.

Sonu was shaking. Bina could hear her heart hammering. Prakash could only stammer: 'Did you see the way he sprang? Wasn't he beautiful?'

He forgot to look at his watch for the rest of the day.

A few days later Sonu stopped and pointed to a large outcrop of rock on the next hill.

The leopard stood far above them, outlined against the sky. It looked strong, majestic. Standing beside it were two young cubs.

'Look at those little ones!' exclaimed Sonu.

'So it's a female, not a male,' said Prakash.

'That's why she was killing so often,' said Bina. 'She had to feed her cubs too.'

They remained still for several minutes, gazing up at the leopard and her cubs. The leopard family took no notice of them.

'She knows we are here,' said Prakash, 'but she doesn't care. She knows we won't harm them.'

'We are cubs too!' said Sonu.

'Yes,' said Bina. 'And there's still plenty of space for all of us. Even when the dam is ready there will still be room for leopards and humans.'

10

The school exams were over. The rains were nearly over too. The landslide had been cleared, and Bina, Prakash and Sonu were once again crossing the stream.

There was a chill in the air, for it was the end of September.

Prakash had learnt to play the flute quite well, and he played on the way to school and then again on the way home. As a result he did not look at his watch so often.

One morning they found a small crowd in front of Mr Mani's house.

'What could have happened?' wondered Bina. 'I hope he hasn't got lost again.'

'Maybe he's sick,' said Sonu.

'Maybe it's the porcupines,' said Prakash.

But it was none of these things.

Mr Mani's first dahlia was in bloom, and half the village had turned out to look at it! It was a huge red double dahlia, so heavy that it had to be supported with sticks. No one had ever seen such a magnificent flower!

Mr Mani was a happy man. And his mood only improved over the coming week, as more and more dahlias flowered—crimson, yellow, purple, mauve, white—button dahlias, pompom dahlias, spotted dahlias, striped dahlias... Mr Mani had them all! A dahlia even turned up on Tania Romola's desk—he got on quite well with her now—and another brightened up the headmaster's study.

A week later, on their way home—it was almost the last day of the school term—Bina, Prakash and Sonu talked about what they might do when they grew up.

'I think I'll become a teacher,' said Bina. 'I'll teach children about animals and birds, and trees and flowers.'

'Better than maths!' said Prakash.

'I'll be a pilot,' said Sonu. 'I want to fly a plane like Miss Ramola's brother.'

'And what about you, Prakash?' asked Bina.

Prakash just smiled and said, 'Maybe I'll be a flute player,' and he put the flute to his lips and played a sweet melody.

'Well, the world needs flute players too,' said Bina, as they fell into step beside him.

The leopard had been stalking a barking deer. She paused when she heard the flute and the voices of the children. Her own young ones were growing quickly, but the girl and the two boys did not look much older.

They had started singing their favourite song again:

Five more miles to go!
We climb through rain and snow.
A river to cross…
A mountain to pass…
Now we've four more miles to go!

The leopard waited until they had passed, before returning to the trail of the barking deer.

THE THIEF'S STORY

I was still a thief when I met Romi. And though I was only fifteen years old, I was an experienced and fairly successful hand. Romi was watching a wrestling match when I approached him. He was about twenty-five and he looked easygoing, kind and simple enough for my purpose. I was sure I would be able to win the young man's confidence.

'You look a bit of a wrestler yourself,' I said. There's nothing like flattery to break the ice!

'So do you,' he replied, which put me off for a moment because at that time I was rather thin and bony.

'Well,' I said modestly, 'I do wrestle a bit.'

'What's your name?'

'Hari Singh,' I lied. I took a new name every month, which kept me ahead of the police and former employers.

After these formalities Romi confined himself to commenting on the wrestlers, who were grunting, gasping and heaving each other about. When he walked away, I followed him casually.

'Hello again,' he said.

I gave him my most appealing smile. 'I want to work for you,' I said.

'But I can't pay you anything—not for some time, anyway.'

I thought that over for a minute. Perhaps I had misjudged my man. 'Can you feed me?' I asked.

'Can you cook?'

THE THIEF'S STORY

'I can cook,' I lied again.

'If you can cook, then maybe I can feed you.'

He took me to his room over the Delhi Sweet Shop and told me I could sleep on the balcony. But the meal I cooked that night must have been terrible because Romi gave it to a stray dog and told me to be off.

But I just hung around, smiling in my most appealing way, and he couldn't help laughing.

Later he said, never mind, he'd teach me to cook. He also taught me to write my name and said he would soon teach me to write whole sentences and to add figures. I was grateful. I knew that once I could write like an educated person, there would be no limit to what I could achieve.

It was quite pleasant working for Romi. I made tea in the morning and then took my time buying the day's supplies, usually making a profit of two or three rupees. I think he knew I made a little money this way, but he didn't seem to mind.

Romi made money by fits and starts. He would borrow one week, lend the next. He kept worrying about his next cheque, but as soon as it arrived he would go out and celebrate. He wrote for the *Delhi* and *Bombay* magazines: a strange way to make a living.

One evening he came home with a small bundle of notes, saying he had just sold a book to a publisher. That night I saw him put the money in an envelope and tuck it under the mattress.

I had been working for Romi for almost a month and, apart from cheating on the shopping, had not done anything big in my real line of work. I had every opportunity for doing so. I could come and go as I pleased, and Romi was the most trusting person I had ever met.

That was why it was so difficult to rob him. It was easy for me to rob a greedy man. But robbing a nice man could be a problem. And if he doesn't notice he's being robbed, then all the spice goes out of the undertaking!

Well, it's time I got down to some real work, I told myself. If I don't take the money, he'll only waste it on his so-called friends. After all, he doesn't even give me a salary.

Romi was sleeping peacefully. A beam of moonlight reached over the balcony and fell on his bed. I sat on the floor, considering the situation. If I took the money, I could catch the 10.30 express to Lucknow. Slipping out of my blanket, I crept over to the bed.

My hand slid under the mattress, searching for the notes. When I found the packet, I drew it out without a sound. Romi sighed in his sleep and turned on his side. Startled, I moved quickly out of the room.

Once on the road, I began to run. I had the money stuffed into a vest pocket under my shirt. When I'd gotten some distance from Romi's place, I slowed to a walk and, taking the envelope from my pocket, counted the money. Seven hundred rupees in fifties. I could live like a prince for a week or two!

When I reached the station, I did not stop at the ticket office (I had never bought a ticket in my life) but dashed straight onto the platform. The Lucknow Express was just moving out. The train had still to pick up speed and I should have been able to jump into one of the compartments, but I hesitated—for some reason I can't explain—and I lost the chance to get away.

When the train had gone, I found myself standing alone

THE THIEF'S STORY

on the deserted platform. I had no idea where to spend the night. I had no friends, believing that friends were more trouble than help. And I did not want to arouse curiosity by staying at one of the small hotels nearby. The only person I knew really well was the man I had robbed. Leaving the station, I walked slowly through the bazaar.

In my short career, I had made a study of people's faces after they had discovered the loss of their valuables. The greedy showed panic; the rich showed anger; the poor, resignation. But I knew that Romi's face when he discovered the theft would show only a touch of sadness—not for the loss of money, but for the loss of trust.

The night was chilly—November nights can be cold in northern India—and a shower of rain added to my discomfort. I sat down in the shelter of the clock tower. A few beggars and vagrants lay beside me, rolled up tight in their blankets. The clock showed midnight. I felt for the notes; they were soaked through.

Romi's money. In the morning, he would probably have given me five rupees to go to the movies, but now I had it all: no more cooking meals, running to the bazaar, or learning to write sentences.

Sentences! I had forgotten about them in the excitement of the theft. Writing complete sentences, I knew, could one day bring me more than a few hundred rupees. It was a simple matter to steal. But to be a really big man, a clever and respected man, was something else. I should go back to Romi, I told myself, if only to learn to read and write.

I hurried back to the room feeling very nervous, for it is much easier to steal something than to return it undetected.

I opened the door quietly, then stood in the doorway in clouded moonlight. Romi was still asleep. I crept to the head of the bed, and my hand came up with the packet of notes. I felt his breath on my hand. I remained still for a few moments. Then my fingers found the edge of the mattress, and I slipped the money beneath it.

I awoke late the next morning to find that Romi had already made the tea. He stretched out a hand to me. There was a fifty-rupee note between his fingers. My heart sank.

'I made some money yesterday,' he said. 'Now I'll be able to pay you regularly.'

My spirits rose. But when I took the note, I noticed that it was still wet from the night's rain.

So he knew what I'd done. But neither his lips nor his eyes revealed anything.

'Today we'll start writing sentences,' he said.

I smiled at Romi in my most appealing way. And the smile came by itself, without any effort.

WHEN THE TREES WALKED

One morning while I was sitting beside Grandfather on the veranda steps, I noticed the tendril of a creeping vine trailing nearby. As we sat there in the soft sunshine of a North Indian winter, I saw the tendril moving slowly towards Grandfather. Twenty minutes later, it had crossed the step and was touching his feet.

There is probably a scientific explanation for the plant's behaviour—something to do with light and warmth perhaps—but I liked to think it moved across the steps simply because it wanted to be near Grandfather. One always felt like drawing close to him. Sometimes when I sat by myself beneath a tree, I would feel rather lonely but as soon as Grandfather joined me, the garden became a happy place. Grandfather had served many years in the Indian Forest Service and it was natural that he should know trees and like them. On his retirement, he built a bungalow on the outskirts of Dehradun, planting trees all around. Lime, mango, orange and guava, also eucalyptus, jacaranda and Persian lilacs. In the fertile Doon Valley, plants and trees grew tall and strong.

There were other trees in the compound before the house was built, including an old peepul that had forced its way through the walls of an abandoned outhouse, knocking the bricks down with its vigorous growth. Peepul trees are great show-offs. Even when there is no breeze, their broad-chested, slim-waisted leaves will spin like tops, determined to attract your attention and invite you into the shade. Grandmother had wanted the peepul tree cut down but Grandfather had said, 'Let it be, we can always build another outhouse.'

Grandmother didn't mind trees, but she preferred growing flowers and was constantly ordering catalogues and seeds. Grandfather helped her out with the gardening, not because he was crazy about flower gardens but because he liked watching butterflies and 'there's only one way to attract butterflies,' he said, 'and that is to grow flowers for them.'

Grandfather wasn't content with growing trees in our compound. During the rains, he would walk into the jungle beyond the riverbed armed with cuttings and saplings which he would plant in the forest.

'But no one ever comes here!' I had protested the first time we did this. 'Who's going to see them?'

'See, we're not planting them simply to improve the view,' replied Grandfather. 'We're planting them for the forest and for the animals and birds who live here and need more food and shelter.'

'Of course, men need trees, too,' he added. 'To keep the desert away, to attract rain, to prevent the banks of rivers from being washed away, for fruit and flowers, leaf and seed. Yes, for timber, too. But men are cutting down trees without replacing them and if we don't plant a few trees ourselves, a time will come when the world will be one great desert.'

The thought of a world without trees became a sort of nightmare to me and I helped Grandfather in his tree-planting with greater enthusiasm. And while we went about our work, he taught me a poem by George Morris:

WHEN THE TREES WALKED

> Woodman, spare that tree!
> Touch not a single bough!
> In youth it sheltered me,
> And I'll protect it now.

'One day the trees will move again,' said Grandfather. 'They've been standing still for thousands of years but there was a time when they could walk about like people. Then along came an interfering busybody who cast a spell over them, rooting them to one place. But they're always trying to move. See how they reach out with their arms! And some of them, like the banyan tree with its travelling aerial roots, manage to get quite far.'

We found an island, a small rocky island in a dry riverbed. It was one of those riverbeds so common in the foothills, which are completely dry in summer but flooded during the monsoon rains. A small mango was growing on the island. 'If a small tree can grow here,' said Grandfather, 'so can others.' As soon as the rains set in and while rivers could still be crossed, we set out with a number of tamarind, laburnum and coral tree saplings and cuttings and spent the day planting them on the island.

The monsoon season was the time for rambling about. At every turn, there was something new to see. Out of the earth and rock and leafless boughs, the magic touch of the rains had brought life and greenness. You could see the broad-leaved vines growing. Plants sprang up in the most unlikely of places. A peepul would take root in the ceiling, a mango would sprout on the windowsill. We did not like to remove them but they had to go if the house was to be kept from falling down.

'If you want to live in a tree, that's all right by me,' said Grandmother crossly. 'But I like having a roof over my head and

I'm not going to have my roof brought down by the jungle.'

Then came the Second World War and I was sent away to a boarding school. During the holidays, I went to live with my father in Delhi. Meanwhile, my grandparents sold the house and went to England. Two or three years later, I too went to England and was away from India for several years.

Some years later, I returned to Dehradun. After first visiting the old house—it hadn't changed much—I walked out of town towards the riverbed. It was February. As I looked across the dry water course, my eye was immediately caught by the spectacular red blooms of the coral blossom. In contrast with the dry riverbed, the island was a small green paradise. When I went up to the trees, I noticed that some squirrels were living in them and a koel, a crow pheasant, challenged me with a mellow 'who-are-you, who-are-you'.

But the trees seemed to know me; they whispered among themselves and beckoned me nearer. And looking around I noticed that other smaller trees, wild plants and grasses had sprung up under their protection. Yes, the trees we had planted long ago had multiplied. They were walking again. In one small corner of the world, Grandfather's dream had come true.

KING BHARATA

1

King bharata ruled over all the world. He was a thoughtful and religious man, and he looked upon the whole world as evidence of the supreme spirit of God.

He worshipped God in the form of Vishnu, the Preserver, and was full of devotion, ruling the earth for one hundred thousand years. He had five sons, amongst whom he divided all his kingdom, and went at last into the forests near the river Gandak, where he lived alone, praying and meditating.

His worship consisted of offering fresh flowers, tender leaves, and wild fruits and roots. He controlled all his senses and never grew weary. There was no one to disturb him, no one to take his mind off the worship of God. He bathed three times a day, and worshipped Vishnu in the golden sun.

One day, while Bharata was bathing in the river, he heard a lion roaring, and saw a deer, which was about to give birth to a fawn, fleeing from the lion and splashing across the river. As it reached the other side, it gave birth to the fawn and then died. Bharata saw the helpless little fawn struggling in the water. Being moved with compassion, he took it in his hands and saved it. Then he took the fawn home and cared for it, and soon began to love it. He became so attached to it that little by little he began neglecting his services to God; but he was quite unaware that this was happening.

'There is no one to care for this deer,' he said to himself, 'and so I will look after it and bring it up. The great teachers say that to help the helpless is a virtue.'

His love for the deer grew, and he used to bring it tender grass to eat, and he would bathe it and keep it near him. Sometimes he would hold it in his arms or on his lap. He loved its company. Often, when performing some ceremony, he would break off in the middle to look for the deer.

But one day, the deer disappeared.

Bharata was overcome with grief and a terrible sense of loss.

'Did I not take care of you in every way?' he mused. 'Now I do not know if some animal has killed you, or if you will one day return to gladden my heart. I remember how you used to touch me gently with your horns as I sat in meditation. I remember how you would playfully trample on the things I brought for worship, and if I spoke to you in anger, you would stand at a distance till I called you again. The other hermits looked upon you as a holy animal. Perhaps the moon has taken you.'

Unable to get over his sorrow, he neglected the religious ceremonies he usually performed. He had renounced his family and his kingdom in order to obtain the spiritual freedom of the hermit. Now, because of his attachment to the deer, all his strivings appeared to have been futile.

Then one day, the deer returned.

Bharata was overcome with joy. He treated it as though it were his own son, and devoted the rest of his days to its welfare.

In his last days, on his death bed, his thoughts were only of the deer; and so, upon his soul leaving his body, he was reborn as a deer. But the memory of his past life remained with him. He felt sorry that he had neglected his duties to God, and regretted his former attachment to the deer. He did not mingle with the rest of the herd, and at last left them and went away alone to his old place, where he had formerly lived and worshipped; and there he remained, bathing in the river and grazing on its banks; and so much did he desire to be freed from the body of a deer that, when he died, he was able to be born again into a Brahmin family.

2

Born to a Brahmin father, Bharata was brought up well; but remembering his former lives, he kept aloof from other people, so that many thought he was half-witted. When his parents died, his brother forced him to do menial work. People made fun of him, but he paid no attention, and took everything that came his way, good and bad. He cared neither for cold nor heat, going without clothes and sleeping on the bare ground, so that his sacred thread became black with dirt.

In spite of these hardships, he remained sturdy and strong.

One day, the king of the country decided to offer a human sacrifice to the Goddess Kali, and hearing from his servants that Bharata was a useless fellow, seized him as being perfectly suitable for the sacrifice.

After a ceremonial bath, Bharata was given fine clothes and decorated with jewels. He was given rich food. Burning camphor and perfumes were placed before him. Then, accompanied by dancers and musicians, he was taken to the temple of Kali.

At the temple the king himself led Bharata to a raised platform. Sword in hand, he was about to cut off Bharata's head when Kali, seeing Bharata and recognizing him immediately as a man of God—a man without hatred in his heart, and with love for all living creatures—was afraid to receive such a sacrifice.

The goddess grew angry with the king. She became visible, and so terrifying was her aspect that the king and his followers fell dead on the spot.

Then Kali turned to Bharata and said, 'No deity will allow any harm to come to you.'

She disappeared, and Bharata, who feared neither the sword nor Kali, remained standing, his mind steadfast in God.

The people who had gathered to watch the sacrifice became greatly afraid. They made way for Bharata, and he returned to watch the fields as before.

NALA AND DAMAYANTI

Long ago, there reigned in Berar a famous king named Bhima. His chief claim to fame was that he had a beautiful daughter named Damayanti. She was waited upon day and night by a band of handmaids of great beauty, but she shone among them like the moon among the stars, and her hand was sought, we are told, by both gods and mortals.

Nala, King of Nishada, came to hear of Damayanti's loveliness and her many accomplishments, and was struck with passion for her. She, in turn, had heard that Nala was brave and handsome, well-read and skilled in arms. They loved each other upon the mere fame of their respective virtues, and Damayanti pined for the presence of her unknown lover.

One day, while Nala was seated in a grove dreaming of his beloved, he saw a flock of swans, with wings all flecked with gold, come to rest close by him.

Nala crept up to the leader of the flock and seized him.

'O mighty king,' said the swan, 'set me free, and I will do your bidding, whatever it might be.'

'If a bird can do a mortal any service,' said Nala, 'fly to my love, Damayanti, and tell her how much I love her!' He released the bird, and it flew off to Berar, rejoicing in its freedom.

When the bird arrived in King Bhima's kingdom, it found Damayanti reclining in her garden, surrounded by her charming handmaids.

'What a lovely bird!' she cried when she saw the swan. 'And look at its wings, all edged with gold!'

The swan came close to her and allowed itself to be made captive.

'Sweet princess,' said the swan, 'I come to you as a messenger of love from Nala, King of Nishada. He is as wonderful to look upon as the God of Love, and has no equal amongst mortals. The union of such a youth and maiden would be a union of perfection.'

Damayanti was struck with wonder at the bird's story, and she set him free, saying, 'Sweet bird! Speak to Nala on my behalf in like manner.' And the swan flew back to Nala with an answering message of love.

Before long, a swayamvara was held for Damayanti.

This was an ancient Hindu rite by which a princess might choose her husband from an assembly of suitors come from all parts to take their chance in the selection. The heroes submitted themselves in silent rivalry to inspection as the princess walked along their line to select from the throng the favoured suitor by presenting him with a garland, or a cup of water, or some such token of regard.

Many were the princes who came to woo Damayanti, attracted by the stories of her beauty. More wonderful still, some of the gods, equally enamoured of her charms, came down to earth to woo her. Most prominent among them were the four great guardians of the world: Indra, God of Heaven; Agni, God of Fire; Varuna, God of the Waters; and Yama, God of Death. What chance did Nala, a mere mortal, have in this assembly?

Damayanti stepped into the swayamvara hall, bejewelled from head to foot, bearing a garland of flowers to place round the neck of the one she would choose for her husband. She was taken round to each of the assembled princes, until she came to where her lover, Nala, was seated; but great was her dismay when she saw not one but five Nalas, each indistinguishable from the other! The gods had assumed his shape to baffle her.

But Damayanti, garland in hand, did not pause for long. She had noticed that the gods cast no shadows, because they were spirits; and that their eyes never winked, because they were the ever-wakeful Guardian Gods; and that their garlands were fresher than most, being woven of the unfading blooms of Heaven. By these tokens did Damayanti tell the gods from her lover; and she threw her garland round the neck of her beloved, the real Nala.

Then, turning to the gods, she said, 'Forgive me, O mighty gods, that I have not chosen my husband from among you. I have long since pledged my heart to this prince, and the vow so pledged is sacred. Forgive me, therefore, for choosing an earthly lord and not one of the rulers of Heaven.'

In this way did Damayanti, the lovely, the peerless, choose Nala for her husband, with the gods themselves as witnesses.

The happy pair then did homage before the gods, and these great guardians of the earth bestowed upon them divine blessings in reward for their constancy.

CHILDREN OF INDIA

They pass me every day on their way to school—boys and girls from the surrounding villages and the outskirts of the hill station. There are no school buses plying for these children: they walk.

For many of them, it's a very long walk to school.

Ranbir, who is ten, has to climb the mountain from his village, four miles distant and two thousand feet below the town level. He comes in all weathers wearing the same pair of cheap shoes until they have almost fallen apart.

Ranbir is a cheerful soul. He waves to me whenever he sees me at my window. Sometimes he brings me cucumbers from his father's field. I pay him for the cucumbers; he uses the money for books or for small things needed at home.

Many of the children are like Ranbir—poor, but slightly better off than what their parents were at the same age. They cannot attend the expensive residential and private schools that abound here, but must go to the government-aided schools with only basic facilities. Not many of their parents managed to go to school. They spent their lives working in the fields or delivering milk in the hill station. The lucky ones got into the army. Perhaps Ranbir will do something different when he grows up.

He has yet to see a train but he sees planes flying over the mountains almost every day.

'How far can a plane go?' he asks.

'All over the world,' I tell him. 'Thousands of miles in a day. You can go almost anywhere.'

'I'll go round the world one day,' he vows. 'I'll buy a plane and go everywhere!'

And maybe he will. He has a determined chin and a defiant look in his eye.

The following lines in my journal were put down for my own inspiration or encouragement, but they will do for any determined young person:

We get out of life what we bring to it. There is not a dream which may not come true if we have the energy which determines our own fate. We can always get what we want if we will it intensely enough... So few people succeed greatly because so few people conceive a great end, working towards it without giving up. We all know that the man who works steadily for money gets rich; the man who works day and night for fame or power reaches his goal. And those who work for deeper, more spiritual achievements will find them too. It may come when we no longer have any use for it, but if we have been willing it long enough, it will come!

◆

Up to a few years ago, very few girls in the hills or in the villages of India went to school. They helped in the home until they were old enough to be married, which wasn't very old. But there are now just as many girls as there are boys going to school.

Bindra is something of an extrovert—a confident fourteen-year-old who chatters away as she hurries down the road with her companions. Her father is a forest guard and knows me quite well: I meet him on my walks through the deodar woods behind Landour. And I had grown used to seeing Bindra almost every day. When she did not put in an appearance for a week, I asked her brother if anything was wrong.

'Oh, nothing,' he says, 'she is helping my mother cut grass. Soon the monsoon will end and the grass will dry up. So we cut it now and store it for the cows in winter.'

'And why aren't you cutting grass too?'

'Oh, I have a cricket match today,' he says, and hurries away to join his teammates. Unlike his sister, he puts pleasure before work!

Cricket, once the game of the elite, has become the game of the masses. On any holiday, in any part of this vast country, groups of boys can be seen making their way to the nearest field, or open patch of land, with bat, ball and any other cricketing gear that they can cobble together. Watching some of them play, I am amazed at the quality of talent, at the finesse with which they bat or bowl. Some of the local teams are as good, if not better, than any from the private schools, where there are better facilities. But the boys from these poor or lower middle-class families will never get the exposure that is necessary to bring them to the attention of those who select state or national teams. They will never get near enough to the men of influence and power. They must continue to play for the love of the game, or watch their more fortunate heroes' exploits on television.

◆

As winter approaches and the days grow shorter, those children who live far away must quicken their pace in order to get home before dark. Ranbir and his friends find that darkness has fallen before they are halfway home.

'What is the time, uncle?' he asks, as he trudges up the steep road past Ivy Cottage.

One gets used to being called 'uncle' by almost every boy or girl one meets. I wonder how the custom began. Perhaps it has its origins in the folktale about the tiger who refrained from pouncing on you if you called him 'uncle'. Tigers don't eat their relatives! Or do they? The ploy may not work if the tiger happens to be a tigress. Would you call her 'aunty' as she (or your teacher!) descends on you?

It's dark at six and by then, Ranbir likes to be out of the deodar forest and on the open road to the village. The moon and the stars and the village lights are sufficient, but not in the forest, where it is dark even during the day. And the silent flitting of bats and flying foxes, and the eerie hoot of an owl, can be a little disconcerting for the hardiest of children. Once Ranbir and the other boys were chased by a bear.

When he told me about it, I said, 'Well, now we know you can run faster then a bear!'

'Yes, but you have to run downhill when chased by a bear.' He spoke as one having long experience of escaping from bears. 'They run much faster uphill!'

'I'll remember that,' I said, 'thanks for the advice.' And I don't suppose calling a bear 'uncle' would help.

Usually Ranbir has the company of other boys, and they sing most of the way, for loud singing by small boys will silence owls and frighten away the forest demons. One of them plays a flute, and flute music in the mountains is always enchanting.

LESSONS IN FUN AND FROLIC

◆

Not only in the hills, but all over India, children are constantly making their way to and from school, in conditions that range from dust storms in the Rajasthan desert to blizzards in Ladakh and Kashmir. In the larger towns and cities, there are school buses, but in remote rural areas, getting to school can pose a problem.

Most children are more than equal to any obstacles that may arise. Like those youngsters in the Ganjam district of Orissa. In the absence of a bridge, they swim or wade across the Dhanei River everyday in order to reach their school. I have a picture of them in my scrapbook. Holding books or satchels aloft in one hand, they do the breast stroke or dog paddle with the other; or form a chain and help each other across.

Wherever you go in India, you will find children helping out with the family's source of livelihood, whether it be drying fish on the Malabar coast, or gathering saffron buds in Kashmir, or grazing camels or cattle in a village in Rajasthan or Gujarat.

Only the more fortunate can afford to send their children to English medium private or 'public' schools, and those children really are fortunate, for some of these institutions are excellent schools, as good, and often better, than their counterparts in Britain or USA. Whether it's in Ajmer or Bangalore, New Delhi or Chandigarh, Kanpur or Kolkata, the best schools set very high standards. The growth of a prosperous middle-class has led to an ever-increasing demand for quality education. But as private schools proliferate, standards suffer, too, and many parents must settle for the second-rate.

The great majority of our children still attend schools run by the state or municipality. These vary from the good to the bad to the ugly, depending on how they are run and where they are situated. A classroom without windows, or with a roof that lets in the monsoon rain, is not uncommon. Even so, children from different communities learn to live and grow together. Hardship makes brothers of us all.

The census tells us that two in every five of the population is in the age group of five to fifteen. Almost half our population is on the way to school!

And here I stand at my window, watching some of them pass by—boys and girls, big and small, some scruffy, some smart, some mischievous, some serious, but all going somewhere—hopefully towards a better future.

ADVENTURES IN READING

1

You don't see them so often now, those tiny books and almanacs—genuine pocket books—once so popular with our parents and grandparents; much smaller than the average paperback, often smaller than the palm of the hand. With the advent of coffee-table books, new books keep growing bigger and bigger, rivalling tombstones! And one day, like Alice after drinking from the wrong bottle, they will reach the ceiling and won't have anywhere else to go. The average publisher, who apparently believes that large profits are linked to large books, must look upon these old miniatures with amusement or scorn. They were not meant for a coffee table, true. They were meant for true book lovers and readers, for they took up very little space—you could slip them into your pocket without any discomfort, either to you or to the pocket.

I have a small collection of these little books, treasured over the years. Foremost is my father's prayer book and psalter, with his name, 'Aubrey Bond, Lovedale, 1917', inscribed on the inside back cover. Lovedale is a school in the Nilgiri Hills in South India, where, as a young man, he did his teacher's training. He gave it to me soon after I went to a boarding school in Shimla in 1944, and my own name is inscribed on it in his beautiful handwriting.

Another beautiful little prayer book in my collection is called *The Finger Prayer Book*. Bound in soft leather, it is about the same length and breadth as the average middle finger. Replete with psalms, it is the complete book of common prayer and not an abridgement; a marvel of miniature book production.

Not much larger is a delicate item in calf leather, *The Humour of Charles Lamb*. It fits into my wallet and often stays there. It has a tiny portrait of the great essayist, followed by some thirty to forty extracts from his essays, such as this favourite of mine: 'Every dead man must take upon himself to be lecturing me with his odious truism, that "Such as he is now, I must shortly be". Not so shortly friend, perhaps as thou imaginest. In the meantime, I am alive. I move about. I am worth twenty of thee. Know thy betters!'

No fatalist, Lamb. He made no compromise with Father Time. He affirmed that in age we must be as glowing and tempestuous as in youth! And yet Lamb is thought to be an old-fashioned writer.

Another favourite among my 'little' books is *The Pocket Trivet: An Anthology for Optimists*, published by *The Morning Post* newspaper in 1932. But what is a trivet? The unenlightened may well ask. Well, it's a stand for a small pot or kettle, fixed securely over a grate. To be right as a trivet is to be perfectly right. Just right, like the short sayings in this book, which is further enlivened by a number of charming woodcuts based on the seventeenth century originals; such as the illustration of a moth hovering over a candle flame and below it the legend—'I seeke mine owne hurt.'

But the sayings are mostly of a cheering nature, such as Emerson's 'Hitch your wagon to a star!' or the West Indian proverb: 'Every day no Christmas, an' every day no rainy day.'

My book of trivets is a happy example of much concentrated wisdom being collected in a small space—the beauty separated from the dross. It helps me to forget the dilapidated building in which I live and to look instead at the ever-changing cloud patterns as seen from my bedroom windows. There is no end to the shapes made by the clouds, or to the stories they set off in my head. We don't have to circle the world in order to find beauty and fulfilment. After all, most of living has to happen in the mind. And, to quote one anonymous sage from my trivet, 'The world is only the size of each man's head.'

2

Amongst the current fraternity of writers, I must be that very rare person—an author who actually writes by hand!

Soon after the invention of the typewriter, most editors and publishers understandably refused to look at any mansucript that was handwritten. A decade or two earlier, when Dickens and Balzac had submitted their hefty manuscrips in longhand, no one had raised any objection. Had their handwriting been awful, their manuscripts would still have been read. Fortunately for all concerned, most writers, famous or obscure, took pains over their handwriting. For some, it was an art in itself, and many of those early manuscripts are a pleasure to look at and read.

And it wasn't only authors who wrote with an elegant hand. Parents and grandparents of most of us had distinctive styles of their own. I still have my father's last letter, written to me when I was at boarding school in Shimla some fifty years ago. He used large, beautifully formed letters, and his thoughts seemed to have the same flow and clarity as his handwriting.

In his letter he advises me (then a nine-year-old) about my own handwriting: 'I wanted to write before about your writing. Ruskin... Sometimes I get letters from you in very small writing, as if you wanted to squeeze everything into one sheet of letter paper. It is not good for you or for your eyes, to get into the habit of writing too small... Try and form a larger style of handwriting—use more paper if necessary!'

I did my best to follow his advice, and I'm glad to report that after nearly forty years of the writing life, most people can still read my handwriting!

Word processors are all the rage now, and I have no objection to these mechanical aids any more than I have to my old Olympia typewriter, made in 1956 and still going strong. Although I do all my writing in longhand, I follow the conventions by typing a second draft. But I would not enjoy my writing if I had to do it straight on to a machine. It isn't just the pleasure of writing longhand. I like taking my notebooks and writing pads to odd places. This particular essay is being written on the steps of my small cottage facing Pari Tibba (Fairy Hill). Part of the reason for sitting here is that there is a new postman on this route, and I don't want him to miss me.

For a freelance writer, the postman is almost as important as a publisher. I could, of course, sit here doing nothing, but as I have pencil and paper with me, and feel like using them, I shall write until the postman comes and maybe after he has gone, too! There is really no way in which I could set up a word processor on these steps.

There are a number of favourite places where I do my writing. One is under the chestnut tree on the slope above the cottage. Word processors were not designed keeping mountain slopes in mind. But armed with a pen (or pencil) and paper, I can lie on the grass and write for hours. On one occasion, last month, I did take my typewriter into the garden, and I am still trying to extricate an acorn from under the keys, while the roller seems permanently stained yellow with some fine pollen dust from the deodar trees.

My friends keep telling me about all the wonderful things I can do with a word processor, but they haven't got around to finding me one that I can take to bed, for that is another place where I do much of my writing—especially on cold winter nights, when it is impossible to keep the cottage warm.

While the wind howls outside, and snow piles up on the windowsill, I am warm under my quilt, writing pad on my knees, ballpoint pen at the ready. And if, next day, the weather is warm and sunny, these simple aids will accompany me on a long walk, ready for instant use should I wish to record an incident, a prospect, a conversation, or simply a train of thought.

When I think of the great eighteenth- and nineteenth-century writers, scratching away with their quill pens, filling hundreds of pages every month, I am amazed to find that their handwriting did not deteriorate into the sort of hieroglyphics that often make up the average doctor's prescription today. They knew they had to write legibly, if only for the sake of the typesetters.

Both Dickens and Thackeray had good, clear, flourishing styles. (Thackeray was a clever illustrator, too.) Somerset Maugham had an upright, legible hand. Churchill's neat handwriting never wavered, even when he was under stress. I like the bold, clear, straightforward hand of Abraham Lincoln; it mirrors the man. Mahatma Gandhi, another great soul who fell to the assassin's bullet, had many similarities of both handwriting and outlook.

Not everyone had a beautiful hand. King Henry VIII had an untidy scrawl, but then, he was not a man of much refinement. Guy Fawkes, who tried to blow up the British Parliament, had a very shaky hand. With such a quiver, no wonder he failed in his attempt! Hitler's signature is ugly, as you would expect. And Napoleon's doesn't seem to know where to stop; how much like the man!

I think my father was right when he said handwriting was often the key to a man's character, and that large, well-formed letters went with an uncluttered mind. Florence Nightingale had a lovely handwriting, the hand of a caring person. And there were many like her amongst our forebears.

3

When I was a small boy, no Christmas was really complete unless my Christmas stocking contained several recent issues of my favourite comic paper. If today my friends complain that I am too voracious a reader of books, they have only these comics to blame; for they were the origin, if not of my tastes in reading, then certainly of the reading habit itself.

I like to think that my conversion to comics began at the age of five, with a comic strip on the children's page of *The Statesman*. In the late 1930s, Benji, whose head later appeared only on the Benji League badge, had a strip to himself; I don't remember his adventures very clearly, but every day (or was it once a week?) I would cut out the Benji strip and paste it into a scrapbook. Two years later, this scrapbook, bursting with the adventures of Benji, accompanied me to boarding school, where, of course, it passed through several hands before finally passing into limbo.

Of course, comics did not form the only reading matter that found its way into my Christmas stocking. Before I was eight, I had read *Peter Pan, Alice,* and most of *Mr Midshipman Easy*; but I had also consumed thousands of comic papers which were, after all, slim affairs and mostly pictorial, 'certain little penny books radiant with gold and rich with bad pictures', as Leigh Hunt described the children's papers of his own time.

But though they were mostly pictorial, comics in those days did have a fair amount of reading matter, too. *The Hostspur, Wizard, Magnet* (a victim of the Second World War) and *Champion* contained stories woven round certain popular characters. In *Champion*, which I read regularly right through my prep school years, there was Rockfist Rogan, Royal Air Force (R.A.F.), a pugilist who managed to combine boxing with bombing, and Fireworks Flynn, a footballer who always scored the winning goal in the last two minutes of play.

Billy Bunter has, of course, become one of the immortals—almost a subject for literary and social historians. Quite recently, *The Times Literary Supplement* devoted its first two pages to an analysis of the Bunter stories. Eminent lawyers and doctors still look back nostalgically to the arrival of the weekly *Magnet*; they are now the principal customers for the special souvenir edition of the first issue of the *Magnet*, recently reprinted in facsimile. Bunter, 'forever young', has become a folk hero. He is seen on stage, screen and television, and is even quoted in the House of Commons.

From this, I take courage. My only regret is that I did not preserve my own early comics—not because of any bibliophilic value which they might possess today, but because of my sentimental regard for early influences in art and literature.

The first venture in children's publishing, in 1774, was a comic of sorts. In that year, John Newberry brought out:

> According to Act of Parliament (neatly bound and gilt): A Little Pretty Pocket-Book, intended for the Instruction and Amusement of Little Master Tommy and Pretty Miss Polly, with an agreeable Letter to read from Jack the Giant-Killer...

The book contained pictures, rhymes and games. Newberry's characters and imaginary authors included Woglog the Giant, Tommy Trip, Giles Gingerbread, Nurse Truelove, Peregrine Puzzlebrains, Primrose Prettyface, and many others with names similar to those found in the comic papers of our own century.

Newberry was also the originator of the 'Amazing Free Offer', so much a part of American comics. At the beginning of 1755, he had this to offer:

> Nurse Truelove's New Year Gift, or the Book of Books for children, adorned with Cuts and designed as a Present for every little boy who would become a great Man and ride upon a fine Horse; and to every little Girl who would become a great Woman and ride in a Lord Mayor's gilt Coach. Printed for the Author, who has ordered these books to be given gratis to all little Boys in St. Paul's churchyard, they paying for the Binding, which is only Two pence each Book.

Many of today's comics are crude and, like many television serials, violent in their appeal. But I did not know American comics until I was twelve, and by then I had become quite discriminating.

Superman, Bulletman, Batman and Green Lantern, and other super heroes all left me cold. I had, by then, passed into the world of real books but the weakness for the comić strip remains. I no longer receive comics in my Christmas stocking, but I do place a few in the stockings of Gautam and Siddharth. And, needless to say, I read them right through beforehand.

MISS RAMOLA AND OTHERS

Though their numbers have diminished over the years, there are still a few compulsive daily walkers around: the odd ones, the strange ones, who will walk all day, here, there and everywhere, not in order to get somewhere, but to escape from their homes, their lonely rooms, their mirrors, themselves...

Those of us who must work for a living and would love to be able to walk a little more don't often get the chance. There are offices to attend, deadlines to be met, trains or planes to be caught, deals to be struck, people to deal with. It's the rat race for most people, whether they like it or not. So who are these lucky ones, a small minority it has to be said, who find time to walk all over this hill station from morning to night?

Some are fitness freaks, I suppose, but several are just unhappy souls who find some release, some meaning, in covering miles and miles of highway without so much as a nod in the direction of others on the road. They are not looking at anything as they walk, not even at a violet in a mossy stone.

Here comes Miss Romola. She's been at it for years. A retired schoolmistress who never married. No friends. Lonely as hell. Not even a visit from a former pupil. She could not have been very popular.

She has money in the bank. She owns her own flat. But she doesn't spend much time in it. I see her from my window, tramping up the road to Lal Tibba. She strides around the mountain like the character in the old song 'She'll be Coming Round the Mountain', only she doesn't wear pink pyjamas; she dresses in slacks and a shirt. She doesn't stop to talk to anyone. It's quick march to the top of the mountain, and then down again, home again, jiggety-jig. When she has to go down to Dehradun (too long a walk even for her), she stops a car and catches a lift. No taxis for her; not even the bus.

Miss Romola's chief pleasure in life comes from conserving her money. There are people like that. They view the rest of the world with suspicion. An overture of friendship will be construed as taking an undue interest in her assets. We are all part of an international conspiracy to relieve her of her material possessions. She has no servants, no friends; even her relatives are kept at a safe distance.

A similar sort of character but even more eccentric is Mr Sen, who used to live in the USA and walks from the Happy Valley to Landour (five miles) and back every day, in all seasons, year in and year out. Once or twice every week, he will stop at the Community Hospital to have his blood pressure checked or undergo a blood or urine test. With all that walking, he should have no health problems, but he is a hypochondriac and is convinced that he is dying of something or the other.

He came to see me once. Unlike Miss Romola, he seemed to want a friend, but his neurotic nature turned people away. He was convinced that he was surrounded by individual and collective hostility. People were always staring at him, he told me. I couldn't help wondering why, because he looked fairly nondescript. He wore conventional western clothes, perfectly acceptable in urban India, and looked respectable enough, except for a constant nervous turning of the head, looking to the left, right, or behind, as though to check on anyone who might be following him. He was convinced that he was being followed at all times.

'By whom?' I asked.

'Agents of the government,' he said.

'But why should they follow you?'

'I look different,' he said. 'They see me as an outsider. They think I work for the CIA.'

'And do you?'

'No, no.' He shied nervously away from me. 'Why did you say that?'

'Only because you. brought the subject up. I haven't noticed anyone following you.'

'They're very clever about it. Perhaps you're following me too.'

'I'm afraid I can't walk as fast or as far as you,' I said with a laugh; but he wasn't amused. He never smiled, never laughed. He did not feel safe in India, he confided. The saffron brigade was after him.

'But why?' I asked. 'They're not after me. And you're a Hindu with a Hindu name.'

'Ah yes, but I don't look like one.'

'Well, I don't look like a Taoist monk, but that's what I am,' I said, adding, in a more jocular manner: 'I know how to become invisible, and you wouldn't know I'm around. That's why no one follows me. I have this wonderful cloak, you see, and when I wear it I become invisible.'

'Can you lend it to me?' he asked eagerly.

'I'd love to,' I said, 'but it's at the cleaners right now. Maybe next week.'

'Crazy,' he muttered. 'Quite mad.' And he hurried on.

A few weeks later, he returned to New York and safety. Then I heard he'd been mugged in Central Park. He's recovering, but doesn't do much walking now.

Neurotics do not walk for pleasure, they walk out of compulsion. They are not looking at the trees or the flowers or the mountains; they are not looking at other people (except in apprehension); they are usually walking away from something—unhappiness or disarray in their lives. They tire themselves out, physically and mentally, and that brings them some relief.

Like the journalist who came to see me last year.

He'd escaped from Delhi, he told me. Had taken a room in Landour Bazaar and was going to spend a year on his own, away from family, friends, colleagues, the entire rat race. He was full of noble resolutions. He was planning to write an epic poem or a great Indian novel or a philosophical treatise. Every fortnight I meet someone who is planning to write one or the other of these things, and I do not like to discourage them, just in case they turn violent.

In effect, he did nothing but walk up and down the mountain, growing shabbier by the day. Sometimes he recognized me. At other times, there was a blank look on his face, as though he was on some drug, and he would walk past me without a sign of recognition. He discarded his slippers and began walking about barefoot, even on the stony paths. He did not change or wash his clothes. Then he disappeared; that is, I no longer saw him around.

I did not really notice his absence until I saw an ad in one of the national papers, asking for information about his whereabouts. His family was anxious to locate him. The ad carried a picture of the gentleman, taken in happier, healthier times, but it was definitely my acquaintance of that summer.

I was sitting in the bank manager's office, up in the cantonment, when a woman came in, making inquiries about her husband. It was the missing journalist's wife. Yes, said Mr Ohri, the friendly bank manager, he'd opened an account with them; not a very large sum, but there were a few hundred rupees lying to his credit. And no, they hadn't seen him in the bank for at least three months.

He couldn't be found. Several months passed, and it was presumed that he had moved on to some other town; or that he'd lost his mind or his memory. Then some milkmen from Kolti Gaon discovered bones and remnants of clothing at the bottom of a cliff. In the pocket of the ragged shirt was the journalist's press card.

How he'd fallen to his death remains a mystery.

It's easy to miss your footing and take a fatal plunge on the steep slopes of this range. He may have been high on something or he may simply have been trying out an unfamiliar path. Walking can be dangerous in the hills if you don't know the way or if you take one chance too many.

And here's a tale to illustrate that old chestnut that truth is often stranger than fiction:

Colonel Parshottam had just retired and was determined to pass the evening of his life doing the things he enjoyed most: taking early morning and late evening walks, afternoon siestas, a drop of whisky before dinner, and a good book on his bedside table.

A few streets away, on the fourth floor of a block of flats, lived Mrs L, a stout, neglected woman of forty, who'd had enough of life and was determined to do away with herself.

Along came the Colonel all the road below, a song on his lips, strolling along with a jaunty air; in love with life and wanting more of it.

Quite unaware of anyone else around, Mrs L chose that moment to throw herself out of her fourth-floor window. Seconds later, she landed with a thud on the Colonel. If this was a Ruskin Bond story, it would have been love at first flight. But the grim reality was that he was crushed beneath her and did not recover from the impact. Mrs L, on the other hand, survived the fall and lived on into a miserable old age.

There is no moral to the story, any more than there is a moral to life. We cannot foresee when a bolt from the blue will put an end to the best-laid plans of mice and men.